The Doctor Orders Christmas

Christmas Town Book 4

by

Ginny Baird

THE DOCTOR ORDERS CHRISTMAS
Christmas Town Book 4

Published by
Winter Wedding Press

Copyright © 2017
Ginny Baird
Trade Paperback
ISBN 978-1-942058-28-1

Edited by Sally Knapp
Cover by Dar Albert

About the Author

From the time she could talk, romance author Ginny Baird was making up stories, much to the delight—and consternation—of her family and friends. By grade school, she'd turned that inclination into a talent, whereby her teacher allowed her to write and produce plays rather than write boring book reports. Ginny continued writing throughout college, where she contributed articles to her literary campus weekly, then later pursued a career managing international projects with the U.S. State Department.

Ginny has held an assortment of jobs, including schoolteacher, freelance fashion model, and greeting card writer, and has published more than twenty works of fiction and optioned ten screenplays. She has also published short stories, nonfiction, and poetry, and admits to being a true romantic at heart.

Ginny is a *New York Times* and *USA Today* bestselling author of several books, including novellas in her Holiday Brides Series. She's a member of Romance Writers of America (RWA) and Novelists, Inc. (NINC).

When she's not writing, Ginny enjoys cooking, biking, and spending time with her family in Tidewater, Virginia. She loves hearing from her readers and welcomes visitors to her website at http://www.ginnybairdromance.com.

Books by Ginny Baird

Christmas Town Series
The Christmas Cookie Shop
A Mommy for Christmas
Only You at Christmas
The Doctor Orders Christmas

Holiday Brides Series
The Christmas Catch
The Holiday Bride
Mistletoe in Maine
Beach Blanket Santa
Baby, Be Mine

Summer Grooms Series
Must-Have Husband
My Lucky Groom
The Wedding Wish
The Getaway Groom

Romantic Ghost Stories
The Ghost Next Door (A Love Story)
The Light at the End of the Road
The House at Homecoming Cove

Romantic Comedy
Real Romance
The Sometime Bride
Santa Fe Fortune
How to Marry a Matador
Counterfeit Cowboy
The Calendar Brides
My Best Friend's Bride
The Borrowed Boyfriend
Tara (Beach Brides Book 2)
Crazy for You

Bundles
Christmas Magic:
The Complete Holiday Brides Series (Books 1 – 5)
The Holiday Brides Collection (Books 1–4)
A Summer Grooms Selection (Books 1–3)
Romantic Ghost Stories (Books 1 – 3)
Real Romance and The Sometime Bride
(Gemini Editions 1)
Santa Fe Fortune and How to Marry a Matador
(Gemini Editions 2)
My Best Friend's Bride and
The Borrowed Boyfriend
(Gemini Editions 3)
Wedding Bells Bundle

Short Story
Special Delivery
(A Valentine's Short Story)

Ginny Baird's

THE DOCTOR ORDERS CHRISTMAS

Chapter One

"Savannah! Wait!"

The handsome Christmas Town doctor approached from behind her, and Savannah's pulse raced. She'd spent all afternoon ignoring Kurt, and trying her hardest not to look into his soulful brown eyes. There was too much interest written there, and too many painful memories.

"You can't keep this up. You've scarcely said a word to me all day."

That was because this day was supposed to be focused on someone else, Savannah told herself rationally. Not twenty minutes ago, Savannah's big sister, Olivia, had married Nick Claus, the attractive new architect in town. They'd held an outdoor ceremony at an area called River Run, where rippling waters skipped over large boulders near the river's banks. Towering mountains on the opposite shore rose in lush summer splendor toward a clear blue sky.

Olivia had considerately planned a June wedding so high school guidance counselor Savannah could attend from Miami. The entire town had gathered for the nuptials, with the friendly small-town minister presiding. Even the woodland animals seemed to appear, huddling near the edge of the woods to catch a glimpse of the happy couple as they exchanged vows.

The ceremony had ended and an al fresco reception had begun, with heavy hors d'oeuvres and dancing to a DJ beneath large white tents, decorated with pretty arrangements of bridal flowers. The wedding party had just finished with photos and Savannah still clutched her bridesmaid bouquet in one hand.

She wore a cream-colored dress with spaghetti straps and a dainty ornamental headband that distinguished her as the maid of honor from the other bridal attendants: Hannah Livingston, who had married Savannah's brother, Carter; Nick's sister, Sandy Claus Winchester, the wife of Hannah's brother Ben; and Jade Smith Scott, whose spouse was named Wendell. Nick had selected Carter, Ben, and Kurt as his groomsmen, with his father, a stout elderly gentleman with a big round belly and a snowy white beard, serving as his best man.

Savannah's parents, Janet and Spencer, were busily chatting with the senior Clauses, Cole and Daisy, and the rest of the group had gone in search of refreshments. Savannah had been halfway to the rustic bathroom building when Kurt stopped her. She'd cried buckets during the ceremony, and was certain her mascara was in need of repair. Just feeling Kurt draw near made Savannah fear she might burst into tears again. As long ago as it had been, her feelings for him still ran deep and they were raw within her.

"Savannah, please." The words were a tender petition. "Don't go."

"Kurt, I…" She inhaled deeply, gathering her resolve. "*We,*" she said more firmly. Though her composure was a farce. "*We've* got nothing to talk about."

"You know I don't believe that. There's a lot more to say, starting with *why*…" Kurt stepped an inch closer and the front of his tuxedo shirt grazed her back. Due to the sweltering heat, he'd removed his bow tie and jacket the moment the photo session ended.

"That was ages ago," Savannah said, even though in her heart it seemed like only yesterday.

"That doesn't mean it doesn't matter."

"We were kids, Kurt."

"That's what others saw," he said hoarsely. "Not the truth that we knew."

"I don't want that truth anymore."

"Don't you…?" His arms slid around her, and Savannah's breath hitched. Kurt was better looking now than he ever was. He stood just over six feet tall with a solid buff frame, and dark blond hair offsetting his rugged features. "Carter tells me that you and James are no longer together."

"That's my business," she said unconvincingly. "Not yours."

"I could make it mine, if you'd let me."

She peered over her shoulder and he rasped in her ear, "We need to talk." Goose bumps skittered down her spine. "We have unfinished business, you and I."

"I think you finished things pretty well." Hurt resonated in her words.

"I don't know what you mean." His face registered surprise and Savannah turned her head. "Savannah?" Kurt tightened his embrace until she felt his heartbeat against her bare back. "Whatever you're thinking," he uttered pleadingly. "It's wrong."

She spun abruptly in his arms to glare at him, and her bridesmaid bouquet spilled to the ground.

"Wrong? Yeah, it was, Kurt! I can't believe you didn't answer! Especially after I said—" A lump welled in her throat and she clamped her mouth shut.

"Said *what*?"

"I hardly see how it matters…anymore." Savannah balled up her fists, biting back her anguish and anger. Part of her wanted to beat on his chest until it became as black and blue as he'd made her battered heart.

Kurt grabbed her wrists in his hands and pinned them against him.

"I wrote to you," he told her. "Many times."

"Yeah? Well…" Hot tears blazed down her cheeks. "I didn't get any letters."

"I'm sorry. You probably didn't know what to think." Emotion threaded his voice as he gently loosened his hold. "I was confused when I didn't hear from you, either. I thought it meant…" His Adam's apple rose and fell. "Well, that you wanted nothing more to do with me. But I never knew the reason…?"

While she'd suffered for an eternity over what she'd imagined as Kurt's neglect, Savannah felt even more perplexed and conflicted by Kurt's current admission. How could it be that he hadn't received her letters and she hadn't gotten his? Even if Kurt was telling the truth, Savannah wasn't certain she could reopen those old wounds now. Not after she'd worked so hard to put those wrenching memories behind her.

"That's in the past," she said, her words warbling. "We can't go back."

"Then, how about moving forward?" He searched her eyes and a tidal wave of emotion crashed over her. "It's not too late, Savannah. Not too late for us."

Savannah had fervently dreamed of this moment, but now that it was real—everything about it felt wrong. Everything but the sultry aroma of his aftershave that reminded her of salty sea breezes and pine, and the heady way he gazed into her eyes. Kurt slowly released her wrists and slipped Savannah's arms around his neck.

As much as she'd tried to fight it, there was no battling her attraction to Kurt. Savannah was as much his at this moment as she'd been as a teen. Maybe more. For time hadn't diminished her craving for Kurt Christmas. Its passage had merely strengthened that yearning.

"I don't want the moon," he sexily whispered. His lips brushed over hers and Savannah's heart fluttered. "I'd settle for seeing the stars with you for just one night."

"One night?" she asked weakly. "And, then what?"

"I'm hoping you'll still be there in the morning."

Kurt cupped her face in his hands and she sighed into his kiss. Deep, heartfelt, and lovely…as the world tumbled around them and the sun slowly set on the horizon.

Then the years fell away and Savannah surrendered to his charms.

Savannah blinked hard and a tear rolled down her cheek. She'd snuck out of Kurt's cozy bungalow early the next morning while he was sound asleep without bothering to say goodbye. A car horn beeped loudly, and Savannah recalled herself to the present, realizing where she was: at the intersection of South Main Street and Santa Claus Lane, where tall streetlamps housing holiday decorations glimmered in the snow. It was after six o'clock on a Saturday, so with the exception of a small grocery store called the Merry Market, the quaint shops that lined the sidewalks had all closed. The tall façade of the Grand Hotel stood proudly to her right. The elegantly restored building towered four stories tall on top of a basement, with an impressive staircase leading to its enormous front door.

Savannah would be working there this winter, helping to establish a children's theater on the Grand Hotel's upper floor. Given Savannah's experience in theater, Olivia, who'd been partly charged with the Grand Hotel's renovation, had begged for her assistance. And, Savannah had eventually run out of excuses for not coming to Christmas Town. She had been able to use a few vacation days to bridge the gap between the Thanksgiving holiday, which she'd spent with her parents in Virginia, and her school's winter break, which began in mid-December. She'd dedicated four whole weeks to completing her task in Christmas Town, and felt confident she could leave things in good order for someone else to take over at the start of the year.

She raised her hand in a wave at the vehicle behind her, and cautiously crossed through the T-intersection, spotting Sandy Winchester's business, the Snow Globe Gallery, on the left-hand corner. The place where she was staying was just beyond that. It was called Sisters' Row and consisted of three townhomes neatly snuggled together. All were pale pink with dark green gingerbread trim. The unit to the far right was a rental, and Savannah had arranged to have it for a month. Given its proximity to the Grand Hotel and the other businesses in town, the location was ideal. Savannah found an empty parallel parking spot across the street, and gingerly navigated into it.

The vehicle that had been trailing hers passed by and its driver gave a sunny wave. Savannah instantly recognized the handsome man in a sheriff's uniform, as he lowered the window on the passenger side of his red pickup truck. "Welcome to Christmas Town!" Carter Livington called, and Savannah laughed at her dark-haired brother.

She slightly lowered her driver's side window. "So you were the one tailgating me!"

"Just trying to get you to mosey along," he said, explaining his earlier honk. He glanced in her direction and his green eyes twinkled. "Need any help moving in?"

"I don't have much other than my clothing."

Carter smiled indulgently. "Don't tell me my kid sister has learned to pack light?"

When Savannah grinned instead of answering, Carter chuckled in reply. "In that case, let me park my truck."

Fifteen minutes later Carter hauled the last of Savannah's luggage indoors. His sheriff's hat was dusted snowy white and small white crystals clung to the shoulders of his uniform jacket. Savannah had been so busy carrying her things inside she hadn't had a moment to look around. The interior of the rental town house was decorated in nice antiques with a small sofa and a few armchairs situated to the left of the living area. A low coffee table sat in front of the sofa and an old walled-up fireplace stood opposite from the seating arrangement.

Savannah noticed a pretty winter scene of a snowy field hanging over the mantel. It appeared to be done in oils and was signed "S. Claus." She turned to her brother with a giggle. "Santa's into artwork now?"

"The artist is Sandy." Carter set down Savannah's final two suitcases with a thud, and shut the door against the brisk howling winds outside. "Sandy Winchester, formerly Claus. Our new sister-in-law, since Olivia married Nick."

Savannah smiled with delighted surprise. "Of course! I should have put it together. Especially since she runs the Snow Globe Gallery."

"It's a great place. You'll have to stop by it sometime."

"I certainly will!" Savannah glanced at the back of the room and the big bay window framing the dining table with four chairs near the stairs. It was snowing even more heavily than before, so it was a good thing she'd packed for winter weather, as well as preparing for other eventualities. Like casual events, business meetings, and that upscale Christmas Town Ball that Olivia had mentioned. Savannah hadn't been able to decide on an outfit for that. So, she'd packed five. *I mean, seriously. A girl can't have too many options!* "Sandy seems really nice," Savannah said to her brother. "But I barely got to know her. We only chatted briefly at Olivia's wedding."

Carter eyed her studiously. "Perhaps that's because your attentions were focused on someone else."

"*Carter*, please."

"It's not like the rest of us couldn't see you talking with Kurt, or dancing with him later."

"Everybody was dancing!"

"Then the next thing we knew, no one could even *find* the two of you."

Savannah's face burned hot. She avoided Carter's gaze as she removed her damp wool cap and peeled off her gloves. "I can't believe that anyone was searching."

"It's more like folks were *talking*," Carter teased her.

"Well, they shouldn't have been," Savannah said with a huff. "It's nobody's business but mine and Kurt's, anyway."

Her brother scrutinized her a beat. "That's exactly what Kurt said."

Savannah pursed her lips, her heart hammering. "You spoke to Kurt?" she asked casually.

"I always speak to Kurt, and—generally—he answers. On one topic, though, he's been decidedly mute." Carter leveled her a look, his green eyes shining. "You."

Savannah pushed her long red hair back over her shoulders, and assumed a disinterested air. "Well, that's just fine, then. Because I feel exactly the same way… Absolutely the same!"

"Meaning, what? That you don't want to talk about him?"

"Or, hear about him, either." She squarely met Carter's eyes. "I'm here to do a job, you know." She unzipped her coat and shook it out over the mat, before hanging it on the rack by the door. "A very specific one having to do with the Grand Hotel."

"Yeah, Olivia told me. You're helping with the theater and that makes sense. You always did have a flair for…" He leaned toward her and whispered, "*drama.*"

Savannah's eyes flashed. "Drama? Ha!" Then she caught a glimpse of herself in the mirror in a painted frame hanging over the entryway table. Her waterproof mascara had run halfway down her face, and Carter hadn't bothered to say a thing! She hastily withdrew a tissue from the purse she'd laid on the foyer table and dabbed at the running dark streaks marring her cheeks. "I can't believe you didn't tell me!"

"Tell you what?" he asked with utmost innocence.

"My makeup's smeared everywhere!"

"Maybe I didn't notice."

When she turned to look at him, Carter added, "Because that's just how you looked the last time I saw you... At the wedding."

Savannah wanted to sock him. Big brothers were supposed to be nice. Protective. Not a major pain in the neck. "People cry at weddings, Carter," she snapped testily. "That is, people with a heart."

Carter tipped his hat in her direction. "I have a heart, Savannah. A fairly big one. Just ask Hannah and Amanda," he said, referencing his wife and one-year-old daughter. When Savannah first met her niece the weekend of Olivia's wedding, the cheerful dark-haired baby was only nine months old and just learning to sit up on her own.

"How is Amanda?"

"Doing great. Thanks!" Carter folded his arms across his chest wearing a proud expression. "She's just started walking."

"That's when the trouble starts."

"For some kids it begins sooner," he answered mysteriously.

Savannah watched him curiously as he continued. "Sandy and Ben's twins were a handful from day one!"

"Lily seems mighty sweet," Savannah said, remembering meeting Sandy's precocious ten-year-old stepdaughter at Olivia's reception. A trusted family friend, Pastor Wilson's housekeeper Mary, had volunteered to look after the twins, while Carter's child stayed with Caleb Smith, who was also babysitting his grandsons: his daughter Jade's boys, Alexander and Josiah.

"Yeah, Lily's awesome. Growing up pretty fast, too. Maybe even faster than her parents realize."

"What's that supposed to mean?"

Carter slowly shook his head. "Nothing really. Nothing concrete I can put my finger on."

Savannah viewed him keenly. "You keep an eye on this town. Don't you? A very close eye, sometimes."

"I do my best." He tamped down his hat and glanced around. "Got everything you need in here?"

"Lou Christmas said the kitchen would come stocked with coffee and tea, and some spices," she answered. "And the Merry Market is right down the street. What time do they close today?"

"Five minutes ago, but I wouldn't worry." He shared a kind smile. "Lou and Sandy will drop by in a bit with supplies. They're on the Christmas Town Welcoming Committee and always make sure newcomers settle in with a few basics, including a home-cooked meal or two."

"Fantastic! How nice!"

"You're going to like them both, once you get to know them better. Lou's a little meddling at first."

"I know, Carter. I remember." As Savannah's mom, Janet, and Lou had been long-term best friends, the two families, the Livingstons and the Christmases, had taken beach summer vacations together for a number of years. That's how Savannah had initially come to know Kurt, and fall for him… He'd been a jaw-dropping teenage heartthrob at sixteen. Not that he looked any worse as an adult. In fact, he looked about a thousand times better, now that he'd matured and had muscled up his formerly lanky teenage frame.

"Lou's the same old Lou," Carter said, speaking of his godmother. "Basically good-hearted. Just be sure to take good care of Mr. Noodles!"

"Mr. Noodles?" Savannah screwed up her face. "Dare I ask?"

"You probably won't have to! Lou will drop by with the Christmas decorations soon enough."

"But I wasn't planning on decorating this place." Savannah quickly glanced around at the nicely furnished rental. "I mean, not for the holidays."

"You, little sister, have a thing or two to learn about Christmas Town," Carter informed her as he walked toward the door. "Everyone decks their halls around here."

"Surely, not *everyone*…"

"Yep. Everyone." Carter laid his hand on the front doorknob and yanked open the door. Then he spoke over his shoulder with a smile. "Even your indelible doctor friend, Kurt Christmas."

"Shut up and get out of here before I throw some luggage at you!"

Carter's gaze roved over the mounds of tote bags, large suitcases, carry-ons, and the single steamer trunk. *Surely, I get credit for only bringing one of those!* "Need any help getting this stuff upstairs?"

"No thanks," Savannah said smugly. "I can do it."

"Olivia says she's meeting you for brunch tomorrow."

"Yes, at the new place in the Grand Hotel."

"Hannah and I would like to have you out to our cabin," he said. "For dinner, maybe one night later this week?"

"That would be nice," Savannah answered. "I'd love to see Hannah and Amanda."

"All righty then. We'll give you a call once you've settled in."

"Thanks, Carter."

"In the meantime, just give me and Hannah a shout if you need anything!"

"Will do, and thanks for the welcome!"

Chapter Two

Early the next afternoon, Kurt Christmas strolled down South Main Street toward the Grand Hotel. He'd just attended the eleven o'clock service at the Corner Church and was headed to the Main Street Café, where he was meeting Eliza Stewart for brunch. Yesterday's heavy snow had converted to a steady dusting, making the visibility better than it had been during Hannah's banner day at the Christmas Cookie Shop. She'd had to close a full hour early due to her selling out of her hottest commodity, her three varieties of Virginia Cookies credited with inspiring good works, forgiveness, and true love.

Folks had come from all around and clamored down Santa Claus Lane, bustling toward the bakery in panicked attempts to buy them. Since Hannah only sold them once a year, word of their legendary powers had grown to great proportions. It had taken Carter and his deputy, Victoria Cho, nearly an hour to clear the crowd that gathered on the street even after Hannah had shuttered her shop!

Kurt mulled over Pastor Wilson's sermon on the gifts of the season, with a focus on hope and renewal.

There was no hope of renewing one thing…that was certain: Kurt's romantic relationship with Savannah. If he'd believed her cold and distant before, Kurt now had evidence she was plain unfeeling. When they'd seen each other at Olivia's wedding, he'd so believed they'd made a connection. And when he'd held her in his arms, old hurts seemed to vanish and a different future seemed possible. The sort of future where he and she—

"Whoa!" Kurt called himself up short, grabbing Kyle's bicycle by the handlebars. It stopped mid-skid, the back wheel of the bike fishtailing against the slick road as Kurt held on tight. His thirteen-year-old nephew had nearly run him down as he crossed Church Street!

The fair-haired boy looked up with flushed cheeks as snow dusted his skullcap. He favored his father, Kurt's brother Ray, and already his features were changing from the smooth contours of a child's into the chiseled outlines of a man's. "Sorry, Uncle Kurt!" he called in a rush above the wind. When he spoke his warm breath clouded the chilly air.

Kurt eyed Kyle's heavy wool jacket, hiking boots, and jeans. The backpack strapped to his shoulders had a few green sprigs with white berries poking out of one pocket. "Where are you off to in such a rush?"

"I…uh…" Kyle scanned the street as a car leaving the church parking lot headed toward them. Kurt steadily tugged the bike toward the curb and released it as Kyle's boots hit the ground. "I'm headed to Uncle Walt's!" he said, referring to Kurt's middle brother, who ran the Christmas Inn. His eldest brother, Ray, ran the North Pole Nursery, where Kyle helped out part-time. Though it was closed for business on Sundays, Kyle had a key.

"Put in an order for some mistletoe, did he?"

Kyle swallowed hard.

A new vehicle rounding the corner crept by them before Kurt continued. As it passed he recognized his friends, Sandy and Ben Winchester, inside. They'd also attended church before retrieving their one-year-old twins from the nursery. Their ten-year-old daughter Lily sat in the back seat next to the toddlers' side-by-side car seats.

She pressed her face to the window and stared at Kyle. The pretty little girl with big brown eyes was maturing, as well. She was in the fifth grade now and had recently cut her hair into a chin-length bob, which made the petite child look much more grown up than she'd appeared in pigtails. Kurt returned Sandy's wave, then set his attention back on Kyle, who appeared transfixed by the departing SUV's taillights.

Kurt pointedly cleared his throat and Kyle whipped his head around. "Mistletoe? Right! He did! Uncle Walt, I mean. His last set of guests ran off with his foyer decoration—"

"Guests?" Kurt interrupted with a smile.

"Had something to do with Mrs. Livingston's Virginia Cookies."

"Ah." Kurt stroked his chin, putting things together. "That would be the commitment kind, I suppose?"

"Wouldn't know!" Kyle shrugged, but the color in his cheeks deepened into a ruddy hue. "Not anything about that."

"No, I suppose you wouldn't." Kurt sagely studied his nephew. "You're far too young for that stuff, anyway. Love…kissing…" Kurt added a sing-songy measure to his voice.

"Yes, sir. I mean, no sir…"

"*Mistletoe…*" Kurt eyed his nephew dead-on.

Kyle blinked and swallowed hard. "I mean, I'm sure you're right!"

Kurt laid his hand on Kyle's coat sleeve, and suddenly Kurt knew for sure. Kyle wasn't exactly telling an untruth, but the boy was definitely up to something.

"Well, I guess I'd better go." Kyle's voice cracked on a high note when he said the last word, and Kurt felt for him. Thirteen. What a difficult age. The good news was that Kyle would live through it. Kurt and his two brothers certainly had.

"All right, then." Kurt gave Kyle's arm an affectionate squeeze. "Just watch where you're going. Okay?"

Kyle nodded quickly and mounted his bike. "Yes, sir!"

Then he was pedaling down Church Street just as fast as his lanky legs could carry him, until he became lost in a swirl of snow.

A few blocks away, Savannah sat with her sister Olivia at the Main Street Café. They'd both ordered mimosas and occupied a cozy two-person table near the fireplace that had a real linen tablecloth and elegant place settings patterned with little pink roses set against bone-white china. Olivia told Savannah that this room had once functioned as the lobby of the Grand Hotel. It was enlarged by removing the wall between it and the hotel's original dining room, which led to the kitchen. She planned to show Savannah around the rest of the building after they had brunch, and was particularly excited to get Savannah's opinion of the fourth floor, where the town hoped to host its children's theater.

The French-style bistro was festive and cheery with holiday decorations adorning the mantel and sconces holding electric candles in glass globes on the walls. The dark pink and magenta striped wallpaper presented a certain old-world charm, with rows of tiny white rose buds on forest-green vines climbing toward the intricately molded ceiling dripping with two matching chandeliers. The enormous windows sweeping the room gleamed in the soft light as snow drifted outside. To the right of the main entrance off the foyer, a harpist plucked out dainty Christmas tunes that seemed to chime from the heavens. All around them, silverware gently clattered as their fellow diners enjoyed muted conversations and exchanged quiet laughter.

Olivia lifted her champagne flute toward Savannah in a toast. She wore a Christmas green sweater above a crisp white blouse and her long red braid was slung forward over one shoulder. She'd clipped a pretty Christmas barrette in her hair that resembled a heart-shaped gingerbread cookie. The tiny green Christmas tree painted on it perfectly complemented her outfit. Savannah was so proud of her sister! She'd never known Olivia to coordinate accessories before.

"Here's to you, little sis," Olivia said, raising her glass. "I'm so glad you said yes!"

Savannah clinked Olivia's glass with hers and grinned. "Let's just hope I haven't gotten in over my head."

"I'm sure there's *nothing* you can't handle in Christmas Town," Olivia answered jovially.

At that exact moment, Kurt Christmas appeared in the doorway, and Savannah's heart thumped. He wore a camel-colored car coat and a tan felted-wool fedora, and looked like a film star out of a movie. Olivia spied her glancing Kurt's way and arched an eyebrow. "Well, *almost* nothing, anyway," she teased in low tones.

Savannah primly straightened her spine and avoided Kurt's gaze as his eyes swept the room. He was obviously looking for someone and hadn't seen her. Maybe he wouldn't notice Savannah at all. She sat very still trying to make herself invisible as she sipped from her mimosa. "I could handle him too—if I wanted," she answered pertly. "But, the fact is, I *don't.*"

"You never told me what happened," Olivia whispered. "After the wedding—"

"Shh!" Savannah cautioned. "He's coming this way."

Kurt strode casually in their direction and Savannah's pulse quickened. Surely, he wouldn't confront her here in this room full of people! Maybe, he wouldn't even want to talk to her at all. Ever again... Which would suit Savannah fine. The more distance she kept between her and Kurt during the course of this month the better off she would be. For a whole lot of reasons, none of which she cared to share with her sister.

The sounds in the room seemed to still as Kurt approached their table with measured footsteps, the soles of his dress shoes gently smacking against the polished wood floor. Then, suddenly, he paused right beside her.

Savannah stared down at Kurt's expensive Italian loafers and her temperature soared. When she glanced up, her face burned even hotter. Kurt had removed his hat and now held it to his chest. He gave a brief nod and suavely issued his greeting. "Ladies."

"Hi, Kurt!" Olivia shot him a friendly gaze but Savannah felt immobilized. She had to know that this would happen. Christmas Town was a very small place so running into Kurt was inevitable. She just hadn't expected it to happen so soon.

"Kurt," Savannah said as calmly as she could. "Nice to see you."

"You too, Savannah." He stared into her eyes, searching for something. Answers, she supposed. Though Savannah wasn't prepared to offer any. "Welcome to town."

Savannah attempted a reply but the words caught in her throat, so she shared a silly plastic smile instead. At least she'd dressed nicely, in a stylish suede mini skirt, brown leggings, and leather boots. And her dusty-rose V-neck sweater showcased the gorgeous pink mother-of-pearl necklace her parents had given her for her last birthday, along with its matching teardrop earrings which nicely accentuated Savannah's flowing red hair. Kurt glanced over his shoulder at a stunning brunette waving at him from a table at the opposite end of the room.

He grinned and casually lifted his hand, indicating that he'd seen her and was on his way. "If you'll both excuse me," he said, tilting his chin at Savannah.

"Uh-huh!" Savannah said, finally finding her voice. Though she croaked it out hoarsely, much to her horror.

"Give my best to Eliza!" Olivia said as he walked away.

Savannah set down her glass, her heart hammering fiercely.

"Oh my gosh." Olivia leaned toward her and whispered surreptitiously. "You're really *not* over him!" Her eyes sparkled with intrigue. "*Are you?*"

"Of course I am." Savannah gave a haughty smirk. "And nothing happened at your wedding, if that's what you're thinking."

Olivia narrowed her dark green eyes. "I wasn't talking about *at*..." she said in low tones. "I meant *after*."

Savannah stared aghast at her sister.

"Come on, Savannah. I'm a grown woman. So are you. Which is why I understand that things sometimes—"

"Oh look!" Savannah interrupted loudly. "Here comes brunch!"

The women paused their conversation while their waiter set two plates of quiche down before them. Each was arranged with a pretty side salad made of field greens and a crystal bowl holding a selection of fresh fruit.

After he left, Olivia persisted doggedly. "It's hard to believe that things went that badly. Surely, there was some kind of spark? Even after all this time?"

Savannah picked up her fork and stared down her sister. "I never said there was no spark." She hung her head and gloomily poked into her salad. "Heat between me and..." She shot a glance in Kurt's direction, seeing him engaged in rapt conversation with his gorgeous companion. "*You know who* has never been the problem."

Savannah noticed Kurt's date had handed him a brown paper package, which appeared to be a gift of some sort. Naturally, Kurt was involved with someone else. What had she expected? Savannah had heard rumors of Kurt seeing a woman named Eliza Stewart long before now. She'd just never seen the woman in person. And, Eliza was exceptionally pretty.

Savannah met Olivia's gaze, feeling oddly unsettled and agitated. "Can we just drop it? Please? I'd really like to enjoy this lovely brunch."

Olivia viewed her with concern. "Oh honey, I'm sorry. I didn't mean to butt in. Not really. It's just that I—"

"Care. Yes, I know." Savannah forced a smile, fighting the burn in her eyes. She was absolutely not going to cry here. Not in this public place, with Kurt sitting twenty feet away from her. Redirecting her thoughts would help. *Focus. Focus, Savannah*, she told herself, taking a deep cleansing breath. *Think about the theater and your mission.* "And I care about you, Olivia. Much more than you know. That's why I decided to come to Christmas Town to help you out."

Olivia's grin sparkled. "And, I'm so happy you're here! It means the world to me, Savannah. It really does." She smiled with big-sisterly affection. "Carter's happy to have you in town, as well."

Olivia took a bite of quiche as Savannah tasted hers. It was made of spinach, portobello mushrooms, and feta cheese, with just the right hint of fresh garlic. The hot morsel melted in her mouth and it was absolutely delicious. "I think Carter's just happy to have someone else around to tease."

"Savannah."

"It's true! He stopped by last night and started in on me already."

"I'm sure it was in jest."

"You'd think he'd have outgrown it by now."

"Family dynamics die hard."

"Yeah." Savannah took another nibble of quiche then sipped from her drink. "The food is really good here." She looked around, taking pains to avoid staring at Kurt again. "This is a very nice place."

"It is nice," Olivia agreed. "I can't wait to show you the rest of the hotel."

"I'm excited to see the upstairs."

"I'll give you a key so you can let yourself in after hours," Olivia offered. "Though I don't want you to take that as meaning anyone on the Town Council expects you to be working late. You go at your own pace. Just submit your hours to Tilly at the end of each week and she'll make sure you get paid."

"Tilly?"

"She's Carter's secretary," Olivia explained. "Wonderful woman and also the treasurer for the Town Council. Since she's the mayor, Lou Christmas will have to sign off on your time sheets, but that shouldn't be a problem." Olivia stopped eating to observe Savannah. "Have you seen Lou yet? She and Sandy are on the Welcoming Committee. They generally—"

"Oh, yeah! They did!" Savannah giggled at the memory of the two women appearing on her doorstep. Sandy in her fluffy white coat and sparkly white earmuffs, holding a brimming gift basket... And Lou in her animal print jacket with the faux fur collar and knee-high leather boots. Despite her eccentricities, Lou was a very convincing woman. Savannah knew she'd been the one to persuade Carter to move to Christmas Town four years ago. Olivia had moved here not long after, and Savannah's siblings had reconnected with the Christmases as old family friends.

"It was great to see Sandy again," Savannah continued. "She's so fun. And Lou—was quite warm and welcoming. Truthfully, I wasn't sure what to expect."

After that one particular summer when Carter had caught Savannah and Kurt making out together, the families had seemed to distance themselves from each other. Gone were the annual seaside holidays, and a more impersonal exchange of Christmas cards had taken their place.

"Naturally, she was welcoming. Lou loves our family. All of us, Savannah," Olivia assured her. "Buddy does, too."

Savannah lifted an eyebrow and said softly, "She just never thought I was right for her son."

"Both sets of parents worried that you and Kurt were too young to become involved." Olivia quietly cleared her throat then whispered, "I mean, that deeply."

Savannah shot a look at Kurt and caught him staring her way. One half of his mouth pulled up in a grin as he raised his cocktail glass her way. He was drinking something in a short glass that looked a lot stronger than a mimosa. Savannah wondered if he thought he needed it, or whether that was his customary drink for Sunday brunch. Not that Kurt's menu choices mattered to her one way or another. She quickly returned her gaze to Olivia. "Well, anyway! That's over now. Isn't it?"

"Don't know. You tell me." Olivia eyed her astutely and heat warmed Savannah's face.

"I'd rather not, thank you." Savannah dabbed her mouth with her napkin. "Talk any more about it, I mean."

"All right," Olivia said, finishing her food. "Then, tell me! What incredible goodies did Lou and Sandy deliver? Those Welcoming Committee baskets are always so cool."

"Oh, lots of good eats," Savannah said, relieved to be talking about something else. "Homemade soups, fruit, nuts, and cheeses! There was even a gorgeous little box of chocolate truffles—"

Olivia gasped in envy. "Not from Nutcracker Sweets?"

"Yes! But, how did you—?"

"That store is my absolute favorite! But the one next door to it, the Christmas Cookie Shop, is pretty special, too."

Kurt finished his scotch and water with one long swig. He generally didn't hit the hard stuff this early, but special occasions called for extra measures. Seeing Savannah here today was certainly a special occasion. He knew he'd see her soon enough. He simply hadn't anticipated running into her within twenty-four hours of her arrival in Christmas Town, while he was having brunch with Eliza Stewart.

Although it was impossible to believe, Savannah was more beautiful than he remembered. In the five and a half months that had passed since Nick and Olivia's wedding, Kurt had convinced himself he'd imagined it. It was unfathomable for a woman to look even better in her early thirties than she had as a teen, but Savannah broke all the rules.

Her emerald green eyes burned brighter. The creaminess of her skin appeared smoother. And her rich red hair seemed incredibly luxurious, inviting a man's touch. Savannah knew how to dress to accentuate her figure, too. And that figure was pretty stunning, settled on her petite five-foot-four frame.

"Go on! Open it!" Eliza nudged his hand and Kurt realized his left palm still rested on that paper bag. Eliza had presented it to him upon their meeting. Now that their brunch dishes were being cleared and coffee was about to be served, she was insisting he "take a peek at dessert."

Kurt eyed the bag then hesitated. The logo from the Christmas Cookie Shop was evident on its seal. "Eliza," he said smoothly. "You shouldn't have."

"Don't flatter yourself, Kurt." She gave a light titter. "You and I have a clear understanding. We enjoy things as they are."

"And, so?" He lifted the bag with his question.

"So…" She gently patted his hand in a congenial manner. "I got you a little gift. Friend to friend… You were working all day yesterday, which means you missed the fanfare."

"Hannah's big day."

"Her unveiling of this year's Virginia Cookies, exactly," Eliza said, her brown eyes sparkling. They reminded Kurt of almonds both in their shape and color. Eliza Stewart really was an elegantly pretty woman. There was no denying that.

Kurt felt lucky to have missed the "fanfare," as Eliza dubbed it. Christmas Town was a zoo the Saturday after Thanksgiving each year. That was, ever since Hannah Livingston had reopened her late great-grandmother's bakery and started selling those legendary Virginia Cookies, based on an ancient—and supposedly magical—recipe. As fortune had it, Kurt had a regular stint that day playing Santa at a nearby children's hospital where he was affiliated.

Kurt filled the role on a regular basis and always looked forward to it. In the past five years, he'd only skipped his duty once, and that had been on account of Della Martin giving birth to her fourth child: a boy named Basil. It had been an emergency situation during a snowstorm and Kurt had performed an at-home delivery. His buddy Carter had substituted as Old Saint Nick with the young patients in the neighboring town.

Eliza watched him expectantly as he unfolded the flap of the bag. "This is unfair," Kurt said. "I didn't bring anything for you."

"I don't *need* anything, darling," she answered in exaggerated tones. "You know how utterly self-sufficient I am."

"Which is why I'm surprised you'd fight the madding crowd. All on account of me?" He paused before opening the bag. "I'm truly touched, Eliza. Thank you."

Kurt figured she'd gotten him one of Hannah's Virginia Cookies, since those were the items that were in high demand. Their sales were so hot they sold out

within a matter of hours of Hannah opening her shop.
For the past few years, she'd had to ration them, only
allowing a certain number per customer. It didn't
appear to matter how many she baked, the number
never seemed to be enough. Hannah had lamented over
this fact to her husband Cater, who in turn had shared
this with Kurt. Though Carter secretly didn't believe
Hannah was sorry. He suspected she was pleased that
her business was doing so well, and Carter was
extremely proud of her. He'd supported Hannah's
endeavor in reopening the shop she'd inherited from the
beginning, so was happy to see her fulfilling her
dreams.

The bag rustled in Kurt's hands as he gently pried
it open, peering down inside. He expected to find a
heart-shaped cookie with a little white angel on top.
That type of Virginia Cookie was meant to inspire good
behavior. Or perhaps the green sort, adorned with a
little Christmas tree and rumored to exact forgiveness.
Instead, Kurt saw…a heart-shaped cookie with a pale
pink icing heart, and dark red lettering stenciled across
it reading: *Forever Yours.*

His head jerked up. "A Commitment Cookie?" he
asked hoarsely. "Seriously?"

"Well, don't look so shocked," Eliza said tellingly.
"It's not meant like *that*, you know."

Kurt swallowed hard. "Then, how *is* it meant?
Precisely?"

"There was only one left, so I took it! At first, I…"
She appeared a bit sheepish about what she was going
to say. "I thought that I might use it. I mean, give it—to
someone else. But then I changed my mind."

"Why, Eliza Stewart," Kurt said in a mock Southern drawl. "Do you have a fellow you've been keeping from me?"

"I'm not the one keeping secrets." Her flippant tone surprised him.

"Oh?"

"I may be crotchety and set in my ways, Kurt, but I'm not blind. I've seen you eyeing that pretty redhead over there." She gestured discreetly toward Savannah.

"When?" Kurt asked, incredulous. He was sure he'd been so subtle.

"Why, all through brunch, you silly man." Eliza laughed lightly and shook her head. "And, anyway. It's not like I mind, or as if it matters."

Kurt set the cookie bag down. "Eliza, look… I'm sorry if I was rude. I didn't mean to be…" he fumbled for the word. "Distracted. That was unconscionable of me while in your company. I apologize." He sent her an earnest look, the one that rarely failed. "Will you forgive me?"

"You know I will." She surveyed him silently. "I'm not angry, if that's what you're thinking. This…" Eliza picked up the cookie bag and handed it to him. "…is for you to do with what you will." She shrugged mildly. "Share it with whomever you want."

"And that's okay by you?" Kurt asked, deadpan.

Eliza twinkled at him. "I'm not the jealous kind." She nabbed her purse off the floor and extracted her wallet, placing some bills on the table. "This is for my share," she said steadily. "I deducted a small amount for the cookie."

"What?"

"This way, I'm not giving it to you. I simply made the purchase on your behalf!"

"Surely, a woman as intelligent as you doesn't believe in that crazy legend?"

Her forehead crinkled. "The one about being forever bound by true love? Of course not, Kurt!" She returned her wallet to her purse and closed it. "I'm just not taking any chances."

She surprised him by standing to go.

"You're leaving? Already? Our espressos haven't even arrived."

Eliza checked her watch and slipped into the coat she'd draped over the back of her chair. "No time for coffee, sorry. I have to get Misha at two." Misha was the five-year-old son Eliza shared with her ex-husband Yuri, a Russian scientist at the university. She was very guarded in the information she shared about her son, and—in their four years of going out—Kurt had never met him. Though Kurt understood and respected Eliza's decision to protect the boy from unnecessary attachments and disappointments.

When they'd first begun dating, Kurt had repeatedly tried to pick up the bill. Finally, Eliza had asked him to please cut it out. She was perfectly capable of paying for herself. Plus, she preferred things that way. Eliza didn't like feeling indebted to anyone. Kurt just hadn't expected being indebted to her—for some unwanted Christmas cookie.

"Well, thanks for the gift!" he said, scanning the bag.

"You're welcome!" As she turned to go, Eliza cut a cursory glance at Savannah then added with a wink, "Use it wisely."

Chapter Three

Savannah and Olivia finished their meal in relative peace. To divert the subject from her, Savannah had begun inquiring about Olivia's state of marital bliss with Nick. And, once Olivia got started, it seemed there was no stopping her. Nick was wonderful and handsome and kind. And oh! Did she mention? Totally great with animals! They were getting two! Of every kind Olivia wanted. She still had her horse, Blaze, and had just procured a second one for Nick to ride. His name was Jim Boy. Olivia would also like two dogs and two cats. Guinea pigs, maybe. A pair of parrots! And…reindeer? Yes! Those would be fun! Savannah's head was spinning so fast she could barely keep up.

"I'm not sure of reindeer in Christmas Town," she commented merrily, finishing her mimosa. "Although I can see where that works with the theme."

Olivia stewed on this a moment. "Hmm. I guess you're right. They're not exactly indigenous to Tennessee. No matter! Reindeer can certainly wait! And anyway, I can't clutter up the shed with outdoor animal supplies. Where else would I store my extra cookie tins?"

In referring to her shed, Olivia meant the one behind the fixer-upper house on Church Street she and Nick had bought and were refurbishing. It was a cute two-bedroom bungalow with a nice slate patio and a huge backyard. But it hardly had room for a menagerie inside. Especially in light of Olivia's incredibly tricked-out kitchen. She had the most elaborate setup Savannah had seen! With a double wall oven and a free-standing range besides. Which seemed a bit excessive for such a small house.

Ever since meeting Nick, Olivia had been seized by this really weird compulsion to bake treats. Christmas cookies, in particular. And at every time of year! When Savannah arrived for Olivia's summer wedding weekend, her sister had been baking darling little gingerbread people all week long. Coupled with butterscotch brownies and Kentucky bourbon balls, and a whole host of fattening things she'd attempted to foist off on Savannah and the other females in her wedding party at every opportunity. Thank goodness for Savannah's restraint in resisting more than just a tiny sampling. Otherwise, she might not have fit into her bridesmaid dress!

Their waiter appeared to take their dessert orders and Olivia recommended the dark-chocolate-cherry mousse, which the sisters decided to split. They also ordered two cups of regular coffee. As soon as their server stepped away, Savannah noticed an empty seat at Kurt's table. She'd been so enchanted by Olivia's happy babbling, Savannah had completely missed Kurt's pretty lunch partner slipping away. Kurt seemed to be mulling something over as he flagged down his waitress and asked for the check.

Though it really wasn't her business, Savannah couldn't help but wonder about the relationship between Kurt and Eliza. At Olivia's wedding, Kurt had intimated to Savannah that he wasn't seriously seeing anybody, and he clearly hadn't had a woman on his arm. Yet, the atmosphere between Kurt and Eliza had seemed particularly cozy today, as if they'd known each other—and perhaps been intimate—for quite a while.

"You really shouldn't do that," Olivia cautioned quietly. "I mean, stare so blatantly. Sooner or later, he's bound to catch you at it."

Savannah scooted over in her chair and flipped back her hair over her shoulders. She hadn't even realized she'd been doing that. Ogling Kurt Christmas in broad daylight! What on earth was wrong with her?

"He's leaving now anyway," Olivia continued in a whisper as their coffees arrived. They each thanked their waiter then Savannah braved a tiny peek. Kurt was slipping into his overcoat all right and placing that stylish fedora on his head. At that precise moment, Kurt looked up and across the room—and straight at Savannah. Their eyes locked and Savannah flushed. Seconds ticked by as Kurt quizzically tilted his chin to one side, his eyes never leaving hers. And, Kurt Christmas had eyes to die for. Dark chocolate pools teeming with heat…emotion…desire. Savannah felt seriously lightheaded, like he'd engaged her in some sort of trance. Then Kurt abruptly broke contact, turning away, and Savannah's heart pinged.

"Whoa! Ow!" Savannah yelped when she realized she'd spilled coffee in her lap! It was as hot as the dickens, too! She'd been holding her cup and had been about to take a sip when she couldn't resist peering over her shoulder at her long-ago ex. And, now look at her skirt! Thank goodness the linen napkin had absorbed most of the splattered liquid.

"Savannah! Oh!" Olivia leapt to her feet to help, quickly dousing her own napkin in her glass of ice water and handing it to Savannah, who rapidly mopped up the mess. "Are you all right? That must have burned!"

"I think I'm okay," Savannah said, flushing, her mind still on Kurt. She stared down at her skirt as he walked out the door. "I hope it won't stain!" she cried, still working furiously at the mess. Their server saw what had happened and hurried over with a rag and a bottle of seltzer water he'd retrieved from the kitchen.

"We can send it out to get laundered," Olivia assured her. "There's no cleaners here, but a laundry in the next town over makes regular pickups and deliveries to the Christmas Inn. I'm sure Walt won't mind tossing one more item into the lot."

"Great thought, Olivia." And it was, too. This skirt was one of Savannah's absolute favorites. "Thanks!"

Once the commotion resolved, Olivia stared past her at Kurt's empty table. "Looks like Kurt and Eliza have gone."

"Yes," Savannah said quickly, before realizing she was ratting herself out. "Eliza left first, and Kurt only minutes ag—" She cupped a hand to her mouth and Olivia arched an eyebrow.

"No wonder you spilled your coffee," she said.

"It was an innocent mistake."

"Harrumph. I'm sure." Olivia studied something carefully in the distance. "It appears that Kurt's just made one, too."

"What do you mean?"

"He's left a little paper bag behind."

Savannah's heart thudded. "Maybe we can catch him?"

"I'll go!" Olivia said, standing quickly. "You grab the bag and meet me on the porch!"

As Olivia darted into the foyer and toward the front door of the Grand Hotel, Savannah beelined for Kurt's table. She snapped up the bag, giving it a cursory perusal. It carried a gold seal with a pretty little emblem that read: The Christmas Cookie Shop. That was Hannah's place, had to be. The one that everyone kept mentioning. Eliza must have bought something for Kurt there and bestowed it as a gift.

Savannah dashed after her sister, telling their waiter as she passed him in the hall that they'd be right back. Next, she was outdoors on the chilly stoop as cold winds roared down the street, sending dancing snowflakes blowing sideways. Only two people were out and in view. One was a tall, slim older gentleman with silvery hair, walking a Pekingese. He wore a heavy dress coat and a hat, scarf, and gloves, and Savannah thought she recognized him as the minister who'd performed Olivia and Nick's ceremony.

The person barreling toward him from the opposite direction was a short, stout middle-aged woman in a red and black plaid ski vest and bright pink leggings and hiking boots. Her bouncy red curls bobbed up and down beneath her lime green cap as she struggled to hang onto her end of the leash holding a small brown poodle.

"Cocoa! No! Heel!" The tiny beast was pulling his hardest on his lead, evidently in an attempt to sniff noses as quickly as possible with the minister's Pekingese.

"Pastor Wilson!" Olivia called loudly from the top of the stairs. He paused briefly and turned her way.

"Hello, Olivia! How are you dear?"

"Did you see Kurt walking that way?"

"Nobody in that direction, I'm afraid," he said, thumbing over his shoulder. "The weather's getting worse out." He viewed her disapprovingly. "You really should learn to start wearing a coat!"

"We're only out here for a second!" she told him, though Savannah agreed Pastor Wilson had a point. Even though the front porch of the Grand Hotel was covered, it was *freezing* outdoors in the elements!

Olivia rapidly turned her attention on the redheaded woman. "Tilly!"

Tilly glanced her way. "Oh, hi, Olivia!" she said with mild surprise, still huffing and puffing in her effort to restrain her small dog.

"Have you seen Kurt Christmas?"

"Kurt?" Tilly screwed up her plump round face, which held a very pleasant appeal. "No! Can't say that I have!" She smiled Savannah's way. "Hi, there! You must be the sister!" While Tilly had been at Olivia's wedding, so had the entire town, so Savannah hadn't had the chance to meet everybody face to face. She might have if she'd actually stuck around, rather than being lured into sneaking out early. Okay, maybe *lured* was too strong a word. *Coerced*? Wrong. *Invited*? Hmm. *Dared*? Yeah, maybe *dared* was more like it.

"Hello!" Savannah shouted back. "Nice to meet you!"

Olivia turned to her sister with a frown. "That's really weird. Kurt just left here seconds ago." She stared straight ahead of her through the T-intersection and down the street that abutted Main Street. "All the shops on Santa Claus Lane are closed on Sundays," she told Savannah. "So it's unlikely he went down there."

"Well," Savannah said, hugging her arms around herself for warmth. "He certainly couldn't have vanished into thin air!"

Olivia thoughtfully set her chin. "No. It's unlikely he did that."

Kurt unwrapped his scarf in his parents' front hall as his mother scuttled toward him from the kitchen in her high-end leather fashion boots. She wore trim blue jeans and a deep red turtleneck beneath a dark green apron. The apron was one of her favorites because she'd made it herself. It sported a hand-cut felt Christmas tree, adorned with multicolored baby pompoms that seemed to spring to life as she approached. The apron was dusted with flour and there appeared to be some in her hair, as well as on the whimsical Santa hat she typically wore this time of year.

"My dear boy!" Lou cried with outstretched arms. "What a delightful surprise!" The slight woman had layered brown and gold shoulder-length hair and light brown eyes. She was of average height and kept herself fit. Thought not really due to exercise. Kurt's mom mostly worked out by running around Christmas Town and butting into other people's business. Still, she was a good-hearted soul and everyone who knew her loved her. Which basically meant everybody in town, since Lou was the local mayor.

"Is Dad around?" Kurt asked, not spotting Buddy in his customary chair by the fireplace in the living room. This weekend Kurt's childhood home had been transformed into a festive holiday display by the addition of several usual Christmas decorations and the inclusion of two large Christmas trees in the living room and front parlor, which always smelled of peppermint and housed Lou's piano. Kurt was glad to see his mom was busy cooking, therefore unlikely to sit down and attempt tinkling the ivories during this particular visit. Not that Lou was *bad* at playing. She just wasn't particularly *good* either. It was a miracle she managed to give lessons and create successful prodigies from her students.

Lou dusted her hands on her apron. "Your dad's in his workshop," she answered with a grin.

Kurt removed his hat and unbuttoned his coat. "More toys?"

"Not this time!" Lou said pertly. "Buddy's making a drone!"

"A drone?"

"One must keep up with the times." Lou authoritatively lifted a finger. "That's what Nick says. And, you know, Nick…" She dropped her voice conspiratorially. "He has an inside track."

"I'm sure that he does." Kurt chuckled warmly and hung up his things in the coat closet under the stairs. "What are you baking?" He detected a familiar scent wafting toward him from the kitchen. "Gingerbread?"

"Gingerbread *houses*," Lou proclaimed, appearing pleased. "For the church bazaar next Sunday! I plan to auction them off."

"Really?"

"Oh, yes! I've made half a dozen, and they're all quite good—if I say so myself."

"I thought you generally left the gingerbread house making to the grandkids," Kurt said as he followed her into the kitchen.

"Well, yes. But now that Noelle and Joy are in college, they say they think they are too old."

"For gingerbread?" Kurt said. "Never!"

"That's what I think, too," Lou answered. "Sadly, Kyle's becoming reticent about it, as well."

"He is a thirteen-year-old boy, Mom."

She widened her eyes in anticipation so Kurt went on to explain. "He likely has other things on his mind."

"Heavens! What could be more important than preparing for Christmas?"

"Maybe he is preparing, but in ways you don't know."

"Now, you're teasing me," Lou said with a light titter. "Kyle is as good as gold! He's never given Ray a lick of trouble."

Kurt shot his mom a sly smile. "Give him time."

"Shush!" She play-swatted him with her hand then gestured around the expansive breakfast room adjoining the kitchen. One end held a big bay window overlooking the backyard, and the opposite wall contained bookshelves cram-packed with cookbooks. A swinging door to their right led into the dining room, and a well-equipped country kitchen with a gleaming white porcelain farm sink and stainless steal appliances stood to the left. A paneled glass door beyond it connected to the mudroom, which had an exterior door and held the washer and dryer, along with cabinets stuffed with Lou's crafting supplies. "Well?" She beamed proudly, viewing her creation on the large breakfast room table before them. "What do you think?"

Kurt stared at the randomly arranged gingerbread "village," struck by the horror of it all. Nothing appeared fitted together properly and the red icing swirls from the rooftops made them all look like they were flaming! Even the poor gingerbread people standing guard seemed eager to flee. Their huge red and green eyeballs fashioned from holiday taffy made them look like eerily creepy guppies. And those little mouths made out of starlight mints seemed to be calling: *Help! Help!*

"Wow!" Kurt set his hands on his hips, biding for time. "I don't know what to say!" Probably not, *This looks like "The* Nightmare *Before Christmas."* Lou might take offense at that.

"Pretty marvelous, isn't it?" Her smile gleamed. "I did it all myself, you know. Right down to the licorice stripes on the windows." Kurt decided not to mention the fact that the barred windows made the houses look like teeny penitentiaries.

"Gee!"

"And, I'm not done yet!"

"No?" Kurt stared at his mom with trepidation. "What are you adding next?"

She raced to a kitchen counter and returned with two bags of red, green, and white cotton candy. Kurt had no idea where she'd gotten it. Maybe at the candy shop in town, Nutcracker Sweets?

"It's Christmas-colored snow!" Lou proclaimed with glee. "Isn't it *sweet?*"

Kurt nodded numbly. "Extra...unusual! Goodness, Mom! You have really outdone yourself."

"Thanks, son!" She glowingly admired her creation. "So! How much do you think it will bring?"

"Bring?"

"At the auction?"

"Oh, tons! Lots of money for charity, I'm certain." And if it didn't, Kurt would put in a private word with Pastor Wilson to take note of a "phantom bidder." Lou had worked so very hard, Kurt couldn't bear to see her disappointed. He also couldn't make the bazaar as it came at the same time of his affiliated hospital's main holiday event for its medical staff and employees. Kurt should probably mention this to his middle brother, Walt. Walt usually attended the annual Christmas event at the Corner Church, so he could help look after Lou's interests, too. Kurt couldn't one hundred percent count on his dad. Buddy was very well intentioned, but also a tad forgetful sometimes. Particularly now that he'd gotten a little older.

"That's what I'm hoping!" Lou said with a sunny grin.

Chapter Four

Since they'd been unable to locate Kurt, Savannah
and Olivia had held onto his bag so they could decide
what to do with it. One of them would return it to him.
The sisters were simply in a debate over which one of
them that might be. As they finished their dessert at the
Main Street Café, Olivia said, "I wonder what's in the
bag?"

"Obviously, a treat from the Christmas Cookie
Shop," Savannah answered.

"Yes, but which kind?" Olivia asked, curiosity
written in her eyes.

"We really shouldn't peek," Savannah said.
Though she was privately curious as well. "It was a gift
from Eliza to Kurt."

"Yeah, well. Maybe he didn't want it?" Olivia
licked the last bit of chocolate off her spoon and
Savannah grimaced.

"Olivia! Ew, gross!"

Olivia retracted her tongue from the top of her
spoon handle. "What?"

"We're in public, you know."

"Fine!" Olivia rolled her eyes in jest. "I wouldn't want to offend Ms. Manners."

"When did you develop such a thing for sweets, anyway?" Her sister had been extremely athletic in high school, when she eschewed eating unhealthy food. Now, just look at her! She was cookied-out to the max. Plus, she'd mentioned something about really loving chocolate truffles.

Olivia set down her spoon and dabbed her mouth with her napkin. "It came on quite suddenly, soon after I moved to Christmas Town. Then, after Nick arrived? Whoa, Nelly! My cravings went absolutely crazy then!" She paused to glance down at her fit figure. "Gosh! I'm not putting on weight, am I?" She sounded both panicked and horrified.

"It doesn't appear you've gained an ounce," Savannah told her truthfully. "I don't know how you do it! If I ate like you do, I'd be the size of a house. Must be all that horseback riding."

"And, training!"

"Training?"

"Nick's…I…er… Never mind."

Savannah leaned closer. "What's Nick training you to do?"

"Family stuff! Hard to say!"

Oh, no. Not that. "Please don't tell me he's teaching you how to 'talk to animals.'" She said that last part with her hands raised and forming quotation marks with her fingers.

"I already talk to animals, Savannah! Most people do! It's just communication the other way that gets tricky."

Savannah shook her head in wonder. "Whatever works for you guys."

Olivia blinked, apparently offended. "It's not what works, Savannah. It's what's real. There's that, and… Well, other things I can't tell you!"

"North Pole secrets?"

Olivia's cheeks colored brightly. "Maybe."

"Let's make a deal, then." Savannah finished her coffee and put down her cup. "You keep your secrets, and I'll keep mine." She gently patted the brown paper bag on the table between them. "We'll let Kurt keep his secrets, too."

"Not on your life!" Olivia impishly grabbed the bag off the table. "I'll have to tell Hannah!"

"Tell Hannah what?"

"That Eliza's trying to catch Kurt!" Her eyebrows knitted together. "Possibly! All depends on what's in the bag." Before Savannah could stop her, she'd already flipped up the flap and peered inside!

Olivia let out a crisp whistle. Then she met Savannah's eyes. "Well, what do you know? No wonder Kurt left it behind."

"You're not making much sense, Olivia."

"It's a Commitment Cookie!" She handed Savannah the bag. "Go on. Take a look."

Savannah did and saw a pretty heart-shaped cookie inside covered in pale pink icing. The dark red lettering across it read: *Forever Yours.* A sweet aroma wafted toward her. Cinnamon, sugar, gingerbread, with a hint of orange and a whole lot of spice.

"It smells divine. Very pretty, too!"

"It's more than pretty," Olivia confided in a whisper. "Some say it's magic."

Savannah lowered the bag in surprise. "Come on." Sometimes she wondered about Olivia's state of mind. She'd seemed a little loopy since coming to Christmas Town. Then again, it was evident that Olivia was extremely happy here. And, Nick apparently understood her. She understood Nick, too, in ways that Savannah could only guess at. Apart from the animal thing and saying Nick *loves cookies* Olivia never mentioned specifics, but she often hinted that Nick was "extra special—even in his family," whatever that meant.

"I'm serious, Savannah," Olivia contested. "It all connects with Hannah's great-grandmother Lena and the legend attached to the Christmas Cookie Shop."

Savannah folded the bag shut again and laid it on the table while her sister continued.

"Years ago, right after World War I, it seems, Christmas Town was in trouble. Many families had lost sons in the war, other community members were taken by disease, and the meager commerce that had existed here was failing. So, Lena, who'd inherited the O'Hanlon bakery from her folks, decided to do something special for the town. She heard about her cousin's query to a newspaper editor in New York about the factual existence of Santa Claus. He answered the child in print, stating the many reasons we should still have faith in the seemingly impossible."

"That story sounds familiar," Savannah said. "I think I might have heard of it. What was it called?"

"It's popularly known by the editor's often quoted reply in the New York *Sun*, 'Yes, Virginia, there is a Santa Claus.'"

"Oh, yeah! And *that* Virginia—the little girl who asked the question—was related somehow to Hannah's great-grandmother?"

Olivia nodded. "The two of them were distant cousins. In any case! That editorial greatly inspired Lena to attempt to renew Christmas Town's faith."

"In?"

"Goodness... Hope... *Love.*" Olivia grinned winningly. "She baked a certain kind of cookie rumored to uplift the heart and inspire change, in the most marvelous and significant ways."

"But that had to have been years ago."

"It was! After Lena grew older and passed away, her shop eventually went out of business. Hannah inherited the store through her family about four years ago."

"I'm guessing Hannah now bakes Lena's special cookies?"

"She does!" Olivia considered this a moment. "Only, she's tweaked the recipe a bit. Lena offered one variety of Virginia Cookie, but Hannah now sells three: a Charity Cookie, a Clemency Cookie, and a Commitment Cookie, like that one right there," she said, indicating the bag. "The Charity Cookie is decorated with a little white angel and is meant to inspire good works."

"I suppose that's cool," Savannah said. "Can't go wrong with that. What does the Clemency Cookie do?"

"Foster forgiveness."

"Does it look like the charity one?"

"They're all about the same shape and size," Olivia answered. "Only the details are different. Maybe a smidgen of the ingredients, too... But Hannah won't say. The recipe is totally…" She lowered her voice and giggled. "Top secret."

Olivia's green eyes sparkled as she recounted her tale. "The Clemency Cookie has a small green Christmas tree painted on it in icing. And, the Commitment Cookie—"

"Yes, yes… I know." Savannah studied the bag. "What sort of 'commitment' is it supposed to bring about? Marriage?"

"That's happened with many more folks in town than you would guess. Lots of people here credit Lena's legendary Virginia Cookies with inspiring true love between their parents, or grandparents."

Something clicked in Savannah's brain. "Called *Virginia* for the little girl who wrote to the paper, right?"

"Bingo."

"That's a darling story, Olivia, but it's hard to imagine that any of it's true."

"It's part of our town history! Even Buddy says he married Lou on account of a Virginia Cookie!"

Savannah eyed her skeptically. "One of Lena's cookies, you mean?"

"Of course. Hannah wasn't even born then. Her cookies have only been around for a few years, though they've already had an effect!"

"On…?" Savannah raised her eyebrows and Olivia blushed.

"Oh! Not me, naturally. Nick's completely immune."

Savannah resisted the urge to fold her face in her hands. "Because he's extra special."

"Yes!" Olivia answered brightly. "That's why!"

"Then, who?"

"I can't say exactly," Olivia confided sotto voce, "but I do suspect they had some sort of impact on Ben."

"Hannah's brother? Ben Winchester?"

Olivia nodded. "The one who married Sandy."

"What makes you think that?"

"Oh, I don't know." Olivia thoughtfully studied the ceiling. "Sandy just seemed awfully interested in those cookies' effects at the time when they were dating. Not that she and Ben aren't perfect for each other. They are!"

"Well, I'm glad Hannah's made her shop a success."

"She has," Olivia stated confidently. "And her success has benefited all of us. Once she reopened her family's shop, business starting booming all over town. Things improved for me at All Things Christmas, too," she said, referring to her knickknack and curio store. "Before Hannah arrived, visitors were uncommon in Christmas Town. The highway bypass going in diverted the previous stream of incidental tourists to the north, so the town was in a sad state. But, it's been coming back little by little! First, Carter moved here. Then, I did, too…" An idea seemed to hit her and she seized Savannah's hand. "Wouldn't it be awesome if you came to join us?"

"I have come." Savannah blinked, taken aback. "I'm here."

Olivia warmly squeezed her hand. "Not temporarily, sis. I mean, permanently! That would be amazing. Carter would love it so much, too."

"That's so sweet for you to say, Olivia."

"We miss having you around," her sister pressed ahead. "Just imagine how much fun we'd have! It would be like old times."

"Sure. With the two of you picking on me."

"We never picked on you," Olivia protested. "Merely looked after you a bit…"

Savannah laughed sweetly and patted Olivia's hand. "I do wish I lived closer. But Miami—"

"Is so hot and overcrowded," Olivia put in. "Loaded with crime!"

"Olivia."

"We have absolutely zero crime here. Just ask our brother, the sheriff!"

"You, sugar, drive a very hard bargain."

"At least tell me that you'll think about it."

"My job is there."

"Who says you won't find another one here?"

"My consultant contract runs for exactly one month, Olivia."

"Yeah, so?" She smiled encouragingly. "Contracts can be renewed."

Savannah sighed heavily. While she appreciated her sister's kindhearted invitation, she couldn't possibly move to Christmas Town. But it was very sweet of her sister to want her here, and Olivia's sisterly love warmed Savannah's heart. "Speaking of work," she said. "Shouldn't we get busy seeing the hotel?"

"Oh, right!" Olivia snapped to attention, suddenly remembering her mission. "Yes, we probably should. This place used to be run by Lena and her husband, Emmet Winchester, you know."

"Really? How very interesting."

"Emmet took over running the hotel from his parents, just as Lena inherited the bakery from hers."

"So they were both entrepreneurs?"

"Yes!"

"I can't wait to explore the rest of the building," Savannah commented. "From the hotel's façade and the way everything looks in here, the restoration is really fantastic."

"There are working artists' studios upstairs," Olivia told her. "They're closed on Sundays, but we can still peek through their windows, and the original ballroom, which is used for community events, is right across the hall. Joy Christmas has an exhibit on display in there now."

"Walt's daughter?" Savannah recalled briefly meeting the attractive twin and her sister, Noelle, at Olivia's wedding.

"Yes," Olivia answered. "She's away at college, but set up her show when she was home for Thanksgiving. Joy's a very talented artist. Her paintings are all about Christmas. You'll love them, I'm sure."

"No doubt."

As they collected their things and prepared to pay the check, Olivia picked up the cookie bag and attempted to pass it to Savannah. "Here, why don't you hang onto this?"

Savannah withdrew her hand. "Me? Why me?"

"So you can give it to Kurt!"

"Nuh-uh!" Savannah scooted back in her chair. "You give it to him!"

"But I can't," Olivia said, trying to foist the bag off on her again. "You take it!"

"Why can't you?"

"I...er..." Olivia bit into her bottom lip. "Won't be seeing Kurt as soon as you will."

Savannah suspiciously eyed her sister. "And, how do you know that?"

"Because he's coming to help you tomorrow!"

"Help me?" Savannah asked, flummoxed. "Do what?"

"Move boxes."

Savannah narrowed her eyes at Olivia.

"Don't give me that look!" Olivia said, befuddled. "It wasn't my idea. Carter thought it up!"

"Carter?"

"Yeah! He, um...said you couldn't possibly clear out that attic space by yourself."

"I'm not a ninety-eight-pound weakling, Olivia. I work out, you know." While it was true that she'd dropped out of Zumba after the first two weeks, her sister didn't have to know that. Signing up had been such an effort. Plus, she'd shopped for three perfectly coordinated Zumba outfits. Which now occupied her bottom dresser drawer back in Miami.

"Nobody accused you of being out of shape, Savannah. It's just that you're a smaller person, and this is a very big job. You'll know what I mean when you see the fourth floor."

Savannah shot her a haughty stare. "Is Kurt aware that he's been called in as my muscle?"

"Of course, he's aware! And, for the record, no one had to call him in. The moment Carter explained the problem, he volunteered."

Savannah snatched back the cookie bag and sighed. "I thought Kurt had doctoring to do. Doesn't he run the Christmas Town Clinic?"

"Since he started opening on Saturday mornings to accommodate working parents, he now takes Mondays off."

"Peachy!" Savannah said.

"Be nice about it," Olivia cautioned lightly. "And be nice to *him*. You two are bound to be running into each other a lot in Christmas Town; it's probably good for both of you to get used to it." She paused to survey Savannah. "You don't have a problem with it?"

"With Kurt coming by the theater?" she asked breezily, though her pulse was pounding. "Of course not."

Olivia's green eyes sparkled. "It was very kind of him to want to help out."

"I'll be sure to thank him when I return his cookie," Savannah answered sassily.

"Would you like something sweet to go with your coffee?" Lou asked Kurt as they settled in at the dining room table. There was no room in the breakfast room due to Lou's gingerbread project. She'd invited him to stay for a short visit and Kurt had easily agreed. There was something he intended to discuss with his mother, anyway.

"No, thanks. I'm cutting back."

"Why, Kurt? You look as handsome as ever!"

"Spoken like a loving mother."

"Spoken like the truth."

Kurt chuckled good-naturedly. "Now that I'm in my mid-thirties, the metabolism's slowing down."

"Heavens! Not already? You're just a spring chicken!"

"Must set the right example for my patients," Kurt said with a wink. "I can hardly lecture about diet and exercise if I grow a spare tire myself."

"Hmm. Yes. Maybe you should talk to your father about that? His…" Lou hesitated a beat. "Excess baggage, that is."

"You know I've tried." Kurt sipped from his cup, thinking of his jolly dad. He had snowy white hair and whiskers, plump red cheeks, and twinkling blue eyes. Lou had convinced him some time ago to relinquish his pipe smoking, but Buddy still had an insatiable hankering for Christmas cookies.

"He claims it's hereditary," Lou informed him. Kurt knew the Claus and Christmas tie went way back. Although one side of their clan had become much better known than the other, they shared certain things in common, including DNA. Buddy and Nick's dad, Cole, were second cousins, yet they still remarkably resembled each other.

"Nature versus nurture," Kurt mused thoughtfully. "Always a tough call." He astutely viewed his mother. "Have you thought of cutting back on your baking?"

Her dark eyes rounded. "Oh now, Kurt! That hardly seems fair. What would I serve for dessert?"

"Not many people besides the Clauses and the Christmases enjoy dessert after breakfast."

She eyed him carefully. "Speaking of families and heredity… Don't you think you should be getting married soon?"

"Mom."

"It's very important, Kurt! To continue the tradition!"

"You have three sons," he told her reasonably. "I don't see how anything comes down to me?"

"Ray's informed me that he and Meredith don't intend to have any more children."

"Why mess with perfection?" Kurt questioned merrily. "Kyle's pretty great."

Lou nodded in agreement and tapped her chin.

"Walt is done, too," she said seriously. "He has his beautiful twin girls."

"He might remarry."

Lou clapped her hands together at the sunny thought. "Wouldn't that be wonderful?"

"She'd have to be the right sort of woman."

"Naturally."

"And unbelievably special."

"Rose is a tough act to follow," Lou said, mentioning Walt's late wife, who'd died of cancer when Noelle and Joy were only eleven.

"It would be nice for Walt to have company," Kurt concurred. "He's poured his whole life into his girls, but Noelle and Joy are growing up. This is their second year of college."

"I know," Lou agreed. "And, they're both doing so well! Joy will be helping Sandy at her gallery again during her winter break from school and Noelle has an internship, too."

"Oh? What's Noelle up to?"

"Since she wants to be a writer, she's located something at the courthouse."

"The courthouse?" Kurt asked with surprise. "What on earth will she be doing there?"

"Working as the court reporter!"

"That could be a boring job," Kurt commented, thinking there was never anything of note going on in court here. Apart from the occasional traffic summons and young couples eloping to get married... Ben Winchester was the Justice of the Peace, a position that didn't keep him terribly busy. This was why Ben had been able to open his pro-bono law clinic for low-income individuals, in conjunction with the law school at the neighboring university.

"It's not boring when we have Town Council meetings," Lou rebuked. "She'll be taking notes during those, too!"

"I just hope Noelle will have enough to keep her occupied."

"Oh, she will," Lou uttered with confidence. "She's a very industrious girl!"

"When do they get home?"

"The middle of next month."

"It will be great to see them, Mom. I know you're proud of them both."

"Just imagine how precious your baby will be!" Lou had an uncanny twinkle in her eye that scared him. "Smart as a whip, too!"

"It's a little premature to be talking babies when I'm not even seeing anybody."

"What about Eliza Stewart?"

Kurt raised his eyebrows. "Eliza and I are friends. Have been for a while now."

"Exactly my point!" She shot him a mournful look. "Don't you think it's time, dear? Time that you moved on? To something more...solidified?"

"Now, Mom—"

"Sandy says Eliza bought a Commitment Cookie!" Lou burst in with glee.

"Sandy?"

"She dropped by the shop to check on Hannah during her new Virginia Cookie debut. And, there—of all people—stood elegantly pretty Eliza Stewart purchasing one particular gift at the counter!"

Kurt frowned at this, thinking Sandy knew better than to start rumors. Particularly unfounded ones… Although Kurt could understand how things must have looked. Everyone in town had seen him and Eliza together many times, since she was his regular dating partner for formal events. "It's not what you think."

"Kurt, listen to me." Lou pleaded with her eyes. "Take the cookie. Don't say no. I'm not an old woman, but I want to see my children settled. And, I yearn to get to know my grandchildren. All of them! Including yours!"

Kurt stared down at his mother, remembering something. That package from the Christmas Cookie Shop! He'd left it on the table back at the Main Street Café.

"As I'm sure you're aware, Eliza wasn't my first pick for you," Lou prattled on. "She's so staid and formal compared to the rest of us! But, as I got to know her, I came to understand her particular charms. She's intelligent, witty, and very, very pretty!" Lou added with a lilt. "You'll make beautiful children together."

Children? Kurt stood abruptly from his chair, and luckily avoided smacking into the table, which held their nearly full coffee mugs. "Mom, please. Stop!"

"*Ho-ho-ho!* What's going on in here?" Buddy toddled into the room with a cheery grin and bear-hugged his son. "Kurt! What a happy surprise! I didn't know you were stopping by."

"I came to talk to Mom."

"Oh!" Lou shouted in surprise and she and Buddy glanced at each other.

"But you're welcome to listen, too," Kurt told his dad. He turned back to Lou and said, "I'm not here to talk about Eliza."

Lou suddenly paled. "No?"

"I came to see you about Savannah."

Buddy's question rumbled. "Savannah?"

Kurt nodded at him and then at Lou. "You both know she's in town to work on the children's theater. You, Mom, helped bring her here, in fact."

"I know. Of course! I just saw her yesterday, and she's looking very well."

"That's my assessment, too," Kurt answered. "Although I don't want you butting in or making trouble."

"Trouble?" Lou asked, incredulous. "Heavens! Me?"

"Mom, you tend to meddle." Kurt heaved a sigh. "I just don't want you meddling this time."

"But you and Savannah are old news," Buddy said from beside him. "You've told us that yourself several times."

"We are; that's true." Kurt shoved his hands in his pockets. "But, now that Savannah's in Christmas Town, she and I are bound to see each other. Talk now and then. And, if we do…" He gave his mom a stony gaze. "That's our business, okay? I don't want anything going out about it by Santa Mail."

Lou flushed at the intimation she'd immediately blab to the town, which Kurt suspected she'd be inclined to do. He knew his mother very well. Kurt also had the sense that Lou and Savannah's mother, Janet, had had something to do with his and Savannah's teenage break-up years before, though he had no way to confirm it. He would know if his mom were deliberately lying. But if she didn't believe herself to be concealing anything untoward, the truth could be impossible for Kurt to detect.

"I'm glad that Savannah's in Christmas Town, Kurt. She's grown into a fine young woman, and I admire her greatly. I'm also quite fond of her, as a family friend, just as I'm fond of her siblings, Carter and Olivia."

Kurt didn't buy that it was quite the same, but he held his tongue.

"I know you're thinking about that falling out that occurred between Savannah's family and ours, but that was years ago, dear," Lou said adamantly. "We've all gotten over it."

Kurt held her gaze. "Have we, Mom?"

"Yes! Indeed! Janet and I smoothed things over at Carter and Hannah's wedding. It appears that all of us have moved on from that, except—"

"Darling," Buddy cautioned quietly and Lou pursed her lips.

"Except for the two people most affected by it," Kurt finished for her.

Lou started to stand, but Kurt stopped her. "Don't bother. I'll see myself out."

"Kurt, please." Tears pooled in Lou's eyes. "Please don't leave like this."

Kurt sadly hung his head, taking pity on his complicated mother. Though she was imperfect, Kurt understood that in her heart she always meant well, which was why he'd continue to adore her regardless. He walked around the table and gave her shoulders a warm hug.

"I love you, Mom. In spite of what you might have done." His subsequent petition was tender yet firm. "Just don't do anything like that again, all right?"

Then, Kurt kissed the top of her Santa hat, and he was gone.

Chapter Five

Savannah decided to get an early start on her day and arrive at the Grand Hotel before its artists' studios opened at ten. She wanted a chance to walk around the building one more time and get a better feel for the place before considering any remodeling recommendations for the prospective theater.

The fourth floor had once been used as living quarters for the hotel owners. It included a small galley kitchen, a bathroom, and a large living room connected to a dining area, with two shotgun-style bedrooms off to one side. Impressively tall windows afforded lots of natural light. And, a hidden staircase behind a door in the kitchen led down to the restaurant's kitchen on the entry level! A small service elevator had been installed beside it, which granted access to every floor, making each handicap accessible. All in all, it was a cool space with lots of historic touches and phenomenal promise. Even if it *was* packed to the gills with mounds and mounds of boxed donations that needed to be sorted through and organized.

Olivia had asked for Savannah's suggestions on how to best convert the former apartment into a theater, and whether she thought any walls needed to be moved. Savannah had said she'd study it and get back to her. Once she had a general plan, Olivia recommended that Savannah consult with Nick, as he was the architect in charge of the upgrade.

Nick had spearheaded the remodeling of the Grand Hotel the previous year, and Olivia, who'd had experience as an interior designer, had worked with him on the project. Apart from the hotel's fabulous restoration, another product of their close collaboration had been them dating and falling in love.

"Welcome to Christmas Town, Savannah!" Savannah looked behind her where she stood in line at Jolly Bean Java. The quaint coffee shop had sleek metallic stools facing a high counter and was filled with café tables, packed with early morning customers. The large picture window overlooking the street showcased Olivia's store, All Things Christmas, across the road.

"Well hi, Nick!" she told her brother-in-law as they exchanged hugs. "I was just thinking about you!"

"All good things, I hope?" Nick gave a wry smile and his blue eyes twinkled. He was dark-haired and buff, and very handsome. Nick was also extremely sunny-natured. It was easy to see why Olivia had fallen in love with him.

"Yes, of course!" Savannah returned cheerfully. The line inched forward and they moved a little closer to the counter. The fellow working behind it was an attractive young guy in his late teens or early twenties with smoky gray eyes and nearly black hair secured behind him in a short ponytail. His nametag identified him as Devon, and Savannah suspected this was the guy Olivia had told her about.

His parents owned South Pole Pottery and Devon apparently was a woodworker. Some of the small furniture items he'd made were available for sale in Olivia's shop, and Devon now occupied the apartment above it. Prior to marrying Nick, Olivia had lived there. They'd kept the property as an investment. Although they charged Devon very little rent, he helped out in other ways by making handyman repairs throughout the building and conscientiously clearing the snow from the sidewalk, both during and after snowstorms.

Olivia felt better knowing someone was around to watch over All Things Christmas after hours. In return, she'd allowed Devon to set up a small workshop on one side of her storeroom, with the condition that he'd only undertake noisy projects when her business was closed. Devon was also supposedly involved with the younger of Walt Christmas's twins, Joy.

"I was contemplating the Grand Hotel and ways to repurpose the space on the fourth floor," Savannah said to Nick.

"It will be wonderful to have a children's theater there," Nick answered. "Olivia's so glad you said yes." His smile sparkled. "All of us are." As they scooted another few paces forward, he asked her, "Any thoughts yet?"

Savannah laughed in reply. "Olivia only showed it to me yesterday, but the ideas are starting to percolate, yes."

"Great!"

"I'll know more later in the week," she told him. "Will you have any time on Wednesday or Thursday to do a walk-through with me? I'd like to get your take on what's possible —structurally and all that. I know it's a very old building."

"I'll take a look at my schedule when I get to my office and have Sara give you a call," he said, mentioning his administrative assistant. Savannah was aware that Nick rented a small office on the second floor above the Holiday Bank. Since the community was undergoing a commercial renaissance of sorts, with businesses booming and tourism on the rise, several of the older buildings in town were benefiting from cosmetic upgrades. His credentials as a restoration architect made Nick the perfect professional to tackle these jobs.

Nick's work kept him busy and happy, according to Olivia, and Nick was grateful to be able to set his own hours. Particularly as certain pressing family matters took him out of town occasionally to where his folks and grandparents lived in Canada.

"Thanks, Nick!" Savannah said, seeing it was her turn to order. "I'd appreciate that." She set her gaze on Devon and he gave a pleasant smile.

"What can I get you today?"

"What's your highest-octane coffee drink?" Savannah definitely needed the caffeine buzz this morning. She'd had such a restless night stewing over that whole Virginia Cookie thing, and her charge from Olivia to return the Commitment Cookie to Kurt. Not that she was nervous about seeing him again. Alone. No, no! Not in the least! After all, Savannah had seen Kurt yesterday, and done just fine with it... Sort of... If you didn't count her sweaty palms, the spilt coffee, or the way her cheeks had flamed each time he'd looked her way.

Devon shook his head with a chuckle. "That would be our Christmas Mud Mocha."

"What's in it?" Savannah asked him.

"Two shots of espresso, an ounce of peppermint syrup, and a whole lot of cocoa."

"Don't forget the whipped cream!" Nick added helpfully from behind her.

"And, white chocolate shavings on top," Devon replied as an additional temptation.

Savannah adored white chocolate, and cocoa and peppermint! And, the double-hit of espresso sounded spot on. So, she grinned brightly at the barista and said, "Sold!"

A little while later, Savannah let herself into the Grand Hotel through its enormous front door. With the restaurant closed, a hushed quiet filled the cavernous hall. The elegant curved staircase led to the upper levels and the doors to the big ballroom were swung open to Savannah's right. She tiptoed into the space, feeling as if she were entering an enchanted realm. The ornate central chandelier dripped with delicate shimmering crystals that sparkled in the morning light beaming in through the windows. The snow had stopped about the time Savannah exited Jolly Bean Java, but the dark clouds moving in promised more flurries in the hours ahead.

There was no furniture in this room as it had been cleared for dancing, and the polished oak floors that appeared to be original to the building gleamed beneath her. Savannah took two sweeping turns around the room and did a simple pirouette. "Don't mind if I do!"

she said, holding out a hand to her imaginary dance partner as she carried her coffee cup in the other. Savannah did one more tiny turn and then stopped herself with a giggle, when she caught her reflection in the gorgeous old mirror in a gold frame hanging over the fancy fireplace.

How silly she would have looked if someone had walked in! And if that someone had been Kurt Christmas... Savannah's cheeks heated just at the thought. She wondered if Kurt would bring Eliza Stewart to the Christmas Town Ball, and guessed that he probably would. Though the notion shouldn't have upset her, in a way down deep part of her soul it did. But it was ridiculous for Savannah to care about who Kurt dated. It wasn't like he was *her* boyfriend. Not even close. Which was good, and Savannah planned to keep it that way. Though it seemed Eliza was already doing that particular job for her, Savannah thought glumly, taking another look around.

Lovely Christmas scenes in matching frames were expertly arranged in an artistic array, dotting the perimeter of the room. These were all part of the holiday show curated by Joy Christmas. Savannah wholeheartedly agreed with Olivia that Joy was incredibly talented, and felt glad for the teen that she'd found her true calling at such a young age. She'd apparently become quite interested in painting during her final year of high school, and Sandy, as an artist herself and the owner of the Snow Globe Gallery, had taken Joy under her wing, offering her an internship there.

Savannah stared at the large wall mural at the far end of the room that was partially cloaked in morning shadows. Upon drawing closer, she saw it was a fanciful rendering of an old-timey Santa Claus and his missus, dancing together sweetly beside a twinkling Christmas tree. Savannah wondered who had done the work, because it was exceptionally good, and the Clauses were so life-like. Almost familiar, in an odd sort of way... Savannah brought her hand to her chin, studying the mural a moment longer. While Joy's work was top-notch, it didn't have the seasoned professionalism of this piece, which left Savannah suspecting that the artist had been Sandy.

A set of doors beside the mural opened into another part of the hotel that had once been a parlor. It abutted the library at the back of the building, and during the hotel's restoration both rooms had been joined together. Now, this larger—yet still cozy—area could be used for smaller events or meetings. Unlike the ballroom, it was carpeted with expensive-looking oriental rugs and filled with comfortable antique-style furniture arranged in various seating groups. There was a huge gas fireplace at either end of the room on the outside wall and a built-in bar in the rear corner overlooking the property's backyard, a portion of which had been converted to gravel parking spaces.

The bar was complete with a sink and a small bank of refrigerators beneath its drink mixing station, two of which were actually cooling compartments for keeping white wines chilled. A high marble countertop divided the bar service section from the rest of the room, and provided a place for the bartender to set down drinks. Olivia said the bar would be open for the first time on Christmas Eve during the first annual Christmas Town Ball. Proceeds from the event would go to the Lena

Winchester Good Works Memorial Fund to further
benefit the community.

Savannah retraced her steps and left the ballroom
with a contented sigh. It was so cool that Nick and
Olivia had been able to bring this historic building back
to life by restoring its innate charms. The glass-paneled
doors to the Main Street Café were closed and the lights
were turned off inside. Savannah saw from a sign on
the door that the bistro was open from eleven to three
each day, hosting a special brunch with live music on
Sundays. Olivia had mentioned that its kitchen facilities
were available to caterers for use during community
gatherings hosted in the ballroom. This was the leasing
arrangement the Town Council had made with the new
restaurant owners, and the Main Street Café was brand
new! It had opened for business at the beginning of
November and was a smash hit already.

Savannah climbed the fantastic old staircase, her
hand gliding along the smooth mahogany banister
railing. She loved every one of the artists' studios
upstairs. There were six occupied on the second floor
and four on the third, with two studios remaining
vacant. There was one person who made jewelry,
another who crafted wood bowls…a weaver, a
printmaker, a book art creator, a textile designer, a
photographer, and a musician who made stringed
instruments…and even a toymaker, and another
talented individual who created puppets!

The Town Council was taking its time in awarding
artists' grants for individuals to fill the last two empty
studios. Olivia shared that they wanted to be judicious
about who they juried in, while making certain each
person's work reflected the local flavor of the

community: both Christmas Town in particular and greater East Tennessee at large. So far, their picks had proven phenomenally successful.

The new studios were a tremendous draw for tourists, many of whom got lured here due to the legend surrounding Hannah's famous cookies at the Christmas Cookie Shop. There were plenty of other fun places to shop in town as well. Apart from Olivia's store and Sandy's gallery, there was the well-stocked Elf Shelf Bookshop, Yuletide Cards and Gifts, South Pole Pottery…the Holly and the Ivy home goods store…Mystic Magi, which sold incense, crystals, and oils, and naturally, the one and only Nutcracker Sweets! Savannah had delved into the box of chocolate truffles from there that Lou and Sandy had brought her, and found them absolutely divine.

Savannah reached the fourth floor and unlocked the apartment door with the second of the two keys Olivia had given her. It was a promising space with large windows and high ceilings, but huge cardboard boxes were piled up everywhere. According to Olivia, they were loaded with donations to the new theater project by Christmas Town's citizens. Once word had gotten out about the planned endeavor, folks had risen to the occasion by contributing myriad interesting and practical gifts.

People dropped items off at the courthouse by the bagful, until both Carter's sheriff's office and Ben's courtroom upstairs were overflowing with the townsfolk's warmhearted generosity. Some brought costumes; others supplied props. Sugar Plum Feed Supply donated sound equipment and stage lighting. Buddy Christmas built a foldable puppet show stage that could be easily broken down, transported, then reassembled. And, Pastor Wilson from the Corner Church personally delivered eighty-nine folding chairs in his old pickup truck! As the church had purchased new chairs as part of its Fellowship Hall redesign, the older ones were no longer needed. Yet, they were still sturdy and in good condition.

Eventually, both Carter and Ben decided that something had to be done about these wonderful *contributions to the arts*—and soon. So, they'd had things boxed up, and moved to the Grand Hotel's fourth floor until Savannah arrived and could decide what to do with them. The only trouble was, Tilly and Lou had volunteered to pack the boxes, and unfortunately none of them had gotten labeled... Which meant Savannah was going to need to open every one and peek inside. *Oh well*, she decided optimistically. *That's one way to jump in and get organized!*

Savannah glanced around at the heaps and heaps of stuff, thinking maybe it wasn't such a bad idea that Kurt was coming over. Some very heavy boxes were piled up high, and she was afraid to try to move them, lest a cardboard tower fall over, breaking something delicate inside. For now, she would leave the tall stacks alone and focus her energy on the short stacks with smaller boxes she could easily manage. Olivia said that the Christmas brothers, Ray, Walt, and Kurt, had helped Ben and Carter with moving these things from the courthouse to the Grand Hotel, and it was easy to guess that was true. Since all of those men stood right around six feet and maybe a little over, these gigantic cardboard mountains probably looked like teeny little molehills to them.

Chapter Six

Savannah was on her twelfth box and her back ached from bending over. Her finds, however, were outstanding. She'd dumped several items from the first few boxes on the floor so she could begin to organize. Costumes would go in one pile, props would go over there—back into those empty boxes, and anything electrical would be left out so it could be repackaged and stored more carefully. Savannah intended to label everything, as well. Since the hotel was too old to have built-in closets, she'd need to purchase a large wardrobe or two, so she'd have a place to hang the clothing. She could ask Olivia if there was discretionary money in the budget for that kind of furniture, but Savannah suspected it wouldn't be an issue.

The next box she opened held a happy surprise: marionette puppets on strings! And, they were holiday puppets, too! Santa in his sleigh and a whole team of individual reindeer… She shuffled carefully through the box and counted. Yep, there seemed to be eight of them. But where was poor Rudolph?

Savannah lifted a reindeer puppet out of the box and gently untangled its strings. Its wobbly reindeer legs with big clunky hooves were so cute! And, its little reindeer smile and big, bright eyes—delightful! Savannah stood up straight and gave the marionette a go, helping it walk across the hardwood floor. *Clip-clop, clip-clop, clip-clop*. Savannah giggled like a gleeful child. Oh, these puppets were fun!

"That one's name is Cupid."

Savannah looked up with a jolt to find Kurt standing in the doorway dressed in an open overcoat and holding his fedora. "How do you know?"

Kurt twinkled in her direction. "There's a name tag around his neck."

Savannah laughed in surprise when she realized it was true. She'd been so busy playing she hadn't even noticed. She peered down in the box, seeing the others also wore collars with names on them.

"Well, I think he's darling." She scooped the puppet up in her hands and carried it over to Kurt. "What do you think?"

"Precious, yes." But his eyes were on her.

"I was talking about the puppet, Kurt."

"I was, too," he lied.

Kurt glanced around the room and the mess Savannah had made. "I can see you're settling in."

"Getting organized is more like it. I'm also taking stock of what we have."

Kurt strolled toward the yellow legal pad resting on the top of a two-box stack and picked it up, leafing through it. "Wow. You've catalogued all these donations already?"

Savannah nodded. "I'm so astounded by everyone's generosity. I really thought part of my job would be procuring things to help establish the theater, but it appears that half of my work's been done for me!"

Kurt's gaze landed on a bowling ball in the corner. "No wonder some of these boxes were so heavy! Who donated the bowling ball?"

"No idea," Savannah said. "But I'm sure there will be a way to use it. Nothing here will go to waste."

"You always were a resourceful person."

"Kurt, I—" He met her eyes and Savannah's heart fluttered. "What I mean is, thanks for coming here to help."

"I don't mind," he told her. "I've got a few extra hours this morning."

"Still, it was very nice of you to volunteer. Particularly after…" Savannah hung her head with a blush and gave a small shrug. "You know."

"Your running out on me?" Kurt blatantly asked. When she looked up, he continued smoothly. "No worries. It happens to me all the time."

"Does *not*."

"That's how I got my nickname, *Love 'im—and leave 'im—Kurt.*"

Savannah resisted a grin. "Stop!"

"What?" he barreled ahead. "Haven't you heard the one about the downtrodden Christmas Town doctor?"

The corners of her mouth twitched harder. "You are one big tease."

Kurt drew his hand to his chest and laid it on thick. "He can cure everything except for his own lonely heart."

"Lonely? You?"

"Every *single* weekend night."

Savannah burst out laughing. "Yeah, Kurt. *Right.*"

Kurt placed his fedora on an unopened box and slipped out of his coat. Even though it was his day off, he was dressed very nicely in navy blue chinos and a gray pullover sweater. Then again, Kurt always dressed well. This was the new Kurt, the grown-up one. As a teen, he'd worn nothing but T-shirts and jeans.

"How's James?" he asked casually, clearly having heard that Savannah and James had gotten back together. Which they had done… Exactly six weeks before Savannah broke it off again. Not that the sorry state of her tumultuous love life was any of Kurt's business. If he was nervy enough to ask, she intended to return the favor by inquiring about his.

Savannah stood up a little straighter, cuddling Cupid in her arms. "How's Eliza?"

Kurt pursed his lips to repress a smile. "Just dandy. Why?"

The mention of Eliza jogged Savannah's memory. The cookie! She'd better give it to him now, before she forgot. "Hold that thought!" Savannah said, passing Cupid to Kurt. "And er…here! Please hold this! I don't want to tangle up his strings."

"Where are you going?" he asked when she darted away from him.

"The kitchen!" Savannah shouted. "I'll be right back!"

Savannah located the Christmas Cookie Shop bag on the counter and returned in record time. To her amazement, it didn't appear that Kurt had moved a muscle. "Why are you standing so still?" she asked him.

"Shh…" He cast a cursory glance at Cupid. "Baby's sleeping."

"Arrgh! Give him to me," Savannah said. "Here, let's trade." She held out his cookie bag and Kurt's forehead rose.

"What's that?"

"Your cookie! You left it behind at the Main Street—"

"First off," Kurt interrupted. "The cookie's not mine."

"Oh yes, it is, Kurt," Savannah insisted. "I saw Eliza Stewart give it to you. Olivia and I both did."

"I didn't realize we had an audience." He viewed Savannah carefully and she felt her color deepen.

"I couldn't help but look! Olivia was…uh…pointing something out on that side of the room!"

"Me?"

Savannah blinked hard. "Not you, you big goof! The um…er…new crown molding!"

"Crown molding?" Kurt asked skeptically. "But I thought that was original? Nearly two hundred years old?"

"That's what Olivia said!" Savannah fibbed. "And it looks fantastic! Really great! Uh-huh! Didn't Nick do an awesome job?"

"On the restoration?" he asked, looking like he was trying hard to follow her convoluted conversation. "Yeah, sure. The best."

"That's what I think, too! I'm so excited to get his input on this space. Now, you just give me that…" She shifted the cookie bag in her hand and gently pried Cupid out of Kurt's grasp. After she laid the marionette down on the box holding the legal pad, Savannah said,

"And, I'll give you—" She held out the bag and Kurt took a giant step backwards.

"No, thanks! Not today!"

"Not today?" Savannah stared at him, flummoxed. "Then, when?"

"Maybe never. I don't know. I don't really eat sweets, Savannah."

"Everybody eats sweets."

"Not me."

"Liar."

"That's a bit unfair."

"When's the last time you had ice cream?" Savannah challenged.

"Nineteen ninety-six…?"

"Candy—of any kind?"

"I can't think that far back."

"Ate dessert?"

Kurt shook his head. "Never touch it."

"Kurt Christmas, I saw you eat a piece of wedding cake."

"Did you?" he asked blithely. "Where?"

"At Olivia's wedding!"

"That was different. I had to."

"Why?"

"Olivia baked the cake herself. I didn't want to hurt her feelings."

Savannah harrumphed and attempted to pass him the bag again. "Well, like it or not, this is yours. You can take it and give it away to somebody else if you don't want it."

"That's a very good idea, Savannah."

Finally, the man was making sense. "Great." She let out a little puff of air. "Here!" She handed Kurt the bag and he took it, then he immediately handed it back to her.

"What are you doing?" she practically screamed.

Kurt shrugged mildly. "Doing just as you advised. Giving it to someone else."

"What if I don't want it?"

"Don't tell me that you don't like sweets?"

Savannah fumed.

"Because just yesterday afternoon I saw you order chocolate mousse."

Savannah arched an eyebrow. "I didn't realize I had an audience."

"I was studying the crown molding," Kurt teased. "On your side of the room."

"You know you make me crazy."

"That goes both ways."

Savannah stared down at the cookie shop bag, recalling Olivia's wild story about Hannah's cookies and their magic. Not that she *really* believed in such things. But, still. "You probably shouldn't have given this to me."

"I didn't. I just gave it back."

"No, *I* gave it back to *you.*"

"Then we're equally culpable."

Savannah threw up her hands. "Fine! I'll keep the stupid cookie. It's not like there's anything to that silly legend, anyway."

"I'm sure you're right," Kurt agreed. "Probably not."

Kurt stared at her and Savannah stared back—extra hard, finally forcing him to look away.

He scanned the cluttered room then casually addressed Savannah. "So! Are you ready for me to move some boxes?"

Savannah shot him an irritated grin and laid the cookie bag down beside Cupid.

"Sure! Why not?"

An hour and fifteen minutes later, Savannah surveyed the decluttered room. With Kurt's help, she'd been able to open and label all the boxes. Savannah was relieved to find that a number of them were actually more organized than she'd first thought. At least they seemed to be categorized, albeit some of them oddly. Like, by color, for example, rather than type. The "white box" held everything from an angel costume to an occasional sofa pillow shaped like a snowflake...a feather duster...and a plastic wedge of fake Swiss cheese.

There were several more boxes she still had to go through, but she'd asked Kurt to move those to the back bedroom where she could deal with them later. She didn't want to detain him any longer than she had to. He'd infuriated her with that business about the cookie, and made her even madder by daring to look so good after all this time. Savannah needed to put Kurt out of her mind and forget him. Really, she did.

James and she were a much better fit. They understood each other and things worked well—when he was actually in town and they were together. Sometimes Savannah wondered if James didn't take some of those trips on purpose. She really couldn't fault him for the mission trips to help needy children abroad, but some of those conferences and meetings he went to…? Savannah just didn't know. Being in Miami tended to make James grumpy. Then, he took his grumpiness out on her. But, things would change! James was basically a good man. Just look at all the good he did for his pediatric patients around the world! No man could hold a candle to that. Not even…

"Savannah?"

"Huh? Yeah?" Savannah turned to find Kurt staring her and realized she'd been standing there meditating on the hunk of fake Swiss cheese.

"Are you all right?"

"Yeah. Why?"

"You just looked a little far away, that's all."

"I was, and I'm sorry."

"Work worries back in Miami?" Kurt guessed.

"Something like that."

"I'm sure you're an excellent counselor."

"I try my best, but some days I fall short," Savannah admitted softly.

Kurt laid his hand on her arm. "Some days we all fall short."

Savannah's smile trembled. "Not the lonely-hearted doctor?"

"Yep. Even me."

"Why are you being so nice to me?" she asked, feeling as if she didn't deserve it.

"I don't know." Kurt shrugged. "Force of habit?"

"That Eliza Stewart is a lucky woman," Savannah told him. "You might have started out a little rough, but you've grown into a very nice guy."

Kurt chuckled at this. "Now, that's a back-handed compliment if I ever heard one."

"I didn't mean it in a bad way."

Kurt fondly squeezed her arm and released it. "I know you didn't."

He looked back over his shoulder toward the main living area. "Need any more help around here?"

"Not today," she answered kindly. "You've done way enough. Thanks so much, Kurt."

"My pleasure, Savannah."

He strode into the other room and picked up his hat and coat. As he walked to the door, Kurt turned toward her. "Good luck sorting things out."

"I'll probably have things better organized by the end of the week."

Kurt placed his hat on his head then said before leaving, "I wasn't talking about around here."

Chapter Seven

A few hours later, Kurt sat at his desk in his office at the Christmas Town Clinic. Though it was closed on Mondays, he often came in when things were quiet to catch up on paperwork. Since it was Christmas Town and it was snowing—more heavily than ever this afternoon—he hadn't bothered to lock the front door. He was so engrossed in his charts, he didn't even hear the entry bell chime, which it must have done minutes ago. Because now his buddy Carter stood rapping at Kurt's open office door.

"Mind if I come in?" Carter was dressed in his sheriff's uniform and was obviously out on patrol.

Kurt grinned broadly and gestured to the chair in front him. "Slow day?"

Carter removed his coat and hat and took a seat. "A whole lot slower than Saturday. That's for sure."

"I heard Hannah sold out of those Virginia Cookies again," Kurt commented.

"The commitment kind were the first to go," Carter said with a chuckle. "A little bird told me that Eliza Stewart bought one."

Kurt thoughtfully stroked his chin, suspecting Carter referred to either Sandy or Hannah. "Was that 'little bird' a blonde or a brunette?"

"I can't rightly recall," Carter fibbed.

"Well, whatever she told you, I'm afraid she was mistaken."

Carter opened his mouth to speak, but Kurt silenced him by plowing ahead,

"Eliza might have purchased a cookie, but it wasn't for the reasons you obviously think."

"And those reasons would be…?" Carter asked leadingly.

"That Eliza was putting the moves on me—for a more permanent relationship." Kurt winked at his friend. "Didn't happen."

Carter's jaw dropped. Kurt rarely saw him surprised yet at the moment he appeared stunned. "Eliza's seeing someone else?"

"Wouldn't doubt it," Kurt said unconcernedly.

"So, she didn't give the cookie to you?"

"Oh, Eliza gave me the Commitment Cookie all right."

"But, you just said—?"

"She just didn't intend for me to keep it. She wanted me to give it to someone else."

"That was magnanimous of her."

"Eliza and I have an understanding."

Carter seemed to be puzzling this out. "That's what you've said…"

"In any case," Kurt continued. "It hardly matters now. I don't have the cookie anymore."

"No?" Carter set his elbows on his knees and leaned forward, intrigued. "Who did you give it to?"

Kurt shuffled some files on his desk, avoiding Carter's gaze. "Somebody who didn't want it, either."

Carter sat back in his chair and hooted. "You know, that's not how those Virginia Cookies are supposed to work. People come clamoring from all around just to try them. They're in incredibly high demand, *and* in short supply."

"If you're thinking that Hannah might want this one back—" Kurt began before Carter stopped him.

"Don't you dare!" Carter spouted jovially. "Hannah would have my head if I told her people were fighting over *not* keeping her cookies."

"Why would Hannah be mad at you?"

"Ever hear of shooting the messenger?"

"Yeah? So?"

"So, I'm not planning to be the party to deliver that sort of news." He scrutinized his friend. "Well? Are you going to tell me who you dumped your cookie on, or am I going to have to pry it out of you?"

"I can tell you, but you might not like it," Kurt said. "Although, it wasn't completely my fault." Kurt met Carter's eyes. "Eliza gave me the cookie yesterday during brunch at the Main Street Café. Unfortunately, my mind was on something else and I—"

"Hang on." Carter seemed to be putting something together. "Didn't Savannah go there yesterday? For brunch with Olivia?"

Kurt blinked hard, feeling caught out. "You know...now that you mention it? I believe that she did!"

Carter blanched. "I can't believe it."

"Now, Carter, don't jump to conclusions."

"You gave my sister a Commitment Cookie?"

"No! The other way around! Initially, anyhow." Kurt drew in a deep breath. "Listen, man. Here's what happened. I honestly forgot and left the cookie bag behind on the table. Savannah picked it up and held onto it, so she could return it to me this morning."

"So, Savannah gave the cookie to you?"

"Sure!" Kurt gave an impish grin. "Only I gave it right back to her."

Carter massaged his temples. "Oh boy, the two of you are in trouble now."

"I don't see how?" Kurt replied. "Last time I checked, Savannah already had a boyfriend: James Peterson."

"Well, pal," Carter said with a grin. "Your information's outdated."

Kurt slapped his desk then muttered to himself, "So *that's* what she was hiding."

"Savannah didn't want you to know?" Carter asked, perplexed.

"Apparently not. At least, she didn't tell me."

"Then, I'm sure she has her reasons."

Kurt pulled himself out of his fog. "Reasons. Right." He hazarded a guess. "Like not wanting me to know she's available?"

"Why?" Carter teased. "Were you hitting on her?"

"I don't hit on women," Kurt stated confidently. "I just sit back and wait for them to hit on me…"

"Watch it. That's my baby sister you're talking about."

"Yes, hmm… Which makes me wonder why you suggested I go by to help her this morning when you clearly knew she and James were broken up?"

"I…uh…" Carter cleared his throat. "*Did* know that, sure. That's what I said."

"And?" Kurt stared at him expectantly.

"And, nothing. Besides, I didn't *suggest* you go. When you heard Savannah might need help you volunteered."

"Yet somehow you knew that I would." Kurt's forehead rose. "I thought you were against me and your sister being together?"

"I was," Carter told him. "Strongly opposed. But that was back when you were kids, and getting yourselves into trouble."

"Grown-ups can get into trouble, too," Kurt bantered.

"The difference now is that you're both old enough to make up your own minds."

"What is this? Guilt talking?"

"I don't know." Carter's shoulders sagged. "Maybe a little."

"Look Carter, you may have ratted on me and Savannah at the beach, but I've never held you accountable for our break-up. There were…" Kurt thought secretly of his mom and of Carter's mother, Janet. "Other players involved." He squarely met Carter's eyes. "Savannah never got any of my letters, did you know that?"

"You sent letters?" Carter asked, evidently surprised.

"Dozens, yes."

"Why didn't you call, then, after she wrote you?"

Kurt sadly shook his head. "I didn't get her letters, either."

"That stinks."

"I know."

Carter viewed Kurt sympathetically. "Both of you must have believed—"

"We did."

"Man oh man." Carter ran a hand through his hair and heaved a breath. "Savannah wasn't allowed to use the Internet much then either. My parents had her on a monitored account."

Kurt pursed his lips. "That's why my e-mails bounced back as spam. At the time, I thought Savannah had blocked me."

"She wouldn't have done that."

"I didn't know." Kurt shared a pained look. "Couldn't fathom at the time what Savannah would and wouldn't do." He gave a melancholy laugh. "I suppose I still haven't figured her out."

"At least now you have time."

When Kurt stared at him in surprise, Carter added, "She's here for a month, Kurt. This is your chance. As your friend, I'm urging you to take it."

"As my friend? Huh." He cautiously studied Carter. "What happened to the protective big brother?"

"He's still here, you better believe it."

"Then, why…?"

"I'm not just thinking of you," Carter told him evenly. "I'm also concerned for Savannah."

"Concerned?" Kurt said, as worry consumed him. "There's not something wrong?"

"I don't know about wrong," Carter answered frankly. "But something hasn't been right with Savannah for quite some time. And, truthfully…? I think it has something to do with you."

"Me?"

"She's still hung up on you, bro," Carter answered hoarsely. "And this time?" He held up his hands as he stood to go. "I'm not getting in anybody's way. Whatever happens—or doesn't—is as it should be. Up to the two of you."

Savannah busied herself with further organizing the theater donations to keep her mind off Kurt. The more focused she remained on the task at hand, the less time she had to think about the handsome dark-eyed doctor. While she'd greatly appreciated his help with the heavy lifting, being around Kurt had also been hard. It was too easy to fall back into that casual way of being with him. The two of them didn't even have to try. They just somehow effortlessly fit together. And, yet... Kurt was with Eliza now, and there were things about Savannah Kurt didn't know. Things that would probably make a difference in the way he felt about her.

Trying to recapture their past was like going down a rabbit hole that grew deeper and deeper as time went on. Savannah couldn't thrust herself into that topsy-turvy world. Nor did she want to drag Kurt down with her.

"Savannah! Oh!"

Savannah straightened with alarm, seeing she'd nearly rammed her shopping cart into Sandy's! They were both at the Merry Market, where Savannah was picking up groceries and Sandy had apparently gone in pursuit of diapers for her twins. She had two cute toddler girls with big blue eyes and curly blond hair in her cart.

The one with a serious expression on her face rode in the baby seat in the front of the cart. She wore a little green dress dotted with Christmas trees and green leggings, and studiously sucked on the pacifier in her mouth as if she were contemplating some earth-shattering problem.

The other child seated in the back of the buggy, amid cereal boxes and clear bags of fresh produce, sported a similar outfit, which was red and bedecked with tiny candy canes. She wore a sunny smile exposing a few toddler teeth, and gurgled contentedly as she played with the groceries packed in around her, lifting and rattling the various items within her chubby-armed reach. Two enormous packages of disposable diapers were crammed onto the low shelf beneath the buggy's basket.

"Sandy," Savannah said, abashed. "I'm so sorry! I didn't see you when I came around the corner."

Sandy smiled pleasantly. "It's all right. No harm done!" She glanced happily at her twins and then at Savannah. "I don't believe you've met my girls. This is Holly," she said, nodding toward the one dressed in green. "And, that's Rose!" she added, grinning at the other child.

"Hi, girls," Savannah said sweetly. "It's nice to meet you."

She turned her attention on Sandy. "They're every bit as darling as I've heard."

"Well, thank you," Sandy answered, understandably pleased. "They're lots of fun!" Then she lowered her voice and leaned toward Savannah, speaking in a whisper. "Most days."

Savannah giggled at this, only able to imagine the challenges presented by a set of twins. Just as she thought this, a box of breakfast cereal seemed to levitate out of the shopping basket. *But that's crazy! Impossible!* Savannah spun quickly on Sandy. "Did you see—?"

"Oh, Rose!" Sandy cried with dismay, as a steady stream of dry cereal tumbled out of the box and onto the floor. "Not again!"

A split second later, the open and newly emptied box crashed down on top of the cereal mound, sending a multitude of minute round balls rolling in all directions.

Holly spat the pacifier from her mouth and began wailing. At the same time, Rose chortled with glee and clapped together her tiny hands.

"Wow," Savannah said, taken aback by what she'd seen. "Here! Let me help with that." She bent down quickly and began scooping up the runaway cereal balls with her hands. Then Savannah glanced around, realizing she had nowhere to put them.

"In the box!" Sandy said, picking up the cereal box and holding it open. But, before she did that, she forcefully popped Holly's pacifier back in the child's mouth. It seemed to work like a charm in stopping the baby from crying. "I plan to pay for it, anyway!"

"How in the world did that happen?" Savannah asked, totally at a loss. "It almost looked like that box was fly—"

"Trouble in paradise?"

Savannah's chin jerked up and she saw Sandy's brother, Nick, standing there with a broom and a dustpan.

"Nick!" Sandy cried with relief. "Where did you come from?"

"I'd just walked in when I spotted Rose…making mischief." Nick's blue eyes twinkled. "The cashier handed me the broom as I passed by."

"Does this happen…often?" Savannah asked with alarm.

"Oh, no—" Sandy started.

But, simultaneously, Nick said, "Yes!"

"I mean, not every day!" Sandy stammered. She shoved the cereal box at Nick. "Do you mind?"

"No worries, sis," Nick replied cheerfully. "I'll take care of it." Then, when he thought no one was watching, Nick narrowed his gaze at Rose and sternly shook his finger. Savannah caught the perplexing exchange out of the corner of her eye.

"That cereal box—" she began.

"Little children are so fast!" Sandy said.

"As quick as lightning," Nick agreed.

"Sleight of hand!" Sandy added, although beads of perspiration were forming at her hairline.

Savannah decided she must have imagined the entire thing. Baby Rose apparently had a reputation for being naughty, but all little children could be that way. Kids loved testing limits and experimenting with different antics to get attention. Rose must have ripped open the cereal box somehow before tossing it out of the basket. The cereal box hadn't been flying, for heaven's sake! Merely *falling*, Savannah thought, trying to reassure herself.

"How are things going at the theater?" Sandy asked Savannah, pushing her cart along. As she did, she peered over her shoulder and whispered to Nick, "Thanks! I owe you!"

Savannah carefully wheeled her cart around the cereal mess and turned it in the other direction to keep up with Sandy. "It's going great! I'm starting to get the donations organized."

Before they left him completely behind them, Nick called out to Savannah, "Sara phoned you, right?"

"Yes, thanks!" she said, turning toward him. "You and I have an appointment on Thursday at four!"

"Good to know!" Nick said with a grin.

"He can't do anything anymore without Sara," Sandy said quietly. "She's worth her weight in gold."

"Sounds like Nick stays really busy," Savannah commented.

"He does! Which is good. More incentive for him to stick around!"

Savannah's brow creased with worry. If Nick left Christmas Town, that meant that Olivia probably would, too. The new couple was just starting to build a life here. Savannah couldn't imagine why either one would think to leave. "Why wouldn't Nick stick around?"

Sandy bit into her bottom lip before saying, "Oh, he will! For a while! A good long while, I'm sure!"

Savannah eyed Sandy curiously. "Sandy, is there something going on that I don't know about?"

"I…er…" Sandy batted her big blue eyes. "You know what? Why don't you talk to your sister?"

"Olivia?" Savannah shook her head in wonder. "Okay, I will."

Sandy picked up a dozen eggs and started to lay them in the back of her buggy. Then, she appeared to think better of it, and wedged the carton in next to Holly in front instead. "You were saying…about the theater…?"

"Oh, just that things are coming along. After I meet with Nick, I'll have a better sense of any structural modifications that can be made. And, once that's done, I'll start the curriculum planning."

"For the theater camps?" Sandy asked, growing animated.

"Yes," Savannah answered. "I've promised to lay the groundwork for the first year of productions, including plays and puppet shows. It should be easy enough for the new director to step in and take over from there."

Sandy shot her a hopeful look. "Any chance that director will be you?"

"Not a very good one," Savannah told her regretfully. "I signed a teaching contract in Miami. And, I help with the high school's theater program there, too."

"Well, darn!" Sandy said, appearing genuinely disappointed. It warmed Savannah's heart to believe Sandy actually cared, which she evidently did. Sandy was a very earthy person, and not the sort to stand on pretense or fake her emotions. "That's too bad."

"Yeah."

"Well, I hope you'll make the most of things while you're here," Sandy continued kindly. "Say…" she said, her blue eyes twinkling. "I've got a great idea! You should come to the bazaar!"

"Bazaar?" Savannah questioned.

"The church bazaar, sure! It's on Sunday and all of the townsfolk will be there." She stopped to ponder this a moment. "I mean, most of them will be! There's a kids' Christmas pageant and everything. A big potluck dinner, too." Sandy grinned good-naturedly. "Ben and I would love it so much if you'd be our guest."

"Well, I…I'd hate to put you out."

"It's not putting us out," Sandy told her. "We're going, anyway. Lily's in the pageant every year!"

Savannah's gaze roved over Rose and Holly, and Sandy giggled. "Not to worry about the twins. They'll be with a sitter."

"I wasn't worried, actually."

"No! Of course you weren't!" Sandy stared into Savannah's eyes then thumped her temples with a perplexed look. "Huh, that's weird."

"What is?"

"Nothing, hon!" Sandy said quickly. Then she clamped her hands around her shopping cart's handle and scurried away. Why was Sandy suddenly so anxious to leave? Only minutes ago, she'd seemed prepared to luxuriate in conversation. "See you on Sunday at five! Okay? I'll drop by to get you!"

"Oh! Okay!" Savannah was overwhelmed by Sandy's warmhearted generosity, and also a little thrown by her sudden departure. "Thanks, Sandy! Thanks so much!"

Chapter Eight

Savannah had just finished unpacking and putting away her groceries when her doorbell rang. She answered to discover a pleasant-looking woman in her late thirties standing outside. She was tall and slender with short curly brown hair and big brown eyes that were flecked with gold around the irises.

"Hi! I'm Liz Martin." The woman jutted out her hand and Savannah saw Liz held a small wrapped package. "I just wanted to say, hello and welcome to Christmas Town!"

"Why, thanks!" Savannah noticed that Liz wasn't wearing a coat. Just jeans and a gray sweatshirt over a red turtleneck top. Her jeans were tucked into furry suede boots that appeared to be a combination of outdoor footwear and slippers, and they had little red pompoms on each side. Savannah peered up and down the street but didn't see any new vehicle parked nearby. "Oh, gosh! You must be freezing! Please come in."

Liz gave a small shiver as sharp winds blew. Beyond her, fast-falling snow coated the pavement, causing the sidewalk to all but disappear. "It is a little cold out," she said with a happy grin. "Six more inches expected!"

"Of snow?" Savannah asked, astounded. "My!"

"That's nothing around here," Liz told her. "It's not even December. Winter's just getting started."

Savannah laughed lightly, grateful she'd packed so much warm clothing. While she didn't have need for it down in Miami, she had a "winter wardrobe" for visiting her folks in Virginia, particularly during the chillier holiday season. She shut the door behind Liz with an observation. "I can't believe you went out without a coat!"

"No coat needed, really." Liz grinned again and Savannah saw dimples settle on each of her cheeks. "I live right next door!"

"Oh, right! Olivia told me. You work at the daycare."

"Jingle Bells Booties, that's right," Liz answered cheerily. Then she dropped her voice in a whisper and spoke behind the back of one hand. "Lou Christmas came up with the name." She rolled her eyes and Savannah giggled, totally able to imagine that. "She didn't realize it might sound kind of lurid."

Savannah laughed harder. "That's Lou!"

"Yeah. Great, isn't she?" Liz beamed her way then glanced around.

"Oh, please!" Savannah said, feeling as if she was forgetting her manners. "Have a seat."

"All right, thanks. But just for a moment." Liz handed the small gift to her. "Here, this is for you."

"How sweet, Liz! Thank you."

Liz took a seat in an armchair and Savannah sat on the sofa. "Would you like a drink?" she asked, thinking it would be polite to offer. "Coffee? Cocoa? Wine?"

"It's a little late in the day for coffee for me. But, I'll take a glass of wine, sure!"

"Red or white?" Savannah asked, setting her package on the coffee table.

"Whatever's open…"

"Lou and Sandy brought by a nice Merlot in their welcome basket."

"Sounds great. Can I help?"

"Nope. I've got it! I'll just be a sec."

Savannah returned a few moments later with two full goblets of wine. While she hadn't been expecting company, it was nice having someone to chat with. She sat back on the sofa and lifted her glass. "Here's to new acquaintances!"

"Here's to new *friends*," Liz corrected with a twinkle. "You can't get off the hook that easily. We're neighbors now, you know." She smiled warmly and Savannah clinked her glass.

"I think I'd like having a new friend in Christmas Town."

"Consider it done." Liz sipped from her wine then eyed Savannah's gift. "You can go on and open it if you'd like."

"Oh yes! Of course." Savannah set her wineglass on the coffee table and giddily picked up the package. She loved getting gifts, especially the unexpected kind. Savannah pried apart the pretty giftwrap finding a small white box inside. When she lifted the lid, she spied three darling barrettes nestled together on a protective cotton pillow. Each one was shaped like a heart and appeared to be made of gingerbread. One had a tiny angel on it. The second one showcased an itty-bitty Christmas tree, and the third contained a facsimile of a pink icing heart with swirly red letters streaming across it. "They're Virginia Cookies!" Savannah proclaimed with delight.

"Yes, indeed," Liz said, looking pleased. "And up-to-date ones, too. These are this year's editions."

Savannah picked up the Commitment Cookie barrette to examine it more closely. "These are amazing! Such intricate work. Kudos to the artist! Do you know who made them?"

"Sure do."

When Savannah looked up, Liz pointed to herself.

"Wow, Liz," Savannah said, eyeing her with admiration. "You've got real talent. These barrettes are beautiful."

"I sell them at your sister's shop on consignment. I started with other kinds of holiday barrettes, and still make those."

"I thought you worked at the daycare?"

"I do my art projects in the evenings, and on weekends," Liz replied. "I've always dreamed that someday... No, never mind," she said, looking abashed. "It's silly, anyway."

"I'm sure that it's not," Savannah said. "There's nothing wrong with dreaming, Liz. All of us do!"

"Yeah?" Liz asked with a sassy grin. "What do you dream about?"

"I...er..."

"A special fellow, maybe?" There was a twinkle in her eye. "Your true Prince Charming?"

Heat warmed Savannah's cheeks. "Okay, you've got me." She pursed her lips then giggled. "Sometimes. Sometimes I dream of a fairy-tale ending, but then— you know, I wake up and I'm back in the real world."

"Where is that?"

"Miami."

"I've never been farther south than North Carolina. Is it unbearably hot there?"

"Yeah, it can be."

"Olivia says you work in the theater."

Savannah laughed good-naturedly. "That's a bit of an exaggeration. I work at a high school as a guidance counselor. I do help out with their theater program though, it's true."

"Well, it sounds like you have the right experience and all," Liz told her. "I was at the Town Council meeting when they discussed your credentials and bringing you in to start the children's theater. Nobody could have lobbied harder for you to get the job besides Olivia and Carter. Except…" Liz pursed her lips and stopped talking.

"Except for who, Liz?"

"Well, you might as well know." Liz shyly lifted a shoulder. "The good doc put in a favorable word for you, too. A very strong favorable word."

"Kurt Christmas?"

Liz studied her briefly. "He sounded like he knew you pretty well."

"Well, maybe…once upon a time."

Liz sagely scrutinized her and Savannah flushed. "We kind of had a thing back in high school."

"High school, huh? That's a long time ago."

"I know, yeah."

"And in all the time since—?"

"Would you like more wine?" Savannah interrupted, even though Liz had only taken a few sips.

"No worries, I gotcha," Liz said with a wink. "Talk about Kurt is off limits."

"I didn't say that…exactly."

"You can just tell me if I'm being too nosy."

Savannah took a sip of wine and shot her a smirk. "Okay, you're being too nosy."

Liz belly-laughed, clearly not offended. "All right then, I'll cut it out."

"What about you?" Savannah asked, enjoying herself. She only had one close friend in Miami, the high school drama teacher Gloria Chavez, and she missed her already. Sharing girl talk with Liz was fun, and helped fill the gap. "Do you have a 'special fellow,' as you put it, here in Christmas Town?"

Liz's lips took a downward turn. "Not yet, and it hasn't been for lack of trying."

"I'm sorry, Liz. Perhaps at the right time—"

"My time's moving on," Liz said, shaking her head. "The old biological clock has already stopped ticking."

"Oh, gosh. But, you're so young?"

"Nearly forty is old enough," Liz said before further confiding, "Going over the hill early runs in my family."

"That doesn't mean you can't find love."

"No, but having babies is probably out. That's one reason I love working at the daycare and being around the little cuties. Living vicariously, I guess."

Liz's stark confession caused Savannah's heart to ache. "There are other ways these days, with technology. There's also adoption."

"Yeah, but here's the thing." Liz smiled sadly. "I don't want to go it alone. I mean…" She viewed Savannah seriously. "Would you?"

Heat unexpectedly surged in Savannah's eyes and she blinked hard, attempting to rein in her emotions. Liz set down her wine and leaned toward Savannah, clasping her hand.

"Oh, no! I've upset you! I'm such a donut head sometimes. Savannah, I'm sor—"

"Donut head?" Savannah grinned in spite of her tears. "Where did you get that?"

"Oh, I don't know…" Liz rolled her eyes, thinking. "Probably back at Santa's Sandwich Shop when I was waitressing there. I thought up all sorts of creative things to say when there were mishaps, so I wouldn't offend the customers."

Savannah dabbed her tears with a tissue from the box on the coffee table, already feeling better. "Oh yeah? Like what?"

Liz grinned impishly. "Like…*jumping jelly beans! Gingerbread snap!* And my personal favorite…*sugar plum fairy!*"

Savannah laughed out loud, her spirits lightened. "Oh, Liz! You're too much!"

"These also come in handy at the daycare," Liz confided. "It's good to have an arsenal of clean expletives at the ready when you're dealing with babies. Most days, they're all little angels. But those Winchester twins… Especially, Rose!" Liz shook her head indulgently. "It used to be that Holly was the troublemaker; now little Rose is giving her sister a run for her money."

Savannah laughed again even harder. This time she nearly snorted wine through her nose, recalling the cereal box episode. It actually was hilarious in retrospect, and Savannah was certain there was a rational explanation for how it happened. "It feels so good to laugh. Really, really good." She stared gratefully at Liz. "Thank you."

"Thank you for hearing all my true confessions in less than an hour."

Savannah liked Liz so much. She was totally genuine and sweet. "Any time you want to confide, I'm here."

"And, any time you need something, I'm right next door."

Savannah checked the clock on the mantel seeing it was nearly seven. "Have you had dinner?" she asked Liz. "I was thinking of ordering something."

"If you were thinking of pizza, I can make a recommendation." Liz beamed her way. "And, the Reindeer Pub delivers."

Liz left a few hours later, after helping Savannah load the dishwasher and wrap up the leftover pizza. Despite her mini meltdown earlier in the night, Savannah was in really great spirits and looking forward to her stay in Christmas Town. She had an exciting job that would keep her busy, and already she was making friends! Though Savannah knew she'd enjoy seeing Olivia and Carter more while in town, meeting friendly Liz had been an added bonus.

Savannah had made decent progress at the theater today, and planned to continue working on things tomorrow. Tonight, though, she intended to relax and maybe peruse one of the tomes on Christmas Town history sitting in the living room bookshelf. The more she learned about the town, the more informed she'd be in creating a unique brand for its theater.

Savannah selected a heavy book and sat down to read on the sofa. *What do you know! It's a story on Hannah's great-grandmother Lena and her founding of the Christmas Cookie Shop!* Someone knocked three times at the front door, then after a short pause began knocking again. Savannah set the book aside and went to open it, thinking perhaps it was Liz coming back to tell her something. But instead of Liz Martin, Savannah spied Lou Christmas outside! She wore her red felt Santa hat, which was completely covered in snow, and an animal print jacket and gloves. In her arms she cradled a huge cardboard box.

"Merry Christmas, Savannah!" Lou called from behind the large package. "I hope I'm not calling too late?"

"No, not at all." Savannah was a little surprised by Lou's impromptu visit. Then she decided that perhaps that's how things were here. People just dropped by! That never happened to Savannah back in Miami. Even with her best friend, Gloria, their social get-togethers were scheduled by text. "Please, come in!" She stepped forward to relieve Lou of the heavy box. "Why don't you let me take that?"

Lou nodded and dusted off her gloves before shutting the door. Night had fallen and a dark richness flooded the inky sky, which was speckled with darting snowflakes that danced and twirled toward the ground beneath the streetlamps' glow. Savannah didn't think much about snow while in Florida, but being in Christmas Town made her realize that she missed it.

Savannah carried the heavy box to the sofa and set it down. "Wow! What have you got in here?"

"Decorations!" Lou sunnily perused the room. "When I stopped by with Sandy on Saturday, I saw you were in need of some."

"I'd only just arrived, Lou."

"All the more reason you could use some assistance." Lou grinned and walked to the box, ripping her gloves off one at a time and shoving them in her pockets.

Savannah hardly knew what to say. Things had been a bit awkward between her and Kurt's mom ever since that beach fiasco. Naturally, Lou had been graciously welcoming in the company of Sandy. But, now that it was just the two of them, Savannah wasn't sure what to expect.

"Meet Mr. Noodles!" Lou said, unfolding cardboard flaps and yanking something out of the box.

Savannah stared in wonder at the odd stuffed creature. It appeared to be made of white…athletic socks? Savannah wasn't sure. One thing she knew, the big bulbous head wearing the felt top hat appeared to be screaming. What with that huge button nose and those terrified-looking button eyes and oddly arched eyebrows… The red plaid scarf around its neck was tied extra tight, as if choking the poor little devil into…uh…happiness? And, *what* was with the stubby arms and legs poking out of the middle round ball and lower one, respectively?

"*Jumping jelly beans!*" Savannah said, when no other words occurred to her. "That's...terrific!"

"I made him myself," Lou announced. "And, he's become a regular fixture around this unit of Sisters' Row. All the renters love him!" Her eyebrows drew together and for a split second she appeared vexed. "Apart from that incident with Hannah and her kittens."

"Kittens?" Savannah asked, perplexed.

"Jingles and Belle!" Lou informed her as she set Mr. Noodles on the back of the sofa and patted his belly twice. "If you've not yet met them, you will soon enough. And, that Jingles hasn't changed his ways."

"I...see," Savannah said, not sure that she did.

"Just mind your shiny things around him," Lou cautioned sternly. "Like that pretty barrette in your hair!"

Savannah fingered the Charity Cookie barrette she'd clipped into her tresses shortly after Liz left. "Oh! This was a gift from Liz."

"Liz Martin?" Lou considered this a moment. "How nice."

"Yes," Savannah said happily. "She stopped by tonight. I'm sure she'll make a very nice neighbor."

"Yes," Lou agreed. "Everybody loves her. She's Stan Martin's sister, you know."

"I'm not sure I've met Stan."

"He works over at the Candy Cane Barbershop and his wife, Della, has a shop right across the street called Mystic Magi."

Mystic Magi Savannah had heard of. It sounded like a fascinating place, and she intended to stop by. Olivia liked some of the soaps sold there and Savannah was considering buying her a gift selection for Christmas.

"Stan and Della have four kids," Lou continued. "Cinnamon, Clove, Sage, and Basil. My Kurt delivered them all."

"That's quite a brood," Savannah commented. "How old are they?"

"Little," Lou answered. "Only the oldest is in school. The others attend Jingle Bells Booties."

Savannah suppressed a giggle hearing Lou mention the name.

Lou dug eagerly into the decoration box and Savannah was almost scared to think of what might come out next.

"Here you are, dear!" Lou said sweetly, handing her a Christmas stocking, which was surprisingly quite nice. It appeared hand-embroidered and everything, with intricate details depicting a horse-drawn sleigh scene in the snow.

"Did you make this, too?" Savannah asked haltingly.

"I wish!" Lou said with a titter. "But, no. I purchased it at Olivia's shop."

She shoved it at Savannah who grasped it uncertainly. "You're being very kind," she said. From her vantage point, Savannah could see the box was loaded with tons of other holiday decorations: wreaths, candles, and lights she could use to adorn the room.

"Of course, dear." Savannah had the sense Lou was a tiny bit nervous. "We like for all our guests to feel welcome in Christmas Town. Not that you're a guest!" Lou inserted suddenly. "More like family, of course! You have kin here, and your family and mine... Well, we go way back. The Christmases and the Livingstons. Your mother and I were very best friends. Still are…" Lou screwed up her face in a regretful pose. "Ever since we reconciled at Carter's wedding."

Savannah laid her hand on Lou's arm. "Lou, I don't want you to worry." Savannah paused and gathered her nerve. "About what happened all that time ago. I'm sure that you and my mother had your—"

"But it wasn't us!" Lou interrupted sharply. Her big brown eyes grew moist. "I mean, at least it certainly wasn't me. I hope that you'll believe that. Because, apparently…" She hung her head. "Kurt doesn't."

Savannah felt a sudden pang of sympathy for the older woman. "What do you mean?"

"I think Kurt holds me accountable for your losing contact with each other," Lou said, meeting Savannah's eyes. "But, sweetheart, I never would have done that. Wouldn't have tried to break the two of you up."

"But you and my mom both agreed—"

"Yes, yes. That you and Kurt were getting in over your heads, and we were worried about your futures… I was particularly concerned—in light of certain things."

Savannah studied her seriously. "What things, Lou?"

Lou solemnly shook her head. "Things that I can't tell you, I'm afraid."

"Not even to this day?"

Lou beheld her worriedly. "You have a kind soul, and you're a beautiful young woman, Savannah. I can understand why Kurt hasn't been able to forget you."

"Hasn't he?" Savannah asked, as a lump formed in her throat.

"I don't think so," Lou answered softly. "There was something more to your relationship with him than the rest of us understood. Perhaps we'll never understand it, will we?" She searched Savannah's eyes, and Savannah swallowed hard.

"Lou, I…"

"It's all right, dear," Lou assured her. "I'm not here to make trouble, or to ask you to back off."

"Back off?" Savannah asked in shock. "But I never said—"

"You didn't have to say a word," Lou replied. "Because I've seen the way you and my son look at each other, when you think no one is watching from across the room."

Savannah's throat constricted as she forced out the words. "When did you see that, Lou?"

"At Olivia's wedding." Lou viewed her kindly. "I may be opinionated and meddlesome. But that doesn't mean that I'd ever stand in the way of true love." She turned her full gaze on Savannah. "Do you love Kurt, Savannah?"

"I…I don't know," Savannah answered, completely broadsided.

"Well, maybe you should make up your mind," Lou advised her. "Because, if you don't? Then I think it's time you let him go."

Chapter Nine

Savannah shifted restlessly under the covers, unable to relax. She'd thought that by going to bed early, she could get a fresh start at the theater in the morning. The only trouble was, she hadn't slept a wink. Savannah's mind raced, as she contemplated Lou's parting words. Lou obviously thought that Savannah had been stringing Kurt along, which she hadn't done. Not on purpose, anyway. How could her failing to contact Kurt after Olivia's wedding be seen as a sign of encouragement?

Kurt hadn't been in touch with her, either. Though, honestly, Savannah kind of understood that. She'd basically walked out on him the next morning, because she'd feared having to explain why she'd completely fallen apart the night before. And, Savannah probably *had* owed Kurt some answers. Only her anxiety over his potential reaction had been far too great.

She reached toward the nightstand and picked up her phone, checking the time. It was a little past midnight, but Gloria was probably up. Her fun-loving Latina friend was such a night owl. Savannah pressed the speed-dial number on her cell and scooted up in bed, propping a pillow between her back and the headboard.

Gloria's reply was immediate, chipper, and characteristically lined with concern.

"*Hola!* What's wrong?"

"Am I calling too late?"

"Ridiculous! No. I was just polishing my nails. Hang on…" It sounded like she'd tucked her phone under her chin. "Let me cap the bottle."

"I don't want to interrupt—"

"Such an important moment! True." Savannah could envision Gloria studying her nails. "But, it's okay. The manicure can wait!"

"What color?"

"Fire engine red," Gloria replied with a playful air. "*Muy dramatica!*"

This drew a chuckle from Savannah. "I'm sorry I won't be there for the holiday play."

"Mr. Scrooge and I will find a way to get along without you."

"I can't believe Principal Clark is playing the lead."

"Fitting, right?" Gloria lowered her voice in a whisper. "No Christmas party this year."

"What do you mean?"

"Mr. Clark's cut the faculty event 'out of budgetary concerns.' As if he ever pays for anything," Gloria added a bit testily. "It's always a potluck!" Gloria heaved a sigh. "One of these days, I'm going to get out of there. If it weren't for the kids, I'd already be gone."

Savannah knew Gloria was an extremely popular teacher, utterly adored by her students and admired by her colleagues, as well. "I know what you mean,"

Savannah said. "Me, too." It wasn't just Mr. Clark; the entire administration was becoming more difficult to deal with. The Parent-Teacher Organization for the school had hired academic consultants charged with bringing up test scores.

The consultants, who apparently had very little experience with public education themselves, had recommended the staff revise their lesson plans to *optimize the classroom learning experience.* This essentially meant a whole lot of busy work for the teachers, who had to document their daily lesson plans on enormous spreadsheets broken down into five-minute increments. And, each little chunk of time had to meet one of the district's numerous curriculum standards. Savannah got a headache just thinking of it! She and her fellow guidance counselors had rallied against the change, saying it would stifle the classroom experience by inhibiting incidental learning while limiting creative freedom for both teachers and students, but their petitions had fallen on deaf ears.

"How are things in Christmas Town?" Gloria asked changing the subject. "How's the theater? *How's Kurt...?*" she asked a little sneakily.

"The theater area is great! There's ample room to work with, and I'm starting to get a sense of how to use the space."

"You didn't answer my last question," Gloria said with a teasing lilt. "You *have* seen him?"

"Yes, but...very briefly. Olivia and I ran into him at brunch on Sunday. And then, this morning, he came by to help—"

"Fabulous!" Gloria shouted with glee. "All on his own?"

"Yes. I mean, no…" Savannah said, growing flustered.

"He brought other people with him?"

"No, he came alone."

"Intriguing."

"Maybe not as much as you think."

Gloria huffed into her mouthpiece. "Then, why are you calling me at midnight, hmm? This has to mean something."

"His mom came by," Savannah confessed.

"What? Lou Christmas? I thought you said the woman didn't like you."

"I know what I said…" Savannah drew her knees up to her chest and tucked the blankets around them. "But it could be I was wrong."

"Really?"

"This new Lou seems different somehow. Softer than I remembered."

"Maybe she's mellowed with age?"

"I don't think the words 'Lou Christmas' and 'mellowed' belong in the same sentence."

"Well, okay. So what did she want?"

"Me to make up my mind about Kurt."

Gloria gasped in disbelief. "She said that? Point blank?"

"Those weren't her exact words, but close enough."

"Wow."

"I know."

"So what was your take on the situation? Protective mom?"

"Yeah, but also? There was something more. I think she wanted to clear the air."

"About what?"

"About my break-up with Kurt back in high school."

"You told me that she caused it."

"That's because I thought that she had."

"And, now?"

"I'm not so sure."

"Who else would have tried to come between you?"

"One of the dads, maybe." Savannah shook her head. "But, that really doesn't seem like Buddy. Doesn't sound like my father either."

"I guess you never know."

"About family?" Savannah said. "That's true."

"Speaking of family…how are your sister and brother?"

"Olivia's doing great, and Carter is, too. He and Hannah are having me out to dinner at their cabin later this week."

"How sweet! I'll bet you can't wait to see the baby."

"Yes. Amanda's bound to have changed a lot since June."

"Children grow so fast."

Just hearing Gloria's voice made Savannah happy. How she wished her friend was here to help ring in the season with her. "I miss you, Gloria."

"Yeah, well. I miss you, too. But this is good for you, being in Christmas Town. Olivia needs your expertise with the theater, and you have a few personal things to settle, too." After a pause, she asked, "Do you have plans to see Kurt again?"

"Not yet, but he gave me his cookie."

"Cookie?"

"It's such a long story, you don't want to know."

"Doesn't Carter's wife Hannah run a cookie shop?"

"Not just any cookie shop," Savannah told her. "It's *the* Christmas Cookie Shop. And, according to folks around here, it's pretty special."

"This Christmas Town sounds like a magical place."

"Will you come to visit?" Savannah asked hopefully. "There are two bedrooms in my rental, plenty of room for you to stay."

"I'd love to honey, but not this year. It's David's first time serving as a senior pastor during the Advent season," Gloria said, referring to her brother. "I kind of promised him I'd attend his holiday services and let him know how he does." Though he was a grown man now, Savannah was aware that Gloria still looked after her extremely handsome sibling. She'd done so since they'd been kids. "Maybe if you go back in the future?" Gloria said. "Or," she added teasingly, "if you decide to stay?"

"I'd never leave you all alone in Miami."

"I wouldn't be alone," Gloria quipped. "I'd have Mr. Clark and his cronies to keep me company."

Savannah hooted at this, but in the back of her mind she'd already begun wondering. Wondering what it would be like to really live in Christmas Town. With her sister and her brother nearby, whimsical holiday shops on every corner, and so many friendly people around. Not to mention all the beautiful snow that made the entire place look like a fanciful winter wonderland. "Thanks for talking with me, Gloria."

"We didn't solve anything, did we?"

"No, but it was still good to hear your voice."

"Yeah, yours too."

"Break a leg this Friday with your opening night."

"Will do. You take care of yourself, now."

"Love you, *amiga*," Savannah said.

"Ditto, Savannah. Kisses from me."

Chapter Ten

Kurt picked up his morning coffee at Jolly Bean Java and headed out the door, nearly trampling over Savannah. "Savannah! Whoa! I'm sorry."

She looked up with a pretty blush, standing there in the snow. She had a green winter hat on and wore a matching green scarf, which picked up the color of her eyes. "Kurt! Good morning."

If Kurt had been watching where he was going rather than reminiscing over the last time he'd seen her, he wouldn't have practically mowed Savannah down on the sidewalk. "Getting an early start on your day?" he asked, since it was barely past seven o'clock.

She locked on his gaze and Kurt's heart stuttered. "Yes, and you?"

"Just grabbing my morning joe," he said, holding up his cup as evidence. The snow started coming down harder, catching them both in its swell.

"On the way to get mine!"

He pondered her pretty face, considering a proposition. If he asked her to lunch, would she go? There were only three places open for lunch and Savannah had already been to the Main Street Café.

"Well, I…" She shifted uncertainly on her feet when he didn't say anything. Why was Kurt finding it so difficult to spit out the words? It wasn't a big deal. Just a midday meal—between friends… Old friends, who had fallen out of touch. "I guess we'd better move along!" Savannah said. "Before the two of us turn into popsicles."

Kurt nodded and tipped his hat. Then, when Savannah stepped past him, he called out, "Hey! Would you like to have lunch?"

Savannah stopped walking and slowly turned on her heel. "Lunch?"

"I mean, take a breather," he explained. "The clinic closes between one and two."

"I'm not sure, Kur—"

"It would be good to catch up," he said.

"We talked yesterday."

Kurt raised his eyebrows. "Yeah, but not a lot."

Savannah seemed to be weighing something. "I've got so much to do."

"Which is why you'll need a break."

"You're not going to give up, are you?"

He locked on her gaze and Savannah's blush deepened. "Nope."

She drew in a quick breath then asked softly, "Where?"

Kurt grinned in satisfaction. "Santa's Sandwich Shop, unless you'd like something fancy?"

Savannah glanced down at her coat, boots, and jeans, then back up at him. "Casual sounds good."

Kurt's heart soared when he realized she'd just accepted. "Perfect. I'll see you there!"

"Where…?"

Kurt thumbed over his shoulder and Savannah saw that Santa's Sandwich Shop was on the far side of Jolly Bean Java. A sign on the restaurant's door said it opened at eleven.

"Oh, gosh!" Savannah laughed, apparently embarrassed she hadn't noticed the sign. "If it had been a snake…"

"Good thing that it wasn't."

"Yeah."

Savannah's eyes sparkled and Kurt was mesmerized, completely unable to look away.

"Yeah," he replied, as his grin broadened.

Savannah blinked hard, then said hastily, "But, this *isn't* a date!"

"Of course not."

"There's James."

"Hmm, yes."

"And he wouldn't want—"

"No." After a beat Kurt added, "I wouldn't either."

"Well, good!"

"Yes, great. I'll see you soon, Savannah. At one o'clock!" Kurt tipped his hat then turned and walked the other way, all the while congratulating himself. *Yes!* She'd said, *yes*! It was only lunch, but that was okay. Lunch might prove a beginning. And, if there was anything Kurt wanted with Savannah, it was a new start.

He'd scarcely slept last night, excited by the possibility that he might actually get to date her. After so many years of waiting, pining, and hoping that blasted James would get out of the way, Savannah's on-again-off-again beau was finally history. Now that he was, Kurt intended to take his opening. Before

Savannah decided to reconcile with James again, which
appeared to be her typical pattern. But, if James were
the one for her, why did Savannah keep leaving him to
begin with? Something was going on there, and that
something didn't spell a future. Not in Kurt's
vocabulary, anyhow.

He approached the roundabout where the library
and courthouse were located. His clinic was west of the
courthouse, just a short ways up on River Road. It was
a three-mile walk from his house on Church Street, but
Kurt never minded getting the exercise. This morning,
especially, he was grateful for the fresh air, and the
wind, and the beautiful, beautiful snow. As he cut
around the corner Kurt's gaze snagged on the sign in
the center of the roundabout and beside the sturdy
flagpole, and his heart skipped a beat.

Welcome to
CHRISTMAS TOWN, TENNESSEE
Where everyday dreams come true!

Kurt had never fully trusted that his dreams could
come true in his hometown, but now he held out hope.
For Savannah was here—and single, Kurt thought with
a grin. The rest would be up to his smoothness and
guile.

Savannah was a nervous wreck sorting through the
rest of the boxes on the fourth floor. While she was
attempting to put things in order, she kept making
mistakes. Like carrying the costumes to the prop room
and the props into the area where she planned to put the

armoires when they arrived this afternoon. She'd double-checked with Olivia this morning about purchasing some, and Olivia had said she'd spotted a few pieces at the Holly and the Ivy home goods store that might fit the bill. Savannah had perused them herself this morning after the shop opened at ten and purchased the pair of cedar-lined wardrobes at once. She'd asked the clerk to send the bill to Lou Christmas, care of the Town Council, at Olivia's instructions. Then, she'd returned here to get to work.

It was easy to see the fourth floor wouldn't need too many improvements to function as a theater. The large room was plenty big enough to hold seating and a stage, and the one unisex bathroom was sufficient, especially since there were additional bathrooms available on the lower floors. Savannah also felt good about repurposing the two shotgun-style bedrooms into a prop room and a costume area that could double as a changing room.

Perhaps it would be nice to have two dressing cubicles installed, similar to what were in department stores. They didn't need to be fancy, but could afford privacy for actors requiring a complete change of costume. She could ask Nick about having those added, as well as several shelving units for the prop area. Savannah didn't imagine either of those would pose a problem.

Her main question involved having a large window cut in the wall between the small dining area and the kitchen. That way a countertop could be mounted on the windowsill and refreshments served to those in the main room from inside the kitchen. Since the entire wall wouldn't have to be removed—only a portion of it—Savannah didn't think this would cause any structural issues, but again she could ask Nick.

She was getting so excited about this project! Savannah had double-majored in theater and psychology in college, and at one point had even dreamed of running her own theater company. That was before she'd volunteered for her campus's women's shelter, after which Savannah decided she wanted a career in counseling. Eager for a sunnier climate than she'd been afforded at the small New England school where she got her B.A., she'd applied to a masters program in social work at a Florida university, where the weather was balmy and warm.

Afterward, she'd been offered the high school counselor position in Miami, and had stayed. Savannah enjoyed her life in Florida, but she did sometimes miss the changing seasons. She'd grown up on her parents' dairy farm in the western part of Virginia, which was lovely. Though she'd never thought of moving back there. Her hometown was really tiny, about the size of Christmas Town. Yet, it didn't quite seem to have Christmas Town's charms… The most *charming* among its residents stood about six foot one, and had chocolate brown eyes.

Savannah heaved a sigh, wondering if she'd made a tactical error in agreeing to meet Kurt for lunch. The more they saw of each other, the more likely it was that they'd become friends. Perhaps even something more. And, if a romantic relationship were to develop… Savannah clasped a hand to her heart to quell its painful pounding. Could she really revisit that heartache? She wouldn't know how. More impossible still would be keeping things from Kurt. If they grew close, she'd have to tell him sometime. She'd never told James. That was one of the stumbling blocks between them.

While James sometimes seemed too preoccupied with his work to care about Savannah's past, at others he appeared perturbed because he believed she was guarding secrets. About what, he couldn't say. He only told her that he sensed something was wrong, and that unless she came clean and told him her whole truth that she and he would never be able to move forward.

Savannah hated being pushed around. More than that, she detested ultimatums. So, she'd hung on to her secrets—all of them. Because the truth was she didn't want to tell anything that personal to James. Way down deep in her heart, Savannah also understood she honestly didn't want to move forward with him, either.

Not when she still desperately cared for someone else.

When Savannah told Kurt everything she'd accomplished at the theater, he was astounded. "Wow. You did all that in just one day?"

"In just one morning," she told him lightly. Savannah spread her paper napkin on her lap and glanced around the homey restaurant that was part sandwich shop and part diner. It had booths that seated four and smaller tables that could be pushed together for larger groups. The tables were all covered with red-and-white checkered plastic tablecloths. Their server had already brought two tall glasses of unsweetened iced tea, and they'd each decided on their picks from the menu. Kurt had ordered a Reuben with potato salad on the side and Savannah had gotten the burger with fries.

"How were things at the clinic?" she asked him.

"Typically eventful for a Tuesday."

"What do you mean?"

"Tuesdays are my pediatric days, the days I see children for their regular check-ups and such. I tackle that in the morning before naptime when everyone's in better spirits," he said with a wink.

"And, after lunch?"

"I leave that available for sick calls. Open to all ages."

"Just anybody can walk in?"

"Is something ailing you, Savannah?" He leaned toward her with a husky whisper and Savannah's pulse raced.

"No, I…was just wondering, that's all!" She took a sip of iced tea, unnerved that Kurt could still do this to her. Just one sultry look, and goose bumps skittered down her spine.

"Because, if you'd like to stop by…?"

"I'm fine!" she replied with a squeak, knowing that was the biggest, fattest lie she'd told in a long while.

"I'm glad to hear you're in the pink of health." He sipped from his tea and set it down. "You're certainly looking well."

"Thanks, Kurt!" Savannah said, grateful she was dressed in designer jeans and her pretty new purple sweater with the dainty pearl buttons. She wore a strand of cultured pearls around her neck to match, and her long red hair was pulled up in a ponytail. She'd added one of her new barrettes as an accent piece.

"I like your barrette," he told her. "Isn't that a Clemency Cookie?"

"The one supposed to bring about forgiveness?" She reflected on what she'd learned. "Yeah, I suppose it is!"

"You planning any naughty deeds today?"

"Now, Kurt!" she said with a chuckle. "Of course not."

"Maybe you should rethink that."

"Maybe you should rethink your flirting."

"Falling flat, is it?" he asked with a mock frown.

"Are you this bad with everybody?"

"Everybody whom?"

"All women."

Kurt thoughtfully stroked his chin. "No, Savannah. Only with you."

"I don't believe that for a minute."

"Where did you get your barrette? I've seen other women wearing them around town."

Savannah didn't know why Kurt mentioning seeing barrettes in other women's hair bothered her. He had eyes, didn't he? And, he was an observant man. There was no reason for Savannah to feel jealous, for heaven's sake. She slunk down a tad in her chair when she realized she actually was. How embarrassing. Thank goodness Kurt couldn't read her thoughts!

"Olivia sells them at her shop, but the artist gave it to me personally," she said, answering his question. "Liz Martin gifted me with a whole set! All three kinds!"

"I didn't realize Liz was the talent behind those little baubles. How long has she been at it?"

"Jewelry making? I'm not entirely sure. But it sounded like for at least a few years."

"Interesting how everybody has their secrets."

Savannah's temperature spiked and her face felt hot. "I'm not sure what you mean?"

"I was talking about Liz, and her *secret* ability for fashioning barrettes," he answered. "I only knew she worked at the daycare. And, of course, I remember her from when she waitressed here." Kurt carefully surveyed Savannah's eyes. "What did you think I was talking about?"

"Oh, er! Liz Martin." Savannah bit into her bottom lip, her heart pounding. "Just like you thought."

Kurt gave her a long steady look. "O-kay."

Their food arrived quickly, providing a distracting exchange with their waitress, who offered to return with a bottle of ketchup.

"This all looks delicious!" Savannah said. "I haven't had a restaurant burger since I don't know when."

"You and James don't go out to eat much?" Kurt asked, fishing.

Savannah flushed when she said, "Not to these kinds of places. James is a vegetarian and into more exotic cuisine. Indian. Thai. That sort of thing."

"I like that food, too," Kurt commented blandly, poking a fork into his potato salad.

"Yeah, so do I," Savannah said. "I just didn't realize how much I missed meat," she continued, sinking her teeth into her burger. Boy was it wonderful, too. Juicy and hot, and cooked just right! "This is so, so good!"

Kurt grinned, pleased. "I'm glad you're enjoying it, because it's my treat."

"Oh no, it's not," Savannah said, setting her burger down.

"Oh yes, it is. And, I insist."

"Why?"

"Consider it my welcome gift to Christmas Town."

"You already helped with the boxes."

"Those were hardly edible."

Savannah giggled, enjoying Kurt's sense of humor. "Kurt—"

"Seriously, Savannah. What's the big deal?" He shrugged charmingly. "I'm the town doctor. You know I can afford it."

"And, I'm the starving theater worker, is that it?" she bantered coyly.

"I'm trying to prevent the starving part. Eat up!" He nodded at her burger and Savannah burst out laughing.

"Oh Kurt, you haven't lost it."

"Lost what?"

"Your way with words. You always could make me laugh."

"They say laughter is the music of the soul."

"Oh yeah?" she asked, nibbling on a French fry. The waitress returned with the ketchup and set it down. "Who says that?"

"All those creative types," Kurt explained, gesturing with his hand. "Poets…troubadours…"

"Troubadours?" Savannah giggled again. "Now, there's a word you don't hear every day."

"That just proves you don't hang out at the Christmas Town Clinic. People show up to sing me their sad songs daily."

"You mean they're not really sick?"

"Some are in need of true medical care, sure. Others though?" He smiled her way. "Simply seem to want a listening ear."

"And you provide it."

"I wouldn't turn paying customers away."

"Stop that, Kurt Christmas. You'll never convince me it's about the money. I'll bet you don't even charge some of those people."

Kurt finished the remainder of one half of his sandwich and wiped his mouth with his napkin. "For a woman who hasn't seen me in years, you seem to know me pretty well."

"Times change, people don't," Savannah said brightly.

"I think that's wrong, Savannah." He shot her a serious look. "In some important ways, I believe we've both changed quite a bit."

"You may be right." Savannah was overtaken by a wave of melancholy. "But you don't seem to have changed. In certain ways, you're just as I remember."

"Not you, Savannah." Kurt's handsome mouth drew up in a smile. "You're better."

Oh, if that were only true. Yet there was so much he didn't know. "Thank you for taking me to lunch," she said. "Being around you, it…helps break the ice. Makes things feel less awkward."

"That's good. I don't want you feeling awkward around me."

"We're bound to keep seeing each around," she told him.

"I'm hoping it won't only be by accident," he replied.

"But, James—"

"You can drop the story, Savannah." Kurt met her eyes. "I know that the two of you aren't together."

"But how? Who?" Olivia's heart hammered. "Did Carter say something? Certainly not Olivia?"

Kurt gently laid his hand on her arm. "Actually, it was you."

"Me?"

"You may not believe this but I can tell."

"Tell what?"

"When you're being truthful."

Savannah gaped at him in alarm. "You can read my mind?"

"No," he said blithely, "that's Sandy's department."

"Sandy Winchester?"

"Formerly Claus."

"Next, you're going to say you can tell who's been naughty and nice."

Kurt's expression was almost mirthful. "Nope, that's Nick."

Savannah was thrown by so much nonsensical talk. "I'm not sure what you're saying?"

"Merely that I have a sense about things—and people. Generally, I'm right."

Savannah pulled back her arm and rubbed the warm place on her sweater sleeve where Kurt's hand had been.

"What does it matter, anyway?" she asked him beseechingly. "About James?"

"It matters to me."

"Well, I don't see why it should," Savannah said, feeling hurt. "That's a bit like the pot calling the kettle black, wouldn't you say?"

He stared at Savannah, waiting for her to continue. "You pester me about whether or not I have a boyfriend, when all the while you're seeing Eliza Stewart?"

Kurt steadily held her gaze. After a few minutes, he said hoarsely, "You're absolutely right, Savannah. My apologies. That was unfair."

They continued their meal in silence, the tension palpable between them. But, seriously? What did Kurt expect? That Savannah would invite romantic attention from a man who was otherwise involved? A man who, Savannah knew from experience, could do so much damage to her still-tender heart? Savannah hung her head thinking this lunch had been a mistake. She'd do well to steer clear of Kurt, rather than wade into these choppy waters. There was only one way things would end: with Savannah getting hurt. And she didn't want to be hurt again. Savannah had endured enough pain on account of Kurt already.

"Thank you for the lunch," she said, laying her napkin on the table. "But I think I'd better go."

"Savannah, no."

She met his eyes, as hers burned hot. "In June, you told me Eliza meant nothing. That things were over."

"In June, you said that you were through with James."

"I was."

"And yet, you went back to him?" He studied her questioningly. "Now, who's the pot calling the kettle black?"

Savannah stood abruptly from their table. "Thanks for the burger."

"You haven't even finished."

Savannah glared fiercely at Kurt, raising her defenses. "Oh yes, I have."

Then she shrugged into her coat and stormed out the door, seconds before she burst into tears.

Chapter Eleven

Savannah withdrew a tissue from her coat pocket and scurried down the sidewalk, racing through the slanting snow. She hadn't gone far when she encountered Sandy on her way back to the Snow Globe Gallery.

"Savannah? Honey?" Sandy gently clasped Savannah's shoulders, as worry filled her eyes. "What's wrong?"

"Nothing," Savannah lied with a sniff. "Nothing at all." She dabbed her cheeks with the mascara-blackened tissue, which was disintegrating in her hand. She was sure she looked a wreck.

"Did you just run out of Santa's Sandwich Shop?" Sandy asked, glancing that way.

"Yes," Savannah said, her breath shuddering. "I was there."

"Well, gosh," Sandy said, trying to lighten things. "The last time I ate there the food wasn't that bad."

"When was the last time?" Savannah asked her.

"Yesterday, at our girls' lunch. Olivia said she invited you, but since it was your first day you wanted to dive into things at the theater."

"That's right." Savannah finished drying her eyes and shoved the tissue back in her pocket.

"Well, I hope you'll join us next time." Sandy gave Savannah's shoulders an affectionate hug. "We meet every Monday at one."

"Thanks, Sandy," Savannah said, genuinely grateful for her kindness.

"Where are you headed now?"

"I was going back to the Grand Hotel."

"Any chance you want to make a pit stop?" Sandy grinned warmly. "I'd love for you to see my gallery. I keep hot cider in a carafe at the ready."

"I love hot cider," Savannah said. "I haven't had it in years."

"Well then, come on over and let me pour you a cup!"

"Thanks, Sandy. I'd love that."

Savannah had passed by the gallery several times since it stood on the corner right beside Sisters' Row. She'd been entranced by the large sparkly snow globe in the front window, but was even more enchanted with the place once she stepped inside. Sandy's gorgeous artwork was everywhere. Oil canvasses of a various sizes hung on the walls, illuminated by tasteful gallery lights. Each scene was a holiday one.

Some portrayed outdoor landscapes set in snowy fields, and others depicted sweet Christmas scenes of families with children hanging stockings from their mantels or decorating Christmas trees. One piece in particular immediately caught Savannah's eye. In it, a cute brunette with apple dumpling cheeks sat with a

handsome fellow in a horse-drawn sleigh. It was a
period piece, probably set in the early nineteen
hundreds, and the woman—who had just taken a bite
out of a cookie—was offering the treat to her
companion.

"Is that a Virginia Cookie?" Savannah asked,
stepping closer. As she did, she saw the painting was
titled *Winter Wedding*.

"It is, indeed," Sandy said pleasantly, slipping out
of her coat. She offered to take Savannah's and hung
them both on a rack by a table holding an assortment of
holiday mugs, including one that contained candy
canes. Sandy poured them each a mugful of steaming
hot cider then unwrapped a candy cane and plopped it
in her drink, while Savannah watched with amazement.
"Want a candy cane, too?"

Savannah laughed cheerily in reply. "I'll just take
mine straight up, thanks." When Sandy handed her the
mug, she asked, "When did you paint *Winter
Wedding*?"

"Oh, some years ago." Sandy thought on this. "It
was before Hannah moved here, though. And, you want
to know a secret?" Her blue eyes twinkled. "I think that
she found it inspiring."

"Hannah?"

"Yeah. When she saw it featured her great-
grandma's cookies, she became very interested in the
legend and learning more about Lena."

"I've heard about that legend," Savannah said. "It
sounds pretty incredible."

"Most great things in life are!" Sandy answered
merrily.

Savannah curiously cocked her chin. "Don't tell me you believe in the story?"

"About the cookies?" Sandy's cheeks colored. "I do know they're special. I can attest to that." She thought a moment before adding, "Olivia probably will, too."

"Olivia?"

Sandy tapped her chin and studied the ceiling. "And Hannah, of course, as well."

"What is it that everybody will attest to?"

"Oh, just that…" Sandy swirled the candy cane around in her mug. "Magical things happen when you open yourself up and believe."

"So, the cookie in my freezer has powers?" Savannah asked jokingly.

Sandy blinked hard. "That depends! What kind of cookie is it?"

"A Commitment Cookie, the sort that says *Forever—*"

"*Yours*?" Sandy yelped joyfully. "What? Who on earth gave you that?"

"Kurt Christmas."

"Kurt?" Sandy appeared delighted. "Awesome." Her eyebrows knitted together, then she viewed Savannah with sympathy. "Oh, dear. Oh, dear. Oh, dear…" Sandy set her mug on the counter to rub her temples.

"Sandy? What's wrong?"

Sandy leaned toward her and whispered. "Eliza's still in the picture, isn't she?"

"Yes, but how did you…?" Savannah abruptly stopped talking, recalling what Kurt had said. Surely, he'd been kidding when he'd intimated that Sandy could read minds?

"Sandy?"

Sandy stared at her innocently. "Huh?"

What am I thinking? Savannah said to herself without uttering a word.

"Now, how would I know that? Ha-ha!" Sandy cupped a hand to her mouth and her cheeks flamed. "Oops!"

Savannah blinked hard, flummoxed. "How did you just do that?"

"I...uh...er..."

"Are you telepathic somehow?"

"Tele...ha! Heavens! No!"

"Then how could you guess—?"

"Honestly, I don't know," Sandy said with panic-stricken eyes. "That wasn't supposed to happen with you."

"What does that mean?"

"It means... Hoo boy." Sandy heaved a breath and sat down on a stool by the counter. Her gaze shot to the door and the street outside. The gallery was still technically closed for lunch for ten more minutes, and no one appeared to be coming. "Nick's going to kill me."

"Nick? Why would he care?"

"Family secrets," Sandy hissed quietly.

"There are more?" Savannah asked, fascinated. "You mean Nick really *can* tell who's been naughty and nice?"

"Who told you that?" Sandy asked with alarm.

"Kurt."

Sandy shook her head in disappointment. "That man is one big blabbermouth."

"It's all right," Savannah said, wondering if Sandy had gone slightly off her rocker. Nick, too. Not to mention Kurt! "I won't tell anybody."

"Good, that's good. Because you can't."

Savannah didn't intend to, lest people think her crazy, as well.

"You can't talk about the Clauses or the Christmases, either!"

"The Christmases?" Savannah asked astounded. "Are you saying they have 'family secrets,' too?"

Sandy's blue eyes rounded. "Nope! Didn't say that! Not me!" She picked up her cider mug, apparently puzzling through something. "That is so odd," she said, musing to herself. "Really, really strange."

"What is?"

Sandy's head jerked up. "Oh! Sorry, Savannah. Just chattering to myself." She stared deep into Savannah's eyes. "You must have *something*, something *very special* calling you to Christmas Town… Otherwise?" She perplexedly shook her head. "No, it doesn't make any sense."

"You and Kurt are cousins, right?" Savannah asked.

"Very distant ones," Sandy said. "Buddy's grandpa and my great-grandma were brother and sister. They were both Christmases then she became a Claus. And the rest is, well…" Sandy shrugged merrily. "History!"

Sandy grabbed onto her candy cane again and swirled it around and around in her mug. It was half as tall as when she'd first dropped it in there, and appeared to be melting. "So," she asked cagily. "What are you planning to do with your Commitment Cookie?"

"I…uh…eat it, I sup—"

"No!" Sandy shouted, surprising Savannah with her energy. "You can't do that. You must *share it.*" Her gaze landed on the painting titled *Winter Wedding.* "Share it with the one who gave it to you."

"Is that what happened with you and Ben?" Sandy was so emphatic about this Savannah was starting to believe she'd had personal experience with these Virginia Cookies.

"Er…um, not exactly!" Sandy beamed a smile. "Our story was slightly different." She stewed on this. "So was Olivia's…and, Hannah's, actually. But don't ask me!" she amended hurriedly. "You'll have to ask them!"

"But, what if I don't want to share my cookie?" Savannah asked suddenly.

Sandy looked like she'd been doused in cold water, then she appeared to shake it off. "That might work, too." She gnawed at her bottom lip. "You never can be sure with those Commitment Cookies. They sometimes have a will of their own."

"We *are* talking about inanimate baked goods? Sugar and flour and spice?"

"And, everything oh so nice—when it comes to matters of the heart," Sandy warned. "You'll have to be careful with yours."

"My heart or my cookie?"

"Both!" Sandy said with renewed vigor. "Absolutely!"

"I'll take your caution under advisement."

"Good!" She narrowed her eyes in thought. "You'd probably better advise Kurt, too."

"I don't expect I'll be talking to him…" Savannah stalled by sipping from her cider. "Anytime soon."

"That's okay," Sandy said with a wave of her hand. "There's no super big rush. You can take it up with him on Friday."

"Friday?"

"Hannah and Carter are having Ben and me out to dinner at their cabin. Hannah said you and Kurt are invited, too."

Savannah was aware that she'd been included, but she'd had no clue that Kurt was coming, as well.

"He *is* Carter's best friend," Sandy explained, even though Savannah hadn't commented.

She set down her mug and carefully observed Sandy. "You're very intuitive, aren't you?"

"Intuition! Uh-huh! That's what it is," Sandy said, her eyes sparkling. "One hundred per cent."

The next evening after closing the clinic, Kurt went to see Eliza at the hospital. Her job as an administrator had her keeping late hours, and he found her in her office busily working at her desk as he'd expected. Kurt had slept on the decision, and was more certain than ever this is what he needed to do. Things had been going on too long with Eliza. A clean break was what they needed. It was the right thing for both their sakes.

She caught him standing in her open doorway when she looked up from typing at her keyboard. "Why, Kurt! This is a surprise."

"Good evening, Eliza," he said, removing his hat. "I hope I'm not interrupting."

"Come now," she said graciously. "I always welcome interruptions from you."

Kurt wondered if she would have said that, if she'd known what was coming.

"Please," she said as he took off his coat. "Have a seat."

Eliza's office was sleek and efficient with stylish metal-frame chairs facing her desk. Their seats and backs were made of red cordovan leather, adding a hint of elegance to the streamlined room. There were two potted plants in the corner by the window and a bonsai tree sat on her desk, which was as clean as a whistle. Eliza never left paperwork lying around. She was an extremely meticulous woman. Plus, she was always fabulously put together, in a tastefully understated way.

"I didn't think you made rounds on Wednesdays?"

"I don't." Kurt took a seat in one of the chairs facing her desk. "This is a social call."

Eliza's grin brightened, then seconds later her lips drew into a thin line. "Something's the matter, isn't it?" Worry registered in her pretty brown eyes and Kurt hated himself for what he was about to do. Then again, he knew he'd despise himself even more if he didn't follow through with the conversation he'd planned. He'd been over and over it during his twenty minute drive here, until he had his speech down cold. Now, suddenly, his rehearsed lines failed him, so he opted for speaking from the heart.

"You know I think you're a wonderful woman."

She viewed him thoughtfully. "And, I think you're a wonderful man."

"It's just that we're—"

"Not right for each other." Eliza stunned him by cutting him off. "Honey…" She perused him affectionately. "I know."

"Eliza—"

"Please, wait and let me finish." She met Kurt's eyes. "You and I have been together a long while, and it's been a good ride. Wait. Correct that." Eliza smiled softly. "A great ride. You and me, the two of us together—we've worked so well. And, do you want to know why?"

Kurt's throat felt raw when he said, "We understand each other."

"Yes, we do." She viewed him compassionately. "We always have."

Kurt slowly shook his head. "It's no good. I can't do this…any longer."

"No," Eliza said surely. "I suspect you can't."

"It isn't about you."

"I know that," she said gently. "It's about someone else, isn't it? That pretty redhead you ran into at brunch."

"Her name is Savannah."

"She's beautiful."

"So, Eliza, are you."

She laughed at this, but not at him. "You can't help yourself with the compliments."

"Not when they're well deserved," he said honestly.

"Have you known her for a while?" Eliza asked.

"Yes."

"Longer than us?"

"Much longer, but we've been out of touch."

"How lucky for you both that you found each other again."

"I'm not so sure it's going anywhere," Kurt admitted hoarsely.

Eliza nodded with understanding. "But you have to try."

"Yeah."

"Then, I wish you Godspeed and good luck."

"What about you?" Despite Eliza's outward strength, Kurt couldn't help but worry about her. She'd been nothing but a class act, and had always treated him so well.

"I can take care of myself," she said with a thin smile. Then she surprised Kurt by mentioning her ex-husband. "Yuri and I are going for coffee."

"Is that right?" Kurt asked with a pleased grin.

"It could mean nothing." Eliza lifted a shoulder. "Then again..." Her eyes twinkled with mischief.

"I wish the two of you well."

"Thanks, Kurt!" She slid open her desk drawer and extracted two tickets. "Here," she said, handing them to him. "You might want to take these."

Kurt saw they were tickets to the Christmas Town Ball. He'd invited Eliza to attend with him in October and she'd accepted. "You can still keep the tickets," he said attempting to hand them back to her. "Take Yuri."

Eliza shook her head. "You're the one with the connection to Christmas Town. You go, and take Savannah."

"If she'll come with me." There was a hint of doubt in his voice.

"Why wouldn't she?" Eliza questioned, and then she asked, "Did you give her that Commitment Cookie?"

Kurt flushed with embarrassment. "Actually, yes...I did."

"Well then," Eliza said with conviction. "It appears you're all set."

Chapter Twelve

On Friday evening, Sandy and Ben offered to give Savannah a ride to Carter's cabin. Ben was stopping by Sisters' Row anyway, to pick up Liz, who'd be babysitting their twins with Lily's capable "mother's helper" assistance. Lily wasn't quite old enough to handle Holly and Rose on her own, but Sandy thought she would be soon. Probably by this time next year. Savannah had been watching from her front window and stepped out onto her stoop when she saw Ben's SUV pull up to the curb. Liz exited her town house at the same time, and the two women nearly knocked elbows in their coats as they latched their front doors.

"Hi, Savannah!" Liz said with a jolly laugh. "Fancy running into you here!"

"Good to see you, Liz."

Savannah felt a little sorry for Liz being stuck babysitting, but Liz assuaged her worries by volunteering that she was really looking forward to tonight. "I of course see the rascals at the daycare," she said, "but it's especially fun spending time with them at night." Liz smiled warmly. "I love reading stories, and the tucking into bed part."

Savannah thought to herself what a great mom Liz would make, and her heart ached for her due to Liz's earlier admission.

Ben stepped from his SUV and gave a cheery wave. "Hello, ladies!" He was tall and dark-haired with dark eyes, well built and very handsome.

"Stay right there!" Liz instructed. "We're coming!"

Savannah had dressed in brown jeans, leather boots, and a sparkly white V-neck sweater. She had a small strand of pearls around her neck that matched her pearl teardrop earrings, and she'd worn her hair long and loose with just one top portion pulled back in an angel cookie barrette.

"I see you're enjoying your accessory," Liz commented, as they descended the short flight of steps and headed for Ben's SUV.

"I'm enjoying all of them," Savannah replied. "Thanks so much!"

"I guess you're planning on being good tonight," Liz said with a wink.

Savannah thought of seeing Kurt again and her face flushed hot. "Why, yes! Of course!" she answered breezily, though her heart hammered harder.

"It's so nice of your brother to have you out to dinner."

"Yeah. I can't wait to see Hannah and Amanda," Savannah said, purposely neglecting to mention that the Christmas Town doctor would also be there. When she called to offer Savannah a ride, Sandy had mentioned that Kurt would be running a little late due to a last-minute emergency at the clinic. He had his SUV with him though, so he would drive directly to the cabin when he could, since it was a straight shot down River Road.

Not that Savannah was keeping things from Liz. It was more like, at the moment, there wasn't much to tell. Savannah additionally felt really awkward about how she'd left things with Kurt at Santa's Sandwich Shop. She'd basically run out on their lunch. Just like she'd run out of Kurt's bungalow the morning after Olivia's wedding.

Ben held open a door for Liz to sit in front then gallantly opened one of the back doors for Savannah so she could climb inside. Before she did, she gave him a quick hug. She'd met him previously at Olivia's wedding, which was where she'd gotten to know Sandy. "It's nice to see you again, Ben!"

"Yeah," he said, cordially hugging her back. "You too, Savannah. It's great having you in Christmas Town."

On the way to Sandy and Ben's house, Liz glanced back over her shoulder at Savannah. "Will Olivia and Nick be there tonight, too?"

"I'm afraid not," Savannah answered. "Nick's trying to wrap up some work before his upcoming family trip, and Olivia's busy baking."

"Baking what?" Liz asked.

"Cookies, apparently!" Savannah said. "Lots of them!"

Ben flipped on his turn signal as they approached Church Street. It was still snowing hard, and his wiper blades were struggling to keep up. "I hear she's going with Nick up to Canada."

Savannah nodded when he viewed her in his rearview mirror. "Yes, it will be her fist time seeing Nick's family's farm."

"That should be exciting," Liz said.

"Very," Ben remarked, as if he knew something that they didn't.

"It's a shame Olivia will be gone part of the time you're here," Liz said.

"I know," Savannah answered. "But it couldn't be helped. Nick's needed in the Maritime Provinces, and Olivia's excited about going with him to support him."

Liz gave a happy sigh. "They're perfect for each other."

"Yeah, they are," Ben wholeheartedly agreed.

Ben pulled into the drive of a cute two-story house that was all decked out for Christmas. Evergreen garlands and Christmas lights shaped like snowflakes draped from the porch railing and there was a pretty wreath with a red-and-green checkered bow hanging on the front door.

Savannah viewed it with admiration. "Darling house!"

"Thanks!" Ben answered happily. He turned to Liz. "Let me walk you inside and get Sandy." Next, he addressed Savannah. "If you just want to wait here, I'll leave the engine running."

"Of course!" she said, as he and Liz exited the SUV.

After a short fifteen-minute ride, Sandy, Ben, and Savannah arrived at Carter and Hannah's cabin out near River Run. It was a cute log-frame house with a tin roof and a broad front porch facing the mountains. A wide snowy field separated the property from the riverbank, and someone had obviously had a good time today building a sturdy snowman in the cabin's front yard.

"He looks like Frosty," Sandy commented with a chuckle as they walked by.

"From the cartoon?" Savannah questioned.

"From our front hall," Ben answered with a smile. "But he's made of wood, not snow, and serves as our entryway sentinel."

"It's true!" Sandy's expression brightened. "I'll show him to you sometime when I have you over. I'm sorry about tonight," she explained apologetically. "We didn't want to get the kids too stirred up by visitors before leaving them with a sitter."

"It's all right," Savannah said. "I didn't mind waiting in the SUV." And she honestly hadn't. Not one bit. Ben had only been gone a few minutes, before he returned with Sandy wearing her puffy white coat, mittens, and shimmering earmuffs.

Ben was just about to ring the bell when Carter pulled open the door. He held Amanda in one arm, and the toddler was adorable. She had wispy brown hair that fell to her shoulders and enormous dark eyes. Her milky complexion was offset by rosy cheeks and plump pink lips tipped up in a grin. She had a few teeth already, and apparently more were on the way.

"Welcome! All of you," Carter said.

Amanda shook the silver rattle she held in one hand and gave a contented chortle.

"She is just precious!" Savannah said, leaning forward and giving her niece a kiss. "You're such a sweetie," she told the child, who stared at her and gurgled happily again.

"Good to see you, sis!" Carter gave her a one-armed hug and then briefly hugged Sandy, before taking Ben's hand.

Ben shook hands then passed Carter a decorative wine bottle package. "It's holiday wine!" he announced merrily. "Meant to be served hot."

"Sounds great. Thank you!" Carter ushered them inside and shut the door. As he did, two adult cats skittered out of the way. One was a curious orange and white striped tabby, and the other a more timid-seeming gray cat with a white blaze on its nose and paws that looked like little white boots.

"These must be the pets I've heard so much about," Savannah said, smiling. She bent low to pet them both on the head, and the gray one cautiously slunk away while the orange fellow eagerly darted forward, his pink nose tilted up and his eyes focused on Savannah's barrette.

"Yes," Carter answered. "Meet Jingles," he said motioning toward the orange one. "And, Belle." He nodded toward the other.

"Mind your jewelry!" Sandy said.

"I'm keeping my keys close this time." Ben patted his pocket and Sandy and Carter chuckled, apparently recalling some previous joke.

"Kurt's running late," Carter said, glancing briefly at Savannah. "But he'll be here in a bit. He just phoned that his patient emergency is wrapping up."

"What happened?" Sandy asked, removing her mittens and earmuffs. "Kurt was dashing to the clinic when he phoned me, so he didn't have time to explain."

"Josiah Smith needed stitches," Carter answered.

"The baby?" Sandy gasped with concern. "Oh, no!"

Ben addressed Savannah. "Josiah's about one year older than our twins and Amanda. He's Jade and Wendell Scott's son. They also have an older boy, Alexander."

"How did it happen?" Ben removed his coat and offered to take Savannah's and Sandy's.

"Apparently, Alexander was trying to teach Josiah how to jump on the sofa."

"Oh, no!" Savannah said.

"Oh, yes," Carter replied, shaking his head. "Josiah bounced off and hit his head on the coffee table."

Sandy clapped a hand to her mouth. "Poor Josiah! How many stitches did he need?"

"Just three." Carter tapped his left temple. "Right here."

"That's mighty close to the eye," Ben said. "It's a good thing it wasn't worse."

"Children tend to have guardian angels that way," Sandy added. Then she spoke to Savannah. "Love the barrette! Is that a Charity Cookie?"

Savannah nodded pleasantly. "It was a gift from Liz."

"Did I hear something about my Virginia Cookies?" Hannah asked, emerging from the kitchen. Her chestnut colored hair was cut in a chin-length bob and her dark brown eyes sparkled. She dusted her hands on her apron and rushed for Savannah. "Savannah! It's so great to see you! Welcome to Christmas Town!" She hugged her warmly then pulled back to examine

Savannah's barrette. "It *is* a Charity Cookie, and a very lovely one at that. Liz Martin does excellent work."

Savannah surveyed the cozy living room that included a small sofa and a couple of reading chairs. A table by a window had seating for two and a high chair was pushed up against it. A woodstove was by another window framing the darkened mountains, their silhouettes barely visible through blasting torrents of snow. Christmas decorations adorned the walls, and a nicely decorated Christmas tree stood in one corner partially obstructing a set of bookshelves. "You have a wonderful place," she told Hannah and Carter. "Very homey."

"Believe it or not, your brother bought most of the Christmas decorations himself."

"Carter?" Savannah asked, blown away. She'd never known Carter to care much about decorating anything. He was a no-nonsense sort of guy who rarely even noticed home decorating details.

"Oh, yes," Hannah said. "He got them when we were dating and completely did this place up!" She twinkled at her husband. "I think he was trying to impress me."

Carter jostled Amanda in his arms, and smiled lovingly at Hannah. "Did it work?"

"You know it did!" she said, striding over to give him a plucky kiss.

"Still newlyweds!" Sandy said with a joyful sigh.

"We are too, dear." Ben brought an arm around her shoulder and held Sandy close, and suddenly Savannah felt like the odd person out.

"Need any help in the kitchen?" she asked Hannah.

As Hannah started to answer, someone knocked at the front door.

"That would be Kurt," Carter said. "Savannah, could you get it? I think Amanda needs changing." Savannah saw that the gray cat had curled up and gone to sleep on the sofa while the orange one was close on Carter's heels.

Sandy and Ben swapped secretive glances, then Ben said, "And, I'll just carry these coats upstairs!"

"I'm helping Hannah in the kitchen," Sandy announced, snagging her friend by the elbow.

"Right!" Hannah said. She grinned brightly at Savannah. "Thanks for answering the door!"

The two women scooted into the kitchen as the men disappeared upstairs, with the orange cat trailing them. Kurt knocked again and Savannah's heart pounded. It was merely dinner at her brother's place. Something casual. No big deal. But when she opened the door she found Kurt standing there, looking more handsome than ever. He held a bottle of bubbly in one hand and a dozen long-stemmed red roses in the other.

Chapter Thirteen

"I'm sorry I'm late." Kurt stepped inside and searched the empty living area. "Have I missed all the fun already?"

"No, not at all!" Savannah took a giant step backwards and her knees wobbled. "Sandy, Ben, and I only just got here a few moments ago." She glanced at the flowers. "How nice of you to bring a hostess gift."

"These aren't for the hostess," Kurt said, meeting Savannah's eyes.

Heat flooded her cheeks. "What?"

Kurt set the bottle of champagne down on a side table then removed his fedora. "The champagne is for dessert. But these?" He moved toward her and offered her the beautiful bouquet. "Are for you."

"I don't understand?" Savannah searched his eyes and Kurt swallowed hard.

"I'm afraid I made a really big mistake on Tuesday. I offended you, and I'm sorry. I hope you'll accept my apologies and these."

Savannah accepted the fragrant bouquet, which was wrapped in green tissue paper and tied up with a silky red ribbon.

"Kurt," she said weakly. "You shouldn't have. Eliza—"

"There is no Eliza," he told her seriously, and Savannah's pulse raced. "Not anymore."

He stared down at her with a longing look. "You were right about what you said, you know. It wasn't fair for me to ask about James, when I was still seeing her. So I went to see Eliza on Wednesday, and we broke it off."

"Was she…?" Savannah caught her breath, her heart pounding. "Upset?"

Kurt gave a melancholy smile. "In a way, she might have been relieved. Things were never going anywhere between us. Both of us knew that."

"I'm sorry, Kurt. That still must have been hard."

"Doing the right thing often is. Don't you agree?"

"How is the patient?" Ben asked, traipsing down the stairs. He took one look at Kurt and then stared at Savannah. Next, his gaze fell on the flowers. "If I'm interrupting…" he said, starting to back up the steps.

"No, stay!" Savannah said, her mind reeling. "I'm just going to…" She shot a quick glance at Kurt. "Put these in water."

As she walked toward the kitchen, Kurt slipped out of his coat and grinned at Ben. "How's our Justice of the Peace?"

"Just great. How's our town doctor?" Ben joined him in the living area and offered to take Kurt's coat, but Kurt declined with a shake of his head. "No worries. I'll take it upstairs myself." He viewed the staircase. "Is Carter up there?"

"He's with Amanda in the nursery."

"Great," Kurt said, heading that way.

Kurt laid his coat on the bed in the master bedroom with the others, as Carter exited the nursery holding Amanda. Jingles was right behind him. Probably due to Amanda holding that bright shiny silver rattle. The tomcat loved all things that glittered, and often got into mischief due to this inclination.

The huge upstairs loft had once been one room with an en suite bathroom. When he and Hannah were expecting Amanda, Carter had partitioned off what had previously served as a sitting area, converting it to a proper nursery with a dividing wall and a door. This afforded him and Hannah privacy, and also provided a quieter sleeping space for Amanda during her naps and earlier bedtime. A baby monitor near her crib connected to a portable receiver in the kitchen that could be carried around the downstairs, so the adults could hear their baby if she needed them. The most amazing thing was, Amanda rarely fussed or cried. She was a very happy-natured child.

"Kurt!" Carter said with a pleased grin. "You made it!"

"Josiah is all stitched up," Kurt said. "And, as good as new."

The friends approached each other and firmly shook hands.

"How did it go with the flowers?" Carter asked sotto voce.

"Well enough," Kurt whispered back. "Thanks for the tip."

When Kurt had confided to Carter about how badly he'd messed up his Tuesday lunch, Carter had reasonably suggested he do two things. Clear the air with Eliza, and then make things up to Savannah. Carter had learned from Hannah that women had a weakness for roses. They were a great way to say so many things, including *I'm sorry*.

"Did you have a chance to talk?" Carter asked him.

"Not much, but I did tell her about Eliza."

"That you broke it off?" When Kurt nodded, Carter said, "Well, good. That's good. That's a start."

Kurt smiled at Amanda and gently pinched her chubby cheek. "Hey, cutie! How are you?"

Amanda cooed at him and shook her rattle.

"She gets prettier every day," Kurt said, smiling at the child.

Carter bounced Amanda contentedly in his arms. "Yeah."

"I've got to tell you," Kurt continued. "So does Savannah."

"You've still got it bad, haven't you?"

"Honestly, man? It's worse than ever."

Carter eyed him curiously. "Why do you think that is?"

"Because, for the first time in forever, I feel like we might have a chance."

"That would be pretty amazing."

"What would?"

Carter's green eyes sparkled and for a split second they appeared moist. "Calling you brother."

"Don't go jinxing things," Kurt warned, as Jingles observed the men curiously. "Savannah hasn't even agreed to date me yet."

"She will," Carter replied knowingly.

"How can you be so sure?"

"Come on." Carter laid a hand on Kurt's shoulder then spoke confidently. "What woman could resist the good doctor of Christmas Town?"

Savannah carried the roses into the kitchen, and Sandy and Hannah turned to her from their work at the counter. "Roses!" Hannah said cheerily. "Well!"

"Kurt brought those for you?" Sandy asked with delighted surprise. "Gosh!"

Savannah's blush deepened. "He brought some champagne for all of us to enjoy later."

"Champagne?" Hannah and Sandy twinkled at each other. "What are we celebrating?" the pair asked in unison.

"I'm not sure," Savannah answered, thinking of Eliza. It felt wrong to celebrate a break-up. Then again, a sneaky little part of her heart couldn't help but rejoice in the idea that Kurt was free.

"He is?" Sandy asked, grinning.

Savannah blinked in surprise, and Hannah scrutinized Sandy. "Nobody said anything," Hannah said suspiciously.

"I...er! Just had a feeling!"

"Intuition?" Hannah quipped in a whisper.

When Sandy nodded quickly, Hannah stared agape at Savannah and just said, "Wow."

"I know, right?" Sandy glanced sideways at Hannah. "It's got to mean something."

Something freaky, yeah. Like Sandy had a strange way of getting into Savannah's head. "But I...didn't even mention Eliza."

Hannah clapped her hands together. "Cat's out of the bag! It's true!" She stepped closer to the others and whispered. "Kurt told Carter he planned to cut things off. A clean break, completely."

Sandy frowned sympathetically. "Poor Eliza."

"Come on!" Hannah cried. "Eliza doesn't love Kurt." When the others looked at her, she continued, "She said so."

"When?" Sandy asked.

"When she came to buy that Commitment Cookie."

"She didn't buy it for Kurt?" Savannah asked, perplexed.

Hannah shook her head. "She intended to give it to her ex-husband, Yuri. If she could get up the nerve. That's what she told Meredith at the register when they were making conversation."

Savannah immediately felt better about the break-up. "So Eliza was still hung up on him?"

"Apparently, yes," Hannah said. "They have a child together and have been spending more time doing things as a family unit."

"Wouldn't that be wonderful for Eliza?" Sandy said.

"Yes!" Savannah agreed, her heart lighter. "Perfect." She nervously surveyed the others' faces. "I didn't want to feel responsible. Not for another person's misery."

"We understand what you mean," Sandy said sweetly. "I had no clue Eliza still pined for her ex, either."

"Me either," Savannah said. "That's interesting."

"Yes." Sandy's eyebrows knitted together. "So, instead of giving the cookie to Yuri she gave it to Kurt?"

"Eliza didn't intend for him to keep it," Hannah filled in. "She suggested he give it to someone else. Kurt told this to Carter when he was explaining how Kurt's Commitment Cookie wound up with Savannah."

Both women grinned sunnily. "My, my!" Hannah said. "It's all coming together!"

"But, I haven't eaten the cookie yet," Savannah said.

"Where is it?" Sandy questioned.

"I popped the bag in my freezer."

"You'd best be careful," Hannah said. "That freezer's not to be trusted at Sisters' Row."

Freezer? Savannah was certain she must have misheard her.

"No, you didn't," Sandy said. "That—" She clamped her mouth shut, and shyly shrugged. "Sorry, Savannah."

Savannah blinked and shook her head.

"Just don't think about anything too personal around her," Hannah suggested. "Think of snow-covered hills, one huge snowy white landscape! A big blank!"

Savannah wasn't quite sure how to respond.

"Here," Hannah said, reaching under the kitchen sink for a vase. Savannah noted she had a number of them. "Let's put those roses in water."

She set the vase down by the sink and pulled open a kitchen drawer, extracting a pair of shears. Sandy picked up the scissors and unwrapped the roses, expertly trimming the bottom of their thorny stems.

Savannah glanced around the kitchen. "Er...can I do anything to help?"

"Why don't you serve the wine?" Hannah said. "You can ask the guys if they want red or white, or if they'd prefer a beer. We have vegetarian lasagna and garlic bread coming and Sandy's made the salad."

Savannah saw that a colorful mixed salad with croutons on top sat by the refrigerator in a large wooden bowl. "It all smells delicious."

Sandy beamed happily. "Hannah's made tiramisu for dessert."

"Yum! I guess that will go well with champagne."

"Then, afterward, we can have the mulled wine!" Sandy added.

"Sure," Hannah said. "Assuming you've picked your designated driver."

"We could all sleep over!" Sandy joked. "It would be like one big slumber party! The girls upstairs and the fellows down here."

"Are you certain that Liz could handle the kids overnight?" Hannah studied her and Sandy puffed out her bottom lip.

"Oh yeah. Probably not."

Savannah was glad that whole idea got nipped in the bud. She started to think about Kurt and her sleeping together under the same roof, but then quickly backed away from Sandy, recalling Hannah's warning. "I'll just go and ask the guys what they want to drink!" she shouted, imagining drifting snow.

The evening passed pleasantly with everyone sitting near the woodstove in the living area. Carter pulled the two chairs from the table over into the seating group, and sat beside Hannah, who was in one of the armchairs. Amanda sat near her feet on a play blanket, happily shaking her toys and flipping through child-sized cardboard books. Jingles crouched contentedly beside her flicking his tail, while Belle had apparently sought out a quieter place to sleep upstairs.

"Is she always so well behaved?" Savannah asked, observing Amanda.

"Yeah," Carter said. "I guess we're lucky."

"Not that all parents aren't lucky!" Hannah rushed in. She smiled compassionately at Sandy and Ben. "All babies are a blessing."

"Even the challenging ones," Ben said with a chuckle. "We know."

Kurt was in the other straight-backed chair next to Savannah and Sandy and Ben sat on the sofa.

"This lasagna is delicious," Savannah said, complimenting Hannah, and everyone readily agreed. The group also thanked Sandy for putting the tasty salad together.

"Be sure to save room for dessert!" Hannah advised them.

"Dare I guess?" Ben teased lightly. "Cookies?"

"Nope, not cookies this time," Hannah replied. "Tiramisu."

"That reminds me of the bottle I put in the freezer," Kurt said. "I'd better go and check on it."

"What are we celebrating?" Sandy called after him.

Kurt turned in the doorway and grinned around the room. "Good friends being together." When his eyes settled on Savannah, he added, "Old and new."

Savannah felt a warm glow envelop her, and for a moment she was lost in Kurt's chocolate-brown gaze.

"I'll drink to that!" Carter said, raising his wineglass, and everyone laughed.

"Me, too," Savannah uttered softly, taking a dainty sip of wine.

As she did, Kurt's grin broadened. Then, when none of the others were watching, he shot her a wink and Savannah's heart fluttered. She'd be here in Christmas Town through the new year, and would have ample opportunity to see him, and get to know him better. As he was now, a completely grown-up and very sexy man... And, there was nobody standing between them. Not James. Not Eliza. Not Lou, nor Carter. The only stumbling blocks that remained were the secrets of her heart. Unfortunately for Savannah, they were pretty big ones.

Chapter Fourteen

As the adults finished their dinner, Hannah excused herself briefly to put Amanda to bed. When she picked the baby up, she glanced around the room. "I wonder what happened to Amanda's new rattle?" Her eyes searched the floor. "Her grandpa just gave it to her this year for her birthday."

The others all helped her look but no one could locate the sterling silver toy. All at once, Hannah met Carter's gaze, then stared around the room. It wasn't only Amanda's rattle that was missing; the big orange furball had disappeared, too.

"Jingles!" everyone cried collectively.

"I think I know where to find it," Carter said, standing.

Hannah carried Amanda and was right behind him on the stairs. "Check under the bed!"

"Right."

While they were gone, Ben started loading the dishwasher and Sandy put away food. Savannah was given the task of serving dessert, which she ladled into clear glass bowls, and Kurt poured the bubbly.

A short time later, everyone enjoyed dessert and champagne in the living room while chatting amicably. It was a fun way to end a companionable evening, during which the married couples had compared baby stories, and the group brought Savannah up to date on the other residents of Christmas Town. When the conversation turned to her, Savannah mentioned she'd finally organized the theater donations and had annotated everything. It would help with her curriculum planning to be able to easily reference what the theater already had on hand. Sandy asked about her meeting with Nick and Savannah explained her vision for utilizing the space. As she was discussing the idea of a serving counter for refreshments, Sandy's cell rang in her purse.

"Excuse me," Sandy said. "I'd better check that. It might be Liz."

When she answered her face hung in a frown. "Oh, no! Oh, dear! Really? When?"

"Is it the twins?" Ben asked, worry creasing his brow.

Sandy clamped her hand over the mouthpiece. "It's Lily. She's apparently come down with some sort of stomach flu, or maybe food poisoning. Liz isn't sure."

"What could she have eaten?" Hannah wondered.

Sandy rolled her big blue eyes and answered, "She and Annabel Slade apparently took a crack at making homemade eggnog this afternoon."

"Uh-oh!" Savannah replied.

"There were at the Slades' house and decided to use some of the fresh eggs they'd gotten from a nearby farm."

"Unpasteurized. That could be the trouble," Kurt said. "Do you want me to stop by and take a look at her?" he offered kindly.

"Let's see how she does tonight with crackers and ginger ale," Sandy answered, ending her conversation with Liz. "If she's not doing better in the morning, I'll call you."

Ben had already dashed upstairs to retrieve their coats. "We're sorry to cut out on you," he said, his mind obviously preoccupied by his daughter.

"Don't mention it," Carter said. "We understand."

Sandy glanced uncertainly at Savannah, who'd only finished half her dessert. "It's okay," Savannah said, setting down her bowl. "I can grab my coat and come—"

"Don't be silly," Hannah replied. "Please stay and finish your tiramisu!" She glanced Kurt's way. "Kurt can drive you home."

"I was just about to offer," he told Savannah. "Seriously, Sisters' Row is right on my way."

"Well, I…"

Sandy and Ben were slipping into their coats and were clearly anxious to get home. "Hannah's right," Savannah told them. "You two run along. I'll ride back with Kurt."

When the Winchesters nodded and prepared to leave, Savannah added, "I hope Lily feels better!"

"Yes, us too," Hannah said on her and Carter's behalf.

"Don't be afraid to give me a buzz if she takes a turn for the worse," Kurt said. "You know you can call me anytime."

Not long after, Savannah and Kurt thanked Hannah and Carter for their hospitality, saying they should be on their way. Carter was on duty tomorrow and Hannah was working, as well. Since Kurt had Saturday hours, he'd be at the clinic for a half day, too. So, nobody wanted the evening to run too late.

As they were leaving, Hannah slapped her forehead. "We forgot all about opening Ben and Sandy's holiday wine."

"Now, that's a shame," Carter lamented.

Savannah held her bouquet of roses in the vase Hannah had insisted on giving her. After all, she said she had plenty more under the sink.

"I have an idea!" Hannah's face lit up in a smile. "Why don't you two take it?"

"Us?" Kurt asked, surprised.

"For a little nightcap later, yeah!"

"I, er…" Savannah stared uncomfortably at Kurt. "I'm sure that Sandy and Ben meant for you two to have it."

"Let me show you a little secret." Carter crooked his finger, drawing their attention to a side cabinet that doubled as his bar. He opened the top door, exposing several wine bottles sporting the very same label.

"Wow, but how—?" Savannah started.

"Everyone working at the courthouse got a bottle this year," he explained. "As a gift from a new local vineyard. Tilly doesn't drink, so she gave me hers," he said, mentioning his secretary. "My deputy Victoria won't drink any wine with 'flavors' so she gave me her bottle, too."

"I'm starting to sense a theme," Kurt said wryly.

"Della Martin only drinks herbal teas and her husband Stan just drinks beer."

"And Della works at the courthouse, too," Savannah surmised with a chuckle. "Liz said she helps out part-time at Jingle Bells Booties."

"Exactly," Carter said, shutting his cabinet.

Then he picked up the bottle Ben had brought by. "My guess is that Ben and Sandy got more than their fair share of holiday wine, as well."

"All right," Kurt said, taking the bottle. "If you insist!" He surveyed Savannah who'd already put on her coat. "Savannah and I can argue over who gets to keep it during our ride home."

"Don't argue!" Hannah encouraged heartily. "*Share*. And, as long as you're sharing things…don't forget about that little treat in your freezer!"

Savannah felt herself color. "Gosh," she whispered to Kurt, as they walked through the snow toward his SUV. "There are a lot of shameless matchmakers around here."

"Yeah." He observed her studiously in the shadows, appearing not the least bit perplexed. "How about that."

Kurt held Savannah's roses for her while she climbed into the SUV and buckled her seat belt. Then, he handed the vase back to her and shut her door, before quickly popping open the back one and sliding the bottle of holiday wine onto the back seat.

"Looks like we have provisions," he told Savannah. "For…whenever."

He strolled around the vehicle and scooted in behind the steering wheel, cranking the engine and turning on the heat. It was below freezing out, but Savannah wasn't chilly. Her skin warmed each time Kurt looked her way.

"Thanks for driving me home," she said. "I hope that Lily will be all right."

"She should be," Kurt answered smoothly. "Most cases of food poisoning aren't truly dangerous. Merely inconvenient." He glanced at Savannah. "Might not even be food poisoning at all, and just a bug."

"It seems so easy for kids to pick things up," Savannah said. "Especially when they're in school. The first year I was a counselor, I got sick constantly. Even with high school kids, illnesses get passed around and I guess I wasn't used to being around so many germs."

"You appear to have toughened up."

Savannah chuckled at this. "I have in some ways." Then her heart sank just a tad. "But, not in all."

"Savannah." Kurt laid his hand on her arm. "Whatever it is that's bothering you, you can tell me. I know it was a long time ago, but I apparently did something—"

"Nothing that was really your fault."

"Well, you certainly weren't to blame, either."

Savannah swallowed past the lump in her throat. "Kurt, I..." She looked down and pulled out of his hold, but when she did Kurt took her hand.

"There's only so much beating ourselves up we can do over yesterday. We had something special once. Something earth-shattering." Kurt searched her eyes. "We pledged ourselves to each other."

"It's not like we were really married."

"I'm afraid I disagree." He kissed the back of her hand, and the warmth of his lips penetrated Savannah's thin leather glove. "Because, honestly? I've always felt like we were." His voice cracked with the admission. "I know that you remember. The moonlight…the stars…our hand-written vows…" His gaze poured over her and Savannah felt swept away. Snow pounded Kurt's SUV, blanketing the windshield and streaking the windows.

She answered in a whisper, the memory crisp and clear. "Yes."

"The tumbling sound of the ocean." Kurt pressed her hand to his heart. "The breeze blowing through your hair…" He cupped her cheek in his hand and Savannah's breath quickened. "The heat of your mouth against mine."

"We were in high school," she said as her lips trembled.

His voice was husky when he said, "Romeo and Juliet were young too."

"And look what happened to them."

Kurt stroked back her hair. "Not all love ends in tragedy."

"Ours did."

Kurt slowly shook his head. "Our story isn't over."

His lips brushed over hers and Savannah's grasp slipped on the vase. She righted it quickly on her lap, her entire universe whirling.

"Do you think it's a mistake that I'm still a bachelor?" He gave her a rose-petal-soft kiss, and Savannah's head felt light. "A man can't give away what's already been taken. Savannah," he rasped. "You still hold my heart."

She wanted to burst from the truth she held inside her. For—as much as she'd tried to deny and fight it— Kurt still held her heart, as well. Her grasp tightened around the neck of the vase as Kurt's kisses deepened and the sweet fragrance of roses filled the air. Kurt's fingers threaded through her hair and he gave her another tender lingering kiss. "Now, what do you say?" he asked with a questioning look. "Should we open that holiday wine?"

Savannah caught her breath. "Not here."

His dark eyes danced. "Your place or mine?"

Chapter Fifteen

Savannah's hand shook as she inserted her key into the front door at Sisters' Row.

Kurt's hand slid down her coat sleeve. "I'll help."

His hand guided hers and the key turned with a click. Sharp winds blew, chasing snowflakes off the porch railing, but with Kurt's arms around her, Savannah felt safe and warm.

"Just one glass of wine," she said as her voice shuddered.

Kurt gently squeezed her hand. "Yes."

She let him inside and switched on some lights, placing her bouquet on the dining room table. Kurt left his hat on the entryway table and carried the wine to the kitchen.

"Corkscrew?" he called, as Savannah removed her coat.

"In the drawer beside the sink!"

Savannah viewed her reflection in the foyer mirror, scarcely able to recognize herself. Her cheeks were flushed and her dark green eyes sparkled. She appeared radiant. Almost like a woman who'd been brought back into the sunshine after a long, lonely winter.

Another masculine query boomed from the kitchen. "Saucepan?"

"Under the stove!"

"Everything's heating…up."

"I…ah!" Savannah turned in embarrassment, seeing Kurt had entered the room. "…was just checking my hair," she said, nervously combing her fingers through it.

"It's never looked lovelier," Kurt said, admiring her fully. "You've never looked lovelier than you do right now." He twinkled her way. "Your cheeks are so rosy."

"Maybe it's frostbite?" Savannah joked.

"I don't think so," Kurt said, drawing near.

"You'd better hang up your coat! It's damp."

"All right." Kurt grinned sexily. "Then what?"

She sent him a spirited retort. "Then, we'll have our mulled wine."

"I was thinking we might have a cookie?"

"Don't push your luck." Savannah wryly twisted her lips. "Besides, you've already had dessert, Mr. I Never Eat Sweets. Ha! Ha-ha!" she said more boldly. "I knew that was an impossible lie."

Kurt smiled unconcernedly and took a seat on the sofa. "So? Maybe I like to limit my sweets to the ones that matter." He patted the cushion next to him. "Come. Sit."

"No, first I'll grab our wine."

Savannah strolled to the kitchen, mildly annoyed that Kurt was ordering her around. She would sit all right, but not *when and where* he told her. The small amount of liquid on the stovetop was already steaming in the saucepan, so she turned the gas burner off and reached into the cabinet for two mugs.

She returned to Kurt and handed him a mug, before taking a seat in the armchair kitty-corner from the sofa. Kurt slowly arched an eyebrow and accepted his wine, thanking her for it.

For a moment, they both sat in silence, sampling their libations.

"You know, this is pretty good," Kurt said.

Savannah primly straightened her spine. "Hmm, yes." She tasted cinnamon and cloves and maybe a hint of nutmeg, too. It was a delicious concoction.

"Savannah," Kurt said after a bit. "You don't need to be nervous."

"Who said I'm nervous?"

"Or afraid."

"I'm not."

"Of me."

When she stared at him, he continued, "All I want is your time. And, not even all of it. Just some." His Adam's apple rose and fell. "As much as you're willing to give me."

"Why the leniency?" she asked him sassily.

"Because, after a while… I'm certain you'll see what I see." Kurt placed his mug on the coffee table. "That things between us are meant to be: inevitable."

"Inevitable?"

Kurt sat back on the sofa and folded his arms across his chest. "Yes." As he spoke two little snowman legs tickled his shoulder.

He spun around with alarm to find Mr. Noodles goggling at him.

"I see you have company?"

Savannah couldn't help but laugh at the shocked expression on his face.

"Don't tell me you two haven't met?" she teased him.

Kurt took the stuffed object in his hands and turned it over, as if trying to decide which end was up. "This looks like one of my mother's creations."

"It is," Savannah said with a giggle. "She brought him by with a big box of Christmas decorations. Actually, it was very sweet."

Kurt studiously surveyed the room. "It doesn't look like you've put any of them up."

"I was intending to, but I was waiting to get a Christmas tree first."

"That sounds like the right idea."

"Most of the items Lou loaned me are ornaments, anyway."

"Ah." Kurt appeared to be pondering something. "Ray owns the nursery, you know."

"Yeah, and it's very convenient, right at the end of Santa Claus Lane. I thought I'd go by this weekend and pick out a small tree."

Kurt's face brightened in a grin. "I have a better idea."

"Oh?"

"Why don't you let me take you out to Ray and Meredith's farm, so you can cut down a fresh one?"

Savannah grew animated just considering the prospect. "Oh, gosh! I haven't done anything like that in years. Not since I was a kid in Virginia."

"I'd be happy to take you."

Savannah considered the size of her compact sedan and the much more ample space in the back of Kurt's SUV. "If it's not too much trouble…?"

"No trouble at all. The pleasure's all mine."

Kurt finished his last sip of wine then got to his feet.

"You're going already?" Savannah asked with dismay. While she'd insisted Kurt not stay long, she was just starting to feel at ease in his company.

"I don't want to overstay my welcome."

Savannah set her mug down beside his. "When should we go?"

"I work in the morning, but I'm free tomorrow afternoon. Say around two?"

Savannah became excited about this adventure, thinking it might be fun. "Two o'clock works for me."

"Perfect." Kurt strode toward the door, nabbing his coat and hat off the rack. "Then, I'll be on my way."

"Kurt, I…" Savannah got to her feet as well, her face warming. "I wanted to say thank you, and not just for driving me home, but also for what you said earlier—in your SUV. I know it took guts and wasn't easy."

"Doing the right thing seldom is," he said, reiterating what he'd told her earlier. Then, he put on his coat and hat. Savannah followed him to the foyer, catching a glimpse of her flowers as she went. She'd been half hoping he'd kiss her again, but it didn't appear that was in the cards.

"Thanks again for the beautiful roses."

"Thanks for forgiving me, Savannah."

"When did I say that?"

His dark brown gaze washed over her, and Savannah felt like he'd seen straight into her soul. "You didn't have to."

Chapter Sixteen

The next morning Olivia called Savannah at a little after six o'clock.

Savannah answered her cell then checked the clock on the nightstand beside her bed. "Wow, the sun's not even up yet."

"I know!" Olivia said, sounding chipper. "I hope you're not busy? Nick assured me that you'd be awake."

"Nick?" Savannah asked, befuddled. "But, how would he—?"

"He's just very, very good at that!" Olivia proclaimed brightly. "Extra sharp. As sharp as a tack! Or, cheddar cheese! Or…or, a forked tongue! Hmm." She paused to reflect a moment. "No, maybe not that."

"Have you had lots of coffee, or something?"

"No, that's what I'm calling about!" Olivia caught her breath then continued, "Want to go?"

"What?" Savannah sat up partway in bed. "Now?

"In about an hour. I thought I'd meet you at Jolly Bean Java on my way to the stables. Say…" she said, apparently as an afterthought. "Maybe you should come with me! You didn't meet my horse during the wedding, and now Nick and I have two! You and I could ride!"

Savannah knew Olivia loved horses and always had; she just stayed away from them herself. Savannah hadn't been on a horse in so many years, she rarely even thought about riding anymore. Which was absolutely for the better. "I'm not sure I'm up for riding today."

"Savannah, come on! You used to love it as a kid."

"I know, but it's been years."

"All the more reason to take it up again."

"I, uh…didn't bring the right clothes!"

"You can just wear jeans and your heavy coat. We've got the rest at the stables."

"Olivia," Savannah said more firmly. "*No.*"

"Well, gosh," Olivia said. "It was just an idea. No need to get testy." She inhaled sharply then asked with concern, "This isn't about…you know? What happened way back then? Because, Savannah. Honey. That is totally water under the bridge."

"It's not that," Savannah lied. "It's just that I'd rather not get all hot and sweaty. I've got plans later today."

"Plans?" Olivia brightened at this. "Do tell!"

But Savannah decided to tell her later, once she had caffeine in her system and could handle Olivia's constant questioning. Olivia, on the other hand, didn't seem to need any extra juicing up. She sounded positively wired—and winded.

"What are you doing, anyway?" Savannah asked her.

"Er…packing! Lots of tins!"

"Cookie tins?"

"Yes!" Olivia exclaimed like Savannah had just delivered a prizewinning answer in a contest. "How did you know?"

"I just had a hunch." Savannah leaned over and turned on the light. It was true that she hadn't been sleeping. She'd woken up around five a.m. and had become restless thinking of Kurt. He'd so unnerved her with his confession out at the cabin, and excited her with his offer of taking her to cut down a Christmas tree. Even though a part of her was still a tiny bit afraid of opening herself up to him, an even larger part of her heart urged her to forge ahead.

She'd trusted Kurt when he'd said she shouldn't fear him. He'd also been correct in assessing that Savannah had forgiven him for his blunder on Tuesday. The only question was, would he forgive *her* if he knew the whole truth about her past? In spite of how wonderful and understanding Kurt seemed, Savannah wasn't sure.

"Anyway," Olivia prattled on, "I was thinking it would be good for us to have some sister time. You know, before I go away."

"I thought you weren't leaving until the twenty-fourth?"

"Change of plans!" Olivia informed her. "Grandpa Claus has had a fall."

"Oh, dear."

"Yeah, I know. It stinks. His blood pressure isn't great, either. Plus, he's got gout," Olivia added, sounding horrified.

"Yikes."

"He does have a pretty big sweet tooth, it's true," Olivia shared. "Which is one reason I've been working extra hard on all the healthy treats I'm taking. Gluten-free! Low sugar! Sugarless sugar cookies—"

"Sugarless sugar cookies?" Savannah asked with surprise.

"Oh, yes; they're quite good." She dropped her voice in a conspiratorial whisper. "I don't like them quite as much myself to tell you the truth, but I'd never say that to Nick. I'm working hard to get him on a healthy eating plan. An ounce of prevention!"

"Yes, yes. I'm sure."

"So, will you meet me?"

"When are you leaving on your trip?"

"In the morning."

"Oh gee, then I guess I'd better."

"I wouldn't go if I didn't feel I had to," Olivia said. "I hate it so much knowing you've just come to town."

"Family emergencies can't be helped," Savannah responded sympathetically.

"I can call some of my friends," Olivia suggested kindly. "Set up things for you to do?"

"I'm already going to the church bazaar with Sandy and Ben tomorrow… Oh, dear," she said, remembering suddenly. "Lily's got a part in the pageant and she's just taken sick."

"That's what I heard," Olivia said. "She normally rides Blaze twice a week on Wednesdays and Saturdays. Sandy texted me late last night saying she wouldn't make it this morning."

"Poor kid," Savannah said. "I hope she's feeling better."

"If Sandy and Ben don't attend the bazaar, maybe Jade can take you?"

"Olivia," Savannah replied sternly. "I'm a big girl. I can take care of myself."

"You'll still be welcome at the Monday lunch!"

"That's great. I plan to go."

After a pause, Olivia said, "I can't wait to hear all about last night and how things went with Kurt! But, wait! Don't tell me yet... Nick's trying to break into my cookies and I need to stop him. *Nick!*" Savannah could hear Olivia shouting. "*Put that lid back on that cookie tin this second!*" Then his rejoinder rang out, "*Ho-ho-ho, dear! I don't know what you mean!*"

Savannah shook her head, thinking her sister and new brother-in-law were an extremely eccentric pair. Lovable, but really eccentric... Savannah supposed it was good they had found each other. They certainly seemed like a happy and well-suited couple.

"Sorry about that," Olivia said. "Can't trust him as far as I can throw him some days. He's really sneaky about suggesting I perhaps miscounted my cookies. Like, hey? I'm not doing the math? I'm great at math! Better now than I ever was! I can bake using the metric system. I do conversions in my head and everything."

"Wow."

"Impressive, yeah. I know," Olivia responded, sounding pleased.

"Okay, then!" Savannah said lightly. "I guess I'll see you at Jolly Bean Java?"

"Perfect! See you there in a few. *Nick, back away from that wire rack! Those cookies are still cooling...*" She clicked off and Savannah burst into giggles. Baking using the metric system? Who knew Olivia had such skill? And, who would have guessed Nick was such a pig? He kept himself in such great shape!

Savannah recalled Kurt's assertion that he didn't eat sweets, and then remembered the Claus and Christmas family connection. Maybe she shouldn't fault Kurt for being careful with his diet, after all. As a medical professional, he—above all people—surely understood the importance of family history.

When Savannah returned from having coffee with Olivia, she passed Liz, who was headed her way loaded down with small packages stuffed into two bulging paper bags with handles.

"You're out early," Savannah said, as they met on the corner of Santa Claus Lane by the Snow Globe Gallery. It was only a little after eight, so the Christmas Town shops were still shuttered.

"More barrettes," she explained with a grin. "Olivia's nearly run out! She had so much success with them last weekend, her stock has run low."

"That's great news, Liz! Only…I'm afraid Olivia's not there. She's headed out to Sleigh Bell Stables."

"I know. She told me last night that she wouldn't be there, but we agreed I'd leave them under the overhang by her shop's front door."

Savannah wasn't sure who would be around to sell the new merchandise, since Olivia was going out of town. Then, Liz filled in the gap for her.

"Olivia and Nick will be in Canada for the next few weeks, but it's such an important season for Olivia's shop, she didn't want to close it. So, Lou offered to step in and oversee things in the interim."

"That was nice of Lou."

"She and Buddy actually used to own All Things Christmas. Buddy seems content enough, but sometimes I wonder if Lou doesn't regret letting it go." Liz's eyes twinkled merrily. "Mrs. Christmas likes to stay busy!"

"Lou does have a lot of energy," Savannah agreed, wondering if being mayor didn't consume enough of it.

"She certainly stays active!" Liz replied. "She teaches piano lessons to kids and loves managing town business. And, I'm not just talking on the Town Council... Lou Christmas is Christmas Town's Number One Matchmaker."

"Is she?" Savannah asked, recalling Lou's advice to her regarding Kurt.

"Oh yeah, it's true. So far, though..." Liz's lips took a downward turn. "She hasn't found a match for me."

"You mean you've let her try?"

"Sure!" Liz shrugged beneath her winter coat as snow dusted her cap. "I mean, I figured...why not? But some of those fellows she picked out?" She shook her head with a grin. "Oh, boy!"

"I'd love to hear about your adventures sometime."

"And I'd love to share them." Liz surveyed her kindly. "Want to have lunch?"

"Today? I...er..." Savannah hedged, knowing she was already committed to seeing Kurt. Still, she really liked the idea of getting to know Liz better. "I'd love to, but can't today."

"Already filling up the calendar," Liz said warmly. "Good for you!"

"How about sometime next week?" Savannah suggested.

"I'm at the daycare Monday through Friday, but have time next Saturday?"

"One week from today sounds great! Where should we go?"

"The Elf Shelf Book Shop just started serving lunch in its café. Nothing elaborate: just soups and sandwiches." Liz pondered her memory of the menu. "Salads too, I think."

"That sounds fun. I haven't been inside the bookstore yet. I'd love to go, and hear about those adventures," Savannah replied with a giggle.

"Super!" Liz said. "Want to meet up there?" She went on further to explain, "I'm helping Della with something at her shop in the morning."

"That would be fine, yeah. What time?"

"How about twelve-thirty? I was planning to do some Christmas shopping in the afternoon."

"Now that you mention it, I need to do that, too."

Liz beamed brightly. "Then, let's go shopping together! We'll have lunch afterwards."

"Thanks, Liz," Savannah answered. "That sounds like the perfect Saturday plan."

Chapter Seventeen

Savannah stared out the SUV's window in wonder as Kurt drove her through Christmas Town. Sidewalks bustled with pedestrians and the shops on South Main Street seemed to be doing a brisk business, including All Things Christmas, which was packed with customers inside. "So many people out for holiday shopping!"

"We're into December now," Kurt answered. "It will only get worse."

Savannah perused his handsome profile and her pulse fluttered. Kurt was such a good-looking man, and each time she saw him he only looked better. He had a very attractive degree of confidence about him, too. While it was true that it sometimes bordered on cockiness, Savannah didn't totally mind that. She could give as good as Kurt gave—any day.

"Thanks for taking me out to Ray's farm," she said as they neared the roundabout. The snow had let up and only the finest of flakes dotted the windshield.

"Maybe we'll get lucky and catch a break in the weather," he said with an appealing grin.

"How did things go at the clinic this morning?"

"Very well. How about you?" He turned to her briefly. "Did you have a good morning?"

"Yes! I met Olivia for coffee." Savannah stifled a yawn. "At the crack of dawn."

"Olivia's an early riser," Kurt said. "I've often seen her headed to Jolly Bean Java when I'm on my way to the hospital to do rounds. And, I leave before seven."

As they neared the courthouse and took a right on River Run, he asked, "How's Olivia doing?"

"Great..." Savannah recalled the frantic look in Olivia's eyes as she'd recanted all the travel preparations she'd yet to do. "And, a bit panicked," Savannah said with a chuckle. "I think she might be a little nervous about meeting Nick's family."

"But his mom and dad came to the wedding?"

"His grandparents, I mean. His grandfather especially is very revered among the Clauses."

Kurt glanced her way and his dark eyes sparkled. "You don't say?"

"Have you met them? I know your families are close."

"Nick's grandparents? No. They pretty much keep to themselves—in certain ways."

Savannah screwed up her face, not understanding.

"Oh, they get out and about. Nick's grandpa is something of a globe trotter."

"Does his wife travel with him?"

"Sometimes. At others, she stays home and mans the family business. Their operation's quite large."

"That's what Olivia said, though she's been pretty cagey about sharing the details."

"Maybe that's because she doesn't know any?"

"Hmm, maybe." Savannah pondered this. "Well, anyway! She's sure to know more after this trip."

"No doubt it will be a learning experience."

They drove for several miles passing turn-offs to various farms, and a low wooden building with an empty gravel parking lot and a large sign proclaiming its name: The Reindeer Pub.

"Liz and I got pizza from that place," Savannah said. "It was phenomenal."

"Their microbrew's pretty good, too."

"Oh?"

"Yeah, they have their own label: Santa's Sleigh Malt."

"I'll have to try it sometime!"

Kurt grinned warmly. "I'll make sure you do."

Savannah spied a hand-painted sign up ahead for the Christmas Farm. An arrow pointing to the left announced the sale of fresh Christmas trees, with an invitation to "Cut your own!" The winding dirt road Kurt took was flanked by a forest on one side, and had a flat snowy field on the other. "My brother plants pumpkins there in the summer," Kurt mentioned. "Makes for a great fall harvest. He and Meredith offer hay rides, and sell hot apple cider along with homemade apple cider doughnuts in late September and October."

"Christmas Town sounds like a great place to live."

"It is." Kurt shot her a soulful look. "I think you'd like it."

"I'm not planning to stay."

Kurt's dark eyes danced. "Plans change." He pulled up to a large barn and parked outside it. Lots of other vehicles filled the parking area and people milled about in winter coats, some of them carrying bow saws. Others toted fresh-cut trees and skeins of twine.

Savannah glanced around at the bustling activity. "Wow! It looks so busy!"

"Christmas trees are big business this time of year," Kurt said with a smile.

"How can Ray run this and the nursery?"

"He hires employees to help him, and both Meredith and Kyle pitch in."

"Doesn't Meredith also work at the Christmas Cookie Shop?"

"Not regularly. Only as a favor to Hannah on special occasions."

Savannah stared anew at the happy people around her carting fresh Christmas tress toward their cars. "Running a family business must be fun."

"Ray and Meredith seem to enjoy it."

"I remember, in high school, Ray wanted to be a botanist or something."

"He's always been fascinated with nature," Kurt said. "Plus, he has an amazing green thumb. So, between the farm and the nursery, he's found his ideal fit."

"And, his ideal match in Meredith, it seems," Savannah said, recalling meeting the tall attractive brunette at Olivia's wedding. Meredith and Ray shared such a relaxed camaraderie it was easy to see that, in addition to being husband and wife, they were also very good friends.

Kurt viewed her thoughtfully and shut off the ignition. "It's nice when that happens, yeah."

A few minutes later, they approached an outdoor stand where several tree shoppers were lined up to pay for their purchases. Meredith worked the register under the covered area while another lady who was middle-aged yet similar in appearance assisted her. Savannah wondered if she was a relative of Meredith's. Perhaps even her mother? Meredith looked up and saw Kurt and Savannah approaching the queue. "Ray's out in the field!" she shouted with a sunny wave. "Why don't you two go and find him?"

Kurt nodded then smiled at a young teen hauling a Frasier fir to a customer's car. "Afternoon, Kyle!"

"Hi, Uncle Kurt!" the boy replied, reddening.

"I'm not sure you've met Savannah," Kurt told the kid. "Savannah Livingston, this is my nephew, Kyle."

"How do you do, ma'am?" Kyle said politely.

Savannah smiled pleasantly at the cute kid who was a smaller version of his dad but with his mother's lighter brown eyes. "Very well, Kyle. Nice to meet you."

"Savannah's Sheriff Carter's sister," Kurt said.

"Oh, right!" Kyle shifted shyly on his feet, balancing the weight of the tree in his gloved hands. "I heard you were coming to town."

The customers he was assisting were nearly to their hatchback and Kyle was lagging behind.

"Please," Savannah said, "Don't let us keep you."

Kyle nodded and lifted the tree. "Nice meeting you."

"Your nephew has really good manners," Savannah commented to Kurt as they walked along.

"Yeah. He's also up to something." Kurt chuckled to himself. "He knows that I know it, too."

"What do you mean?"

"I caught him barreling down the street on his bike the other day," Kurt replied. "His backpack was brimming with mistletoe."

"Mistletoe?" Savannah's eyes widened at the thought. "But, who—?"

"Can't say for sure, but I do know who fancies him." Savannah's brow rose and Kurt continued. "Lily Winchester's had a raging crush on Kyle for years and everyone in town knows it." He shrugged nonchalantly. "Unfortunately for her, I think Kyle still views her as a kid."

"What grade is she in?"

"Fifth."

"And, Kyle?"

"Seventh, at the Christmas Town Consolidated School. It houses both the middle and high schools here. According to my brothers, the school system's very good. One of the best in the area."

Just as Kurt mentioned his siblings, they spotted Ray a little ways up ahead of them. He strolled down a row of Christmas trees, checking them carefully on either side by pausing to examine their branches. These appeared to be shorter Frasier firs that were not fully grown. The largest one was only about three feet tall. Kurt called out to him and Ray turned with a grin.

"Kurt! Savannah! Welcome!" Kurt's older light-haired brother had a pleasant smile and handsome features that appeared weathered due to him spending so much time outdoors. He ambled in their direction dressed in heavy winter gear, meeting them halfway down the row.

"I hear you're in the market for a Christmas tree?" he asked Savannah with a twinkle.

"Yes! I'm excited about cutting down a fresh one."

Ray glanced at Kurt, seeing he was empty-handed. "You'll probably need a bow saw to help you."

"I figured we could borrow one," Kurt said. "I know you stock plenty."

"Sure do!" Ray said cheerfully. He turned toward the barn. "Why don't you let me go grab one for you while you two look around. You might want to check the next row over, or the one after that. This one here is still coming along." He glanced at Kurt who nodded knowingly.

"Thank you," Savannah said. "This will be really great! I suppose we pay after we cut our tree down?"

"No charge," Ray said with a wink. "Not for an old friend of the family."

Then he ambled away whistling a holiday tune. Savannah thought it sounded an awfully lot like, "O Christmas Tree."

"Shall we?" Kurt asked, motioning in the opposite direction. His dark brown eyes sparkled and Savannah felt herself flush.

"Sure!"

Kurt stepped aside so Savannah could go first, then she heard a strange rustling noise. It sounded like brisk winds rifling through fluttering tree boughs. Savannah spun on her heel only to be slapped in the face by a blast of icy cold air. "Oh!" She brought her hands to her cheeks, her eyes stinging.

Kurt placed a hand on her shoulder. "Savannah? Are you all right?"

"Yes, I just thought I heard…and felt…" She blinked hard to clear her eyes, and her heart hammered. It seemed impossible, but the Frasier firs on their row were suddenly taller than Kurt!

"Those…trees!" she stammered, still unable to believe what she'd seen. Surely, she'd been mistaken, or had experienced an odd sort of illusion. Or, maybe she'd gotten mixed up and they'd somehow already meandered into a different row?

Kurt reassuringly squeezed her shoulder. "I told you Ray has a green thumb."

"But you can't mean that he…?" Savannah shook her head, unwilling to believe it. Kurt and Ray had to be playing a joke on her. But why would they do that? What would they gain?

"You don't need to be afraid, Savannah." Kurt viewed her longingly. "Of anything in Christmas Town. There's nothing here but love."

"Love, and what else?" Savannah challenged.

"If I told you now, you probably wouldn't believe me."

"What other secrets are you keeping?"

He brought his arms around her and gazed into her eyes. "I'll tell, if you will."

Savannah swallowed hard. "I'm not keeping any secrets."

Kurt dipped his chin toward hers and whispered. "Aren't you?" He drew nearer and the heat of his breath warmed her lips. "Because I think you are."

"Oops! Uh!" Savannah and Kurt abruptly broke apart and Kyle gawked at them with an embarrassed flush. "Sorry, Uncle Kurt," he said, his voice rising sharply. The kid held up the bow saw in his hands, and his face was beet red. "Dad asked me to bring this to you."

They located Savannah's top-pick Frasier fir and she and Kurt cut it down. Well, it was more like she got things started, then he finished the heavy work for her. Bow saw cutting was a lot tougher than it looked! That tree trunk was deceptively dense, too! Even with the two of them working, it had taken ten minutes to saw through it. Kurt carried the tree back to the parking area, and the scent of fresh pine filled the chilly air. As Kurt had hoped, they'd gotten a break in the weather. The heavy snow had abated, with only the occasional light flake spiraling by on the wintery wind. When they reached the SUV, Kurt popped open the trunk and loaded the tree inside it.

"Are you ever going to tell me how Ray did that?" Savannah asked, still puzzling over the dramatic occurrence.

"It has to do with the Christmases' DNA," Kurt said like he had this conversation every day, although Savannah was pretty certain he didn't. "Somewhere down the line a bit of magic came into play, and it's been working its way through the descendants of the early Christmases and Clauses, for oh…?" He studied the gloomy horizon in thought. "Roughly the past one hundred and twenty years."

"Magic?" Savannah asked doubtfully. "Sure."

Once they'd climbed into the vehicle and shut their doors, Kurt said, "I'm not supposed to tell anybody, but I don't have a problem with telling you."

"Why not?" Savannah scoffed. "Because you already think I'm wack?"

"No, because I trust that you are sane," Kurt said seriously. "And, highly capable and intelligent. It helps a lot that you're imaginative, too."

"I did *not* imagine that," Savannah said, referring to the episode with the rapidly growing Christmas trees.

"Never said that you did."

She viewed him perplexedly, deciding this must be some sort of ruse after all. Something that he and Ray had concocted. Savannah had no idea why they'd go to the trouble, or how they had accomplished it, but maybe this was one of the weird ways the Christmases welcomed newcomers to town. By playing practical jokes on them.

"Well, honestly? I don't think it was funny." Savannah folded her arms in front of her and looked away. "I don't enjoy being made the subject of a joke."

"It wasn't a joke, Savannah," Kurt said hoarsely. She turned to find an unsettling mixture of emotion in his eyes: frustration, worry, and dismay. "I'm sure Ray didn't even mean for you to see that. For better or worse, we can't always control our abilities, or schedule when—"

"*You* have abilities?" Savannah's jaw dropped. "Like what?"

Kurt wrapped his hands around the steering wheel and sadly hung his head. "Never mind. Let me drive you home."

Something jostled Savannah's memory then she asked on a tentative breath, "Like knowing when someone is lying?"

He turned slowly to look at her. "Yes."

Savannah's heart hammered. "What else?"

Kurt cranked the ignition without answering her. "I think you've learned enough family history for one day," he finally said.

"Yeah," Savannah said, her thoughts churning wildly. "Maybe I have."

Kurt carried Savannah's tree inside her rental and she thanked him numerous times for their outing. Yet, he appeared defeated at worst, and saddened at best. Savannah sincerely regretted upsetting him, but she hadn't been able to help her visceral reaction to the outlandish things he'd said. What did that mean, that his family had *abilities*? Kurt was starting to sound like Olivia had when she'd gone off her rocker while falling for Nick!

Savannah reflected on her morning conversation with Olivia over coffee. Apart from wanting to know every little detail about how things had gone with Kurt on Friday, Olivia had peppered Savannah with questions about her feelings. Was she still attracted to Kurt? Did she think it was mutual? Could Kurt and Savannah, as adults, renew and build upon that early teen romance?

She'd basically ignored her sister, by refusing to answer her nosy questions. Savannah definitely wasn't about to share any telling truths with Olivia, when she hadn't reconciled with what was going on herself. So, she'd turned the conversation around instead, inquiring numerous times about Nick's family and what Olivia expected their home in the Maritime Provinces to be like. This kept Olivia tap-dancing around while avoiding offering her own answers, which had basically gotten Savannah off the hook—and out of the inquisition.

"Well, I guess I'd better get going." Kurt stood by her front door looking dispirited, and Savannah felt partially to blame. At the same time, she wasn't entirely certain what she was expected to say? *Sorry I overreacted? Of course you must be right! It's natural that the Christmases would all have abilities. What a unique and interesting birthright!*

"Thanks again for helping me get the tree," Savannah tried to insert brightly. "And, for putting it up in the corner." Her eyes darted to the spot by the rear bay window where Kurt had situated the nice lush specimen on the far side of the dining table.

"No problem," he said with a hint of melancholy. "I was happy to do it."

Kurt was dressed more casually today in a field coat and boots, forgoing the more formal car coat and fedora he typically donned for work. But, dressed up or dressed down, Kurt Christmas was a heartthrob in whatever he wore. Savannah was just sorry he'd developed these mild delusions about his family and their powers, and was worried that he might need help.

Was that what Olivia had tried to warn Savannah about? She hadn't said anything directly, but had hinted strongly that Kurt might be "special"… But *special in a good way! The best way! Just like Nick! No, not like Nick, exactly. Nobody's quite like Nick. Not even his dad. Certain things skip generations.* Olivia had lost Savannah with her nonsensical talk, but now Savannah wondered if her sister had discreetly been trying to tell her something. But, if Olivia was trying to warn

Savannah off of Kurt, then why was she encouraging her to date him? Savannah's head ached trying to sort it out. Her heart felt a bit bruised, too. Because...she'd been falling for Kurt and falling fast. Even harder than she had the first time, all those years ago. Perhaps because she'd never completely gotten him out of her system.

When he turned to go, Savannah called to him. "When will I see you again?"

He answered without turning. "Not sure."

"Are you going to the church bazaar tomorrow? I'm going with Sandy, and—"

He cut her off solemnly by saying he had to work.

When he finally peered over his shoulder, Kurt said, "I'm not crazy, Savannah. I'm just a man." He seemed to gather his nerve. "Living with the deck I was dealt."

Then, he stepped outside, and was gone.

"Kurt, wait!" Savannah raced after him and threw open the door. But, though she scoured the sidewalk every which way, she didn't see a trace of him.

Chapter Eighteen

Kurt stopped by Carter's office at the courthouse building on his way to the hospital for the annual staff event. Unfortunately, it always coincided with the Christmas pageant at the Corner Church. Otherwise, Kurt would have liked to attend the Advent celebration with his family. Carter typically had to miss it too, because he gave his deputy, Victoria, the day off so she could watch her son, Bobby, play one of the wise men. Carter was sorting through his e-mail when Kurt arrived. His secretary Tilly had a habit of printing it out for him to read, and then insisting on typing up his handwritten replies.

Though Carter had tried to maintain it was just as easy for him to answer his business correspondence himself, Tilly wouldn't hear a word of it. So, Carter indulged her in abiding by her system. Mostly, because it helped provide Tilly with enough work hours to maintain her part-time job. Business at the sheriff's office wasn't typically hopping. This was Christmas Town, after all, where the most pressing legal concern had become traffic control during Hannah's seasonal sales of her Virginia Cookies.

"Kurt," he said, with a smile. "Good to see you!" Then he noted Kurt's dour expression and motioned toward a chair in his office. "What's up?"

Kurt took a seat and set his fedora on his knee. He still wore his car coat but it was unbuttoned. "I'm afraid I might have blown things with your sister."

"Blown things?" Carter asked, astounded. "But, how? On Friday I thought it was going great?"

"So did I." Kurt heaved a sigh. "But that's before I took Savannah shopping for Christmas trees."

"It's hard to see how that alone—"

"It's not just that. It's everything." Kurt paused to run a hand through his hair. "I'm not sure Savannah's going to be able to accept me for who I really am."

"Accept you?" Carter placed his elbows on his desk and leaned forward. "What's so hard to accept? You're single, eligible, rich—most likely, and—from a woman's perspective, I suppose—not a total loser in the looks department."

"Thanks, Carter."

"I mean it, friend. I can't fathom what's gone wrong."

Kurt seriously met his eyes. "Have you ever had something…? Something so deep and personal, you were scared to share it with anyone?"

Carter pushed back in his chair looking caught out. "Well, I…"

"I mean, everybody has secrets, right?" Kurt gave a pained laugh. "Surely, even you?"

Carter pursed his lips and viewed Kurt thoughtfully. "All right, I'll admit it. I might have a secret or two."

"Maybe even some you haven't shared with me?" Kurt carefully scrutinized Carter, and Carter shifted in his chair.

"Look, what's this all about?"

"I just wonder sometimes," Kurt said, "about the fine line between love and acceptance."

"Seems to me that line gets blurred," Carter told him. "If you love someone, you accept them—warts and all. Isn't that what love's about? I mean, according to the philosophers and such," Carter amended quickly, lest Kurt think he was waxing mushy.

"Yeah, I suppose." Kurt's brow rose with the question. "Is that how it is with you and Hannah? Warts and all?"

"Hannah doesn't have any warts." Carter smiled fondly. "She's absolutely perfect."

"How about you?" Kurt asked.

"I've got some battle scars, that's for sure. But, once I shared them with Hannah—"

"So, you did share?" Kurt interrupted. "And she was okay with it? Whatever it was?"

"She was okay with *me*, Kurt. Therefore, very loving and supportive. Just like I would have been with her. Still *am* with her. Hannah and I can tell each other anything."

"That's how it should be," Kurt said with a touch of longing. "To tell you the truth, I think even my mom and dad are that way."

Carter gave a stunned laugh. "Lou and Buddy? Well, good for them!"

"Yeah."

They were both silent a while and Kurt could tell that Carter was thinking. He was probably wondering about what was really wrong, and trying to concoct ways to bolster Kurt's spirits. Carter was a good guy and Kurt admired him greatly. To Kurt, he was practically another brother, especially since Ray and Walt were older and Carter was closer to his age. This was what had caused them to get close as kids during the time their families took all those joint summer vacations at the shore.

"Chin up, my friend," Carter told him. "Whatever it is, it can't be as bad as you think. Savannah and you...? There's been something going on there for a long while. Something that time and distance couldn't erase. That tells me something, and it should also say something to you." He waited until he was sure he had Kurt's full attention. "It's worth the fight, bro."

"But I don't want to fight with Savannah."

"I was talking about the battle within yourself."

Before Kurt could answer, Carter continued, "This could be your chance, Kurt. But, you can't go in halfway. You have to jump in with both feet. Give it your all."

"And if that still doesn't work?

"Then, at least you'll know you tried."

On the other side of town, Savannah and Liz strolled through the snow to the church bazaar. Sandy had called to say Lily was still recovering, so Ben would be staying home with her and the twins. Sandy, however, had a booth to man during the craft time following dinner. She helped kids paint colorful Christmas tree ball ornaments, and didn't want to let anybody down by missing the evening.

Since Ben was staying home, that freed Liz of her prearranged babysitting obligation. Though it had apparently taken some arm-twisting by Sandy to convince Liz to attend the bazaar, she'd eventually agreed. Liz typically didn't like big crowds and felt more comfortable in small groups.

"I'm not much of a mingler," Liz confessed to Savannah as they strolled along. Sandy had offered to pick them up, but they'd insisted on walking the short way.

"Really, Liz? I wouldn't have figured you for shy?"

Liz's high cheekbones colored at this. "I'm not shy, exactly." She hesitated a beat. "It's more like certain types of social conversations intimidate me."

Savannah couldn't imagine anyone purposely making someone else feel uncomfortable in Christmas Town. "I'm sure the people here are very—"

"Oh, they are! As nice as can be! There's no doubt about that, and everyone is really friendly. It's just that…" She timidly lifted a shoulder. "I often don't know what to say."

"You seemed to do just fine the other evening when we had pizza."

"Yeah, but that was one on one." She shot Savannah a smile. "Plus, it was girl talk."

"Well, I'm glad you're stepping out tonight," Savannah said.

"Me, too." Liz wistfully glanced at some children crossing the street up ahead of them with their parents. All were bundled up for the weather and dressed nicely, apparently also headed for the church. "I haven't seen my nieces in the pageant before, and all three play sheep!"

"How cute!"

"This year," Liz added with a chuckle. "Their baby brother, Basil, will play the part of a little lamb."

"I'm sure it will mean a lot to them to have you there. Stan and Della will appreciate it, too."

"Yeah."

They reached the corner with Church Street and crossed over, noting the full parking lot. Parishioners carried covered dishes from their vehicles in through a rear door of the church, chatting merrily with each other as they scuttled through the snow.

"Looks like a full house," Savannah said, as they drew nearer.

Sandy emerged from the church to hold back the door for a pleasant-looking couple in their thirties with dark hair and honey colored skin. The woman was slight and fit, and wore her hair in a tight black chignon, while the boisterous husband sported a megawatt grin. Savannah recognized them from Olivia's wedding as Victoria and Frank Cho. The precious seven- or eight-year-old boy with them was evidently their child. Bobby was the spitting image of his dad.

Frank held a huge cardboard box loaded with short beeswax candles. All had small cardboard aprons around them to keep melted wax from dripping onto people's hands, when they were lit. Victoria grasped Bobby's mitten and hurried him along, while carting a covered casserole. "Savannah, hi!" she said, spotting her. "And, hi, Liz! So nice you both could make it!"

"Absolutely!" Frank crowed. "This is the show of the season! Not to be missed!"

"I'm one of the wise men," Bobby told Savannah with earnest dark eyes.

"How great!" Savannah said. "I can't wait to see your performance." She smiled warmly at the family. "I love performances, you know. All kinds."

"Welcome, ladies!" Sandy said cheerfully, as they stepped inside and out of the elements. She gave them each a warm hug, and Savannah glanced around at the large Fellowship Hall. Several long tables had been pushed together near an open door to the kitchen to form a buffet line. Round tables with seating for eight had been established nearby. On the other side of the room, additional tables held craft supplies, and a final bank of tables closer to the door to the sanctuary displayed all sorts of interesting items, from baked goods to household knickknacks, and jewelry and books. Savannah saw there were white sheets of paper and pens situated in front of each offering and assumed this was a silent auction. Likely, to benefit the church. *But what is that odd collection of brown houses all about?*

Sandy spied Savannah staring that way and quietly explained, "Lou Christmas made an entire gingerbread town for the auction! Isn't that great?"

Savannah was tempted to say, *That's edible?* But she opted for a much more tactful, "How terrific!" The display was a little terrifying, too. Those poor gingerbread people appeared to be fleeing burning buildings. None of them seemed particularly jolly about it, either.

"That certainly looks like Lou's work!" Liz said. "Very creative."

"Did I hear my name?" the older woman asked, shuffling over. In lieu of her usual Santa hat, she wore a dark green elf hat instead. It had a large bell on the end of its tip that jangled as she moved.

"Welcome, Savannah!" she said, giving her a hug. "And, Liz!" Lou's face lit up as she clasped Liz by the shoulders. "I don't believe I've ever seen you here before!"

"I'm usually babysitting."

"Babies, bosh! It's time you had some fun for yourself."

"Yeah," Sandy quipped. "Especially since they're my babies."

"Are they?" Lou's eyes rounded. "Oh! Oh, dear. Sorry, Sandy—"

Sandy chuckled good-naturedly. "It's fine, Lou. And, for the record, I agree. It's nice to see Liz out and about."

"I get out!" Liz swallowed hard then added awkwardly, "And, about."

"Of course you do, dear." Lou viewed her sagely. "And, you'd likely enjoy getting out some more. Did I tell you my friend Mary has a nephew coming to town?"

"Now, Lou," Sandy said. "Let's give Liz an evening off without trying to overwhelm her."

"But, I—" Lou started to protest, when Buddy ambled over with a deep "*Ho-ho-ho.*"

He offered to hang up Savannah's and Liz's coats, then went off to help Ray and Meredith who were carting in greens to make advent wreaths.

"Everyone seems so busy and happy here," Savannah said to Liz.

"I know! This place is buzzing with Christmas cheer!"

Sandy spotted Jade placing some more books on the auction table and waved her over. The pretty woman with a caramel complexion and friendly brown eyes came and took Savannah's hand. "It's so good to see you. I'm glad you got to join us tonight." She turned with delight toward Liz. "You too, Liz! I hope you'll both sit at our table. It will be Wendell and me," she said referencing her husband, "Frank and Victoria, Sandy and Hannah, and hopefully the two of you!"

"What about your boys?" Savannah asked, remembering Jade and Wendell had two young sons.

"Alexander likes to sit with Bobby, and some other kids their age at their own table. We'll pull up a high chair for Josiah, and Amanda will have one, too. So, the little ones can keep each other company. That is…" She glanced at Liz. "Unless you'd like to sit with Stan and Della and their kids?"

"I'm guessing they might already have some regulars they sit with," Liz replied. "They weren't expecting me to come tonight."

"Then please," Jade petitioned warmly. "Sit with us!"

"Sounds great," Savannah said. "Thanks, Jade."

"Yeah, Jade," Liz agreed. "Thank you."

The evening passed by much more quickly than Savannah expected, and the silent auction was an enormous success. At the last minute, Pastor Wilson announced that an anonymous donor had put in a five hundred dollar bid for Lou's gingerbread town, and everyone gasped. As Savannah and Liz helped Sandy and the others clean up and pack away craft supplies, Walt Christmas approached her. Though they were all over six feet, the middle boy Walt was the tallest of the Christmas brothers. He also was the only one with a mustache and beard, and stunning blue eyes. His twin girls had apparently inherited the blue eye color but their late mother's blond hair. Sandy had told Savannah that Noelle and Joy were away at college taking their final exams, and that they'd be home next week.

"I couldn't let the evening pass without saying hello." Walt gave her a cordial hug then grinned, holding her gaze. "You're looking well, Savannah. It's nice to have you home for the holidays."

"Christmas Town isn't my home," she told him kindly.

Walt's blue eyes twinkled. "Don't be so quick to judge."

Savannah laughed lightly at this. "You're looking well, too. I hear your girls are coming home soon."

"Yep. I'm counting the days."

"I look forward to seeing them again. I was stunned when I saw them at the wedding. Both have grown into such great beauties, and they're such accomplished people! I saw Joy's show at the Grand Hotel. It's really marvelous."

"She's very talented," Walt agreed. "Both the girls are. Only Noelle's art is more literary."

"I know you're proud."

"Yes. Thanks, Savannah."

She studied the handsome bachelor, thinking what a fine catch he'd make for just the right woman. But, Walt was apparently picky. Olivia said he'd barely dated at all since losing Rose when his girls were young. Lou had apparently attempted to fix him up, but he'd used the excuse of being a single dad to deflect forming romantic attachments. Now that his girls were grown and in college, Savannah wondered why he was still holding his heart at bay. This made her think of her best friend Gloria, who was also the perfect woman for just the right man. A fabulous idea formed in Savannah's brain as she gazed up at Walt.

"Are you dating, yet?"

He appeared completely caught off guard. "Dating? Who, me?"

"Yes, you. You big silly." She nudged him warmly, trying to picture him and Gloria together in her mind's eye. And what a stunning portrait they made!

"Not exactly…a lot." Walt uncomfortably cleared his throat. "Why?"

"No reason in particular," Savannah said, her mental wheels turning. She was certain Walt would love Gloria. She was so warm, and loving and funny! And, also really outgoing. The perfect person to draw Walt out of his more subdued shell. The only problem was, Savannah would have to get Gloria to Christmas Town. Then, she'd have to convince her to stay. It was doubtful Walt Christmas would move anywhere. His family roots were here and he'd raised his kids in this place. But, Gloria…was always saying how she was itching to get out of Miami…that she'd always dreamed about having a really white Christmas… *What's it like, Savannah?* she often asked her. *Frolicking like a child*

212 The Doctor Orders Christmas

in the snow? Feeling the sharp winter wind nip your nose? Tasting itty-bitty, icy snowflakes on your tongue…?

"Savannah?" Walt asked her, pulling Savannah out of her reverie. "What on earth are you doing?"

"Huh?"

He screwed up his face in confusion. "It kind of looked like you were sticking out your tongue?"

"I…oh! Did I?"

"I don't know how to say this, but…" Walt shifted on his feet then leaned toward her, speaking in a husky whisper. "I'm not interested in you in that way."

"What?"

"And, even if I were, I wouldn't act on it."

"Walt—"

"Kurt would have my head and I wouldn't blame him. Not that you're not a beautiful woman," he stammered awkwardly.

"Walt," Savannah hissed sharply, whispering in his ear. "I wasn't making a play for you, all right?" What kind of person did he think she was? They were in church for heaven's sake!

He eyed her skeptically. "Well, you sure could have fooled me. You were sticking out your tongue and rolling it all over the place. Left then right, and up and—"

Savannah clamped a hand over Walt's mouth when Sandy approached them. Walt blinked and stared down at her as Sandy did a double take.

"Oh hi, Sandy!" Savannah said, trying to think of nothing but snow. That's all she needed now. For Sandy to get the wrong impression, too… *That I'm interested in Walt!*

"Oh! Oh gosh!" Sandy gave a little jump and pressed her hands to her temples. Then she raised her eyes to Savannah's in disbelief.

"No!" Savannah cried defensively. "No, really!"

Walt pried her hand from his mouth, and Savannah was stunned to learn she'd left it there.

"It's not Walt; it isn't!" she said, as Liz approached.

Liz surveyed the scene then asked softly, "What's not Walt?" She took one long look at Savannah's paralyzed expression and another at Walt's petrified stance. "*Sugar plum fairy!*"

"Noooo…"

"Savannah," Sandy scolded sternly. "This is really not ideal. Walt is Kurt's *brother*."

The world was closing in on her, along with the encroaching hubbub from all around. Everywhere Savannah turned there were eyes and more eyes, and totally shocked faces—judging her for what she'd done. Savannah felt like the scarlet woman dressed in Christmas red. Why couldn't she have worn green tonight? *Why, why, why?* Instead of this sultry, come-hither, crimson V-neck sweater and her short suede skirt, which hadn't seemed improper at all until this very moment.

People must be thinking she'd dressed this way on purpose. All done up and sexy, in an effort to attract a man. And, not just any man, but one who had been single for nearly a decade! *Oh, woe is me…* The doubt in the air was palpable as her friends viewed her perplexedly.

She could hear the whispers starting to circulate...

"Isn't that Kurt's old girlfriend?"

"Would a man betray his brother?"

Then, with a hint of disapproval, "What about *her*?"

How could folks believe that of Savannah, when her heart exploded with one overwhelming truth? It was working its way out of her. Bursting forth like an erupting geyser! Until Savannah was unable to tamp it down. It didn't matter if Kurt had troubles, he was undeniably the man for her. She had to find a way to help him and bring him into the fullness of mental health with her love. *And, okay, all right...maybe a good dose of psychiatry if he needs it.* And, Savannah was relatively certain he would.

She was a counselor, for heaven's sake. Wasn't that what she was meant to do? Help people in need? Who could need her more than the man who'd professed his undying love for her? Savannah felt it in her soul as the truth resonated through her, worming its way to the surface and struggling to break free. She balled her hands into fists and shut her eyes, throwing back her head as she wailed at the ceiling. "But I don't *want* Walt!" she proclaimed much more loudly than she intended. "It's *Kurt* I love!"

Savannah's heart pounded at the stunned silence that followed. It was so quiet she could only hear her own panicked breathing and her pulse drumming in her ears.

Thump-thump, thump-thump, thump-thump...

Then the faintest tinkling of a jingle bell sounded from the next room. "Hello? What's happened?"

Savannah opened her eyes in horror to see Lou Christmas standing on the threshold to the kitchen. Pastor Wilson was behind her, peering over her shoulder and into the Fellowship Hall, where the entire world seemed frozen in place. Nobody spoke and no one moved a muscle, not even the little children.

"What are y'all staring at?" Liz asked, unprompted. "Haven't you ever seen performance art before? Improv! Ad lib! Just like in New York!"

A murmur began around the room as people exchanged puzzled glances. At length, Hannah stood and took the floor, clapping her hands together. "Hear! Hear!" she encouraged. "Let's hear it for our new children's theater consultant!"

Jade clapped loudly next, and Sandy shot to her feet and announced, "Stunning! Absolutely fabulous! Such drama and class! World's best!"

As the thunderous applause died down, Savannah and Liz slipped into their coats, then Savannah made her excuses to Sandy and she and Liz quickly left.

"You may not think you're great in social situations," she told Liz as they scurried out the door. "But you just saved my life!"

"You mean that wasn't performance art?" Liz asked with a teasing lilt.

Savannah elbowed her playfully and nudged her along. "Come on, let's go. Before my adoring public arrives and starts asking for my autograph."

Chapter Nineteen

Savannah was almost afraid to meet Sandy, Hannah, and Jade for their girls' lunch on Monday. Given her humiliating declaration at the church bazaar, she wasn't sure what to expect. After saying goodnight to Liz and thanking her again for racing to her rescue, Savannah had been tempted to call Gloria and confess her whole embarrassing ordeal. But since thoughts of Gloria had inspired the episode, she hadn't wanted Gloria to feel responsible. Nor was she prepared to let on she was thinking of fixing Gloria up with Kurt's older brother! *One relationship at a time, Savannah. Wow.* She didn't even know whether Gloria would be interested. Or Walt, for that matter. Though, the more Savannah thought about it, the more perfect the two seemed for each other. Savannah brought a hand to her forehead, wondering if she was catching some of that Christmas Town matchmaking bug? Olivia had told her it was rampant around here.

"Are you feeling all right?" Sandy's brow's knitted in concern and Savannah realized she'd missed the last part of the conversation, which had turned to fitness and exercise apparently. Fortunately, her new friends had been extremely polite, choosing to ignore Savannah's faux pas the night before completely.

"Yeah," Savannah said. "Sorry! What were you saying about snow skiing?" she asked Hannah. "That really sounds like fun. Olivia says there are some great cross-country trails around here."

"There are!" Hannah replied, then she said lightly, "They're just not for me."

"Not much of a skier?" Savannah asked and Hannah laughed.

"Let's just say I get my exercise being on my feet all day baking cookies, and racing after Amanda once I get home."

"Wendell and I ski," Jade volunteered. "We're just now teaching Alexander. For a kid, he's really quite good."

"That's because kids have no fear about anything that can go wrong," Hannah answered.

"Childhood innocence!" Sandy said wistfully. "Isn't it the best?"

The others stopped to consider this.

"The hopeful outlook is to be admired," Hannah replied.

"And, the optimism!" said Jade.

All eyes turned on Savannah. "How about you, Savannah?" Jade asked. "Are you outdoorsy like your sister?"

"Well, I do like to ski, although I haven't done it in a while. Not enough snow in Miami," she added and everybody laughed.

"What about horseback riding?" Hannah wanted to know. "Olivia and Nick keep horses at Sleigh Bell

Stables and there are others there you can take riding for a day?"

"Horseback riding?" A wave of nausea roiled over Savannah and she suddenly felt very, very faint. "Oh, I…" Her stomach was in an upheaval, as if she were about to lose her recently finished lunch. "Don't…" Savannah slumped forward, holding her head in her hands.

"Savannah!" Hannah cried with alarm. "Are you all right?"

"Oh goodness." Worry lined Jade's voice. "Look, she's as white as a sheet."

Sandy laid a hand on her shoulder. "Do you need to visit the ladies'?"

Savannah nodded numbly, her head filled with dark clouds and glittery white stars.

"I'll help you." Sandy got to her feet and took Savannah's elbow.

But, once Savannah had stood as well, she said, "That's all right. I…I'll go."

Savannah staggered to the restroom on wobbly knees as the others watched her with worried expressions. She had to get herself under control. She was having another panic attack, and couldn't do this every time somebody mentioned horses. Savannah pushed into the small bathroom with two stalls, grateful to find it empty. She stumbled to the sink and ran the water cold, splashing the icy water onto her face with her hands—again, and again, and again. At last, the room stopped spinning, and Savannah grabbed some paper towels from the dispenser nearby to dry her face.

But, when she looked up in the mirror, Savannah didn't see a successful adult woman in her thirties; she saw a terrified and heartbroken teen.

Later that afternoon, Kurt completed Buddy's annual physical exam at the clinic. He removed the stethoscope from his dad's chest with a frown. Since Buddy refused to don what he called the "dressing gown," he still wore his plaid flannel shirt and jeans, which was no problem for Kurt. After years of practice, he'd learned to work around Buddy's wardrobe restrictions. Plus, he had the blood work to rely on.

"You haven't taken my advice, have you?" he asked his father.

"Which advice would that be?" Buddy asked as if he didn't know.

"About cutting back on the sugar."

"Well now, son… You know how I like my cookies."

"Yeah, but here's a tip." Kurt patted Buddy's big round belly. "They don't like you."

Buddy's forehead rose in surprise. "That's a bit harsh, wouldn't you say?"

"No, Dad."

"Because I was quite sure that sweets and I had a very decent relationship!"

"I think 'decadent' is the word you're searching for." Kurt began counting things off, enumerating them with his fingers. "Plum pudding, rum balls, peppermint chocolate lava cake…"

"Oh yes! That one's delicious! Have you tried it at the Peppermint Bark?"

"*No-ho-ho*, Dad," Kurt said, intentionally mimicking his father. "And, I don't plan to."

"Well, you might as well have fun, son! Thirty-five years old and still not married. Why, by the time your brothers were your age they already had child—"

"Ray and Walt didn't go to medical school," Kurt interrupted.

"What difference does that make?"

Kurt sighed heavily and packed his stethoscope away. "Here is a leaflet on healthy eating," he said, handing Buddy some flyers. "And, another on lowering cholesterol. Oh, and you're going to love this one." He gave Buddy one more pamphlet. "Suggestions for senior citizen exercise."

Buddy harrumphed. "I stay plenty active for a man my age."

"Building toys doesn't count."

"Says who?"

"Says the American Medical Association."

"You always were too smart for your own good, not to mention too big for your britches."

Kurt glanced down at his dad's bulging waistline and coughed pointedly.

Buddy took that as a sign to scoot off the examining table. "Thanks for the check-up, Kurt! It's always good to see you."

"You too, Dad." He laid his hand on Buddy's shoulder. "I just wish you'd take my advice."

Buddy smiled jovially. "It's good to see that Savannah's taking your mother's..."

"What?"

"Lou talked to her, you know."

Kurt stared at his dad, stunned. "No, I'm afraid nobody told me that part. I know that Mom dropped by to bring Savannah some Christmas things, but I had no idea she—"

"Don't go getting that gloomy expression on your face," Buddy warned. "You know that Lou meant well. And, anyway! It appears that old girlfriend of yours took it to heart, as she's apparently your new girlfriend now."

"Savannah Livingston?"

"She's the only Savannah in town, as far as I know."

"But how can she be my girlfriend? How in the world did that happen?"

Buddy viewed him perplexedly. "You're a little old to be requiring that talk about the birds and the bees."

"I don't need that talk, Dad. And haven't in quite a while. I'm just not understanding why you're so convinced that Savannah's into me all of a sudden."

"Because!" Buddy proclaimed cheerfully. "She told the entire congregation!"

"Told them what?"

"Why, that she's in love with you, my boy! Desperately, apparently. She shouted it at the top of her lungs." Buddy eyes twinkled merrily. "She tried to pretend that she was play-acting. But once that cat was out of the bag, there was *no-ho-ho* putting it back in!"

"She did that in church?" Kurt asked, amazed.

"Well, not in the sanctuary, naturally. It was in the Fellowship Hall while she was talking to Walt."

"What's Walt got to do with any of this?"

Buddy shifted sheepishly on his feet. "I'm not one hundred percent sure about this, so don't go getting your hackles up, but…"

Kurt leaned toward him, anticipating the worst. And then, he got it.

"I think your brother might have made a play for her."

"He wouldn't."

Buddy stroked his snowy beard. "Your mother and I were surprised by that, too. Could be Walt's been a bachelor too long, because that didn't show very good judgment."

"No," Kurt said stonily. "It didn't."

Though his insides were churning, Kurt tried to get through the rest of his afternoon appointments with a professional smile on his face. Beneath his outwardly pleasant demeanor, his emotions roiled furiously, tumbling up and down like tumultuous waves at the ocean during a storm. If what his dad said was true, Savannah had announced her feelings about Kurt to everyone in town! Everyone, that was, except for to him—personally, which would have been greatly appreciated and probably the most appropriate gesture.

Then, there was Walt… *How could he? Why would he?* What's more, Walt was so mild mannered, this just didn't seem like the type of thing he'd do. He wasn't the wolfish kind of guy who preyed on women. All the opposite! Ever since losing Rose, it had appeared Walt was determined to avoid them. Or, at least, avoid becoming involved with any in a serious romantic way.

Kurt decided the best thing to do was talk to Walt and clear the air, because surely there'd been some kind of misunderstanding. Next, he needed to see Savannah. And the two of them were going to have a long talk. Whether Savannah wanted to or not.

At this point? She definitely owed him.

Chapter Twenty

Kurt found Walt at the Christmas Inn putting up more holiday decorations. Although the place was plenty decked out already, Walt was adding extra touches to the Christmas tree in the library. He'd also hung three stockings from the mantel there: one for each of his twins, Noelle and Joy, and one in honor of his late wife Rose. Kurt knew that Walt and his girls had a special tradition. Each year they wrote personal notes to the girls' late mother and Walt's former wife and stuffed them into her stocking on Christmas Eve. On Christmas morning, when they all enjoyed cinnamon rolls and coffee, each cast his or her individual missive to Rose into the roaring fire and shared a brief moment of silence in her memory, before beginning their annual celebration.

While the tradition seemed a bit maudlin to Kurt, it had become an important ritual for Walt and his daughters. It was also one that appeared to bring each of them peace. They'd lost Rose on Christmas Day, so that made the family holiday especially hard. But, as the years went on, happy memories began to replace the painful ones, so they all could look back on their time spent with Rose with tenderness, laughter, and love.

Though the Christmas Inn entertained a steady slew of lodgers during most of the year, Walt kept Christmastime sacrosanct, by leaving his business closed to visitors from mid-December though mid-January. In a way, it was ironic that a place called the Christmas Inn didn't operate at Christmas. But that was how Walt wanted it, and what made sense for his family. Particularly now that the girls were in college, Walt valued providing a special place for them to come home to that they could call their own.

He draped a pretty blue-and-green hand-painted ornament from a bough of the Christmas tree, and turned to Kurt in surprise. "I didn't hear you come in."

"Holiday music," Kurt explained.

Walt glanced at his open rolltop desk and the laptop on it. A Bluetooth device connected the streaming music channel he'd programed to a couple of speakers nestled among books on the built-in shelves.

"Ah, so," Walt said, grinning. He crossed to his desk and turned down the volume.

"I did knock twice." Kurt shrugged. "Then I remembered you never lock the door."

"I do lock it. But not until very late at night." He smiled warmly at his brother. "Force of habit, I suppose, from having paying guests here."

Kurt knew Walt's rule was that everyone turned into pumpkins at midnight. He used to tell that to his girls when they were teens and operating under curfews. As far as Kurt knew, they still did. Walt was a loving, but fairly strict, dad.

Walt motioned toward the wing chair by the fireplace, which was currently unlit. "Can I fix you a drink?" he offered. "I was just about to make one for myself."

"Sure," Kurt answered, taking a seat.

"What's your pleasure?"

"Whatever you're drinking is fine."

Walt's blue eyes twinkled. "Kentucky bourbon it is!"

Kurt almost felt foolish for coming here. He glanced at the mantel, perusing Rose's Christmas stocking and his heart sank on Walt's behalf. Of course Walt hadn't been hitting on Savannah. How much sense did that make?"

Walt poured their drinks then took the chair opposite Kurt's on the other side of the hearth. When they were both settled in with their bourbons, Walt surveyed Kurt carefully. "Is everything all right?"

"Yeah, yeah. Fine."

"It's not like you to make house calls after nine p.m."

"I just had something on my mind."

Walt took a slow sip of his drink. "Care to share it?"

"I saw Dad at the clinic today."

"Routine physical?"

"That's right."

"How's he doing?"

Kurt swirled the ice in his drink. "How do you think?"

Walt frowned at this.

"I tried to talk to him about diet and exercise."

"I'm sure that went far," Walt said with a laugh.

"Yeah, well. I plan to keep after him."

"Good for you!" He studied Kurt a beat. "You want my help? Is that why you're here?"

"It's not about Dad. At least, not about his health." Kurt set down his drink. "It's about something else. Something he told me."

Walt lifted his brow. "Oh?"

"Something about Savannah."

"Oh yeah..." Walt pursed his lips, attempting to repress a grin but failing miserably. "That."

"What happened at the church bazaar?"

"Sounds like you've already heard."

"Dad was fuzzy on the details."

"You could probably...oh...ask just about anyone else in town."

"That bad, huh?"

Walt chuckled. "Let's just say, Savannah hasn't lost her flair for drama."

"I want you to level with me," Kurt said, chancing it. One way or another he had to know. "Did you make a play for Savannah?"

"Me?" Walt blanched in shock. "*No.*"

"The other way around?"

Walt considered this a little longer than Kurt would have liked. "I can't imagine why she would have. She must have been thinking about something else."

"Like what?"

"You!" Walt's blue eyes sparkled with mischief. "She proclaimed her undying love, you know   before at least two hundred witnesses."

"Wow."

"You could have heard a pin drop in that Fellowship Hall."

"But, why there?"

Walt took another swig of bourbon. "Perhaps she felt moved to confession?"

Kurt strummed the arm of his chair with his fingers, staring at the hearth. Walt had laid a fire in it, which was ready to go with one strike of a match. "Still seems a little strange. Especially since she hasn't said anything to me."

"I guess she never got over you," Walt teased warmly. "Which makes me wonder why she broke things off to begin with?"

"She didn't," Kurt answered solemnly. "It was all a big misunderstanding over some lost letters."

"Letters? What do you mean?"

"I didn't get hers. She didn't get mine." Kurt heaved a breath. "It hardly seems to matter now, does it?" Kurt met Walt's eyes, still feeling astonished by the news himself. "Savannah's apparently put that behind her."

Walt laughed and set down his drink. "It certainly looked that way to me! And to…well, all of us." He lifted a crystal candy dish beside him, removing its lid. Next, he leaned forward, offering Kurt a piece of peppermint bark from inside it. "The man is always the last to know."

Kurt absentmindedly took a piece of the white-chocolate and mint candy, popping it in his mouth and rolling it over on his tongue. "Yeah."

Walt selected a treat for himself then set the dish back on the table beside him. "So, now that you *know*…" he prompted. "What do you intend to do with the information?"

Kurt swallowed his chocolate and picked up his drink. "See if she's got the nerve to say it to my—" Kurt's throat constricted suddenly, and he gave a violent cough. "Whoa!" He covered his mouth with one hand, as his drink sloshed over the other.

Walt shot to his feet, handing Kurt a napkin. "What happened? Did you choke—?"

Kurt shook his head then used the napkin to dry his hand after placing his glass on the table. "No, I…" He drew in a breath and his lungs wheezed. "Wow." Kurt sat back in his chair with a puzzled look. "I think I just had an allergic reaction."

"To peppermint?" Walt stared at the candy dish then met his brother's eyes. "Uh-oh."

"I know, right? That's never happened to me before, and I've been exposed to it plenty."

Walt nodded sagely. "Maybe that's because you haven't met the right woman, at just the right time."

"I've known Savannah forever."

"Yeah, but before you were kids." Walt viewed him haltingly. "Surely, you didn't experience anything then?"

Kurt looked away, avoiding his brother's gaze.

"That only would have happened if…"

Kurt stood abruptly. "Thanks for the drink and the conversation, Walt. But I've got to go."

"Where are you going?

"To see Savannah," Kurt said hoarsely. "And straighten a few things out."

The next day on his lunch hour, Kurt visited Savannah at the theater. He caught her rearranging costumes in the new wardrobes she'd procured. "Kurt!" she said, jumping in surprise. "You startled me!"

Kurt suavely removed his hat and laid it on a table stocked with wands and scepters.

"Seems we both have a way of surprising each other."

She blinked at him and attempted to hang a velvet purple cape in an armoire. Unfortunately, she completely missed the bar with the hanger and the garment fell in a heap at her feet. "Oh!"

"Here, let me."

"No, I—"

Kurt bent to help her and Savannah stooped low at the same time. Suddenly they were both crouched near the floor, their knees nearly knocking each other's. She wore stretch blue jeans, worn leather boots, and a feminine-looking midnight blue blouse printed with a glistening star pattern that underscored the gleam in her emerald green eyes.

"I've got it," she finished unsurely.

Savannah twisted the hem of the cape in her hands as Kurt held onto its other end, his fingers gripping the furry white neckline. He still wore his coat, but he'd unbuttoned it upon entering the Grand Hotel.

"If you're sure?"

Savannah licked her pretty pink lips. "Yes."

Kurt tightened his hold on the cape and rolled a bit of fabric forward in his hands. The cape lifted off the floor, pulled taut between them. "This could be a two-person job."

Her cheeks colored sweetly. "Hardly."

Savannah attempted to tug the cape in her direction, but Kurt tugged back, rolling the fabric forward another turn. The length of velvet between them stretched into a tight plane.

"You're going to break it," she said, but her words were a little breathy. Like she'd struggled to say them.

"I'll be careful." Kurt slowly cocked an eyebrow. "Promise."

He turned the fabric another revolution in his hands and Savannah's boots scooted across the hardwood floor, bringing her a few inches closer to him. "What are you doing?" she asked, attempting to maintain her balance.

"Picking up your mess," he said.

"Funny."

Kurt used his maneuver to bring her even closer. Savannah's knees bumped the side of his leg, and her breath quickened. "Kurt—"

"Yes?"

"Let go of this cape!" she demanded. "Now!"

"Now?"

"Ye—" Before she could finish, Savannah stumbled backward onto her bottom and the cape tumbled into her lap. "Ow!"

Kurt stood and offered her a hand.

"Sorry," he said. "I didn't mean to throw you off balance."

Savannah draped the cape over one arm and he tugged her to her feet with her other hand. Suddenly she was in his arms, her sweet womanly body pressed to his.

"I don't like being thrown off balance." Kurt tightened his arms around her. "Do you?"

Her face burned bright red as she stared up at him. "Is this about the bazaar?"

"Normally, Savannah, relationships progress in a certain way," he said huskily. "Boy meets girl... Boy dates girl... They grow to care for each other... Those emotions deepen." He tugged her in tighter and Savannah gasped. "Eventually they talk to each other—"

"You're the one who told me..." Emotion threaded her voice. "Told me you still cared."

"Yes, that's true. But, I said it to you, and not to an entire congregation."

"I don't know what came over me," she said with a blush. "I was lightheaded! Low blood sugar!"

"You mean, you didn't eat any dinner?"

"No, I..."

"Skipped dessert?"

"Not that, exactly."

He narrowed his eyes and tilted his chin. "Did you put the moves on my brother?"

"No! Heavens! I was only thinking about Gloria!"

"Gloria?"

"She's my best friend in Miami, and... And, perfect for Walt."

"I see." His gaze poured over her and Kurt couldn't help but think about how lovely she was. Beautiful, with her long red hair spilling past her shoulders. He ached to kiss her—badly. But he wasn't going to yet. "You're into matchmaking now?"

"Not every day," she said hurriedly. "It's just that I thought—"

"That's a malady, you know. One that affects the good citizens of Christmas Town."

Savannah licked her luscious lips again. "That's...what I've heard."

"I'm a pretty good doctor."

He traced her moist lips with his thumb and Savannah caught her breath.

"I've heard that, too."

Kurt lowered his mouth toward hers. "I could help you with your problem."

"How?" she asked, and her breath shuddered.

His lips hovered over hers as he whispered, "Let me take you on a date, Savannah. Let's do this right."

"A date?" She stared up at him dazed, but there was womanly interest in her eyes.

"I'll take you anywhere you want to go."

"I…uh…"

"The Peppermint Bark?"

"*Yes*." She said it weakly, like her head was spinning.

"Friday?"

"Okay…"

Kurt wondered if this was what it was like to make a woman swoon. Despite his ample experience with women, he'd never had this level of an impact on anyone. And, he kind of liked it. But only because this was Savannah… Kurt needed her to want him. Burned to make her weak with desire. "You *do* want to do this?"

Color swept her cheekbones and crept down her neck.

"Oh boy, do I ever."

"Eight o'clock?"

"Uh-huh."

A grin warmed his face. "Terrific."

He prepared to release her, but Savannah clung on tight. "Wait! Don't…"

Kurt eyed her curiously.

"I might…" Her blush deepened. "Might fall."

Kurt viewed her with a mixture of affection and longing.

"I'll let you in on a little secret," he said. "I already have."

Chapter Twenty-One

Savannah was rushing to get ready for her date when her telephone rang. She nabbed her cell off the dresser, seeing it was Gloria calling.

"Gloria, hi!" Savannah ran her fingers through her hair and examined her reflection in the mirror. Wearing the Commitment Cookie barrette was probably too much. Even if the pale pink background behind the dark red lettering did match her pretty pink cashmere cardigan sweater. It had small pearl buttons and she'd worn it over a white silk blouse. Her ankle length peasant skirt was charcoal gray, and she wore dark leggings and black leather ankle boots beneath it. A small gold pendant shaped like an open heart hung from a gold chain around her neck, and her pearl post earrings complemented the pearl accents on her sweater.

"Sorry to call on a Friday night," Gloria quipped. "You're probably getting ready for a hot date or something."

"I, er…" Savannah gasped and blinked at her reflection. "How did you know?"

"Seriously?" Gloria asked with gleeful delight. "You're going out with somebody?"

Savannah saw herself blush and turned away from the mirror. "Not just anybody. I'm having dinner with Kurt."

"Interesting."

"Yeah, I know." Savannah fiddled with a lock of hair, wrapping it around her finger. "It's pretty impossible to refuse one of his invitations."

"When did all this happen?"

"On Tuesday. He dropped by the theater, and um…popped the question!"

"*You're getting married*?" Gloria asked in shrill tones. Though she was obviously pleased.

"No! Not *that* question. The other one…about going to the Peppermint Bark."

"The Peppermint Bark sounds cute."

"It is, at least from the outside. I've seen it from the street since it's right across from the church."

"Since when do you go to church?"

"Since…always!"

"You never go here."

"Christmas Town is different. Everyone here is connected to that congregation. Almost everyone I've met, anyhow."

"Sounds like a tight-knit community."

"It is! And, all of the parishioners are…" Savannah stalled, trying to block the memory of her most embarrassing moment. "Very understanding, it seems."

"What have they got to be understanding about?" Gloria questioned. "You've practically just arrived! It's not like you've done anything…" She paused in thought. "*Amiga*… Have you?"

"Have I what?"

"Done something already you needed to apologize for?"

"No!" Savannah's pulse drummed in her ears. "Why would you think that?"

"Why would you go to church?" Gloria mused thoughtfully. "Hmm."

"It was a church bazaar, okay? With a silent auction, a Christmas pageant and everything. One of my sister's friends, Sandy, invited me to go and I couldn't say no."

"That was a nice way to get to know more people in town."

Yeah, Savannah thought, flushing heatedly, *and for them to get to know me—personal secrets and all!*

"Yes, well, it was," Savannah said. "And speaking of that...I wanted to mention—" The doorbell rang before she could say, *Walt Christmas*. "Oh! Oh my goodness! That must be him!" Savannah checked the clock on the nightstand, seeing it was five minutes past eight. "I'm sorry, Gloria, but I've got to run!"

"Okay! Well, have fun!"

"Thanks."

"And, don't forget to call and tell me *everything*!"

Savannah did one last check in the bedroom mirror and dashed down the stairs, deciding she didn't have time to change things. She looked good enough, and the barrette matched besides. It was just an accessory after all. It's not like anyone would read anything into it! Savannah hadn't been this excited about a date in years. She felt expectant and joyful, yet her nerves were on edge with little prickly tingles radiating from her fingers and toes inside her lace-up boots.

Kurt Christmas was here to take her out to dinner. While he'd treated her to lunch, that meal had ended in disaster. She'd been upset with Kurt then, because he was still seeing Eliza. Savannah also hadn't fully made up her mind regarding her feelings for him. Now that she'd announced them to every member of his family and most of the citizens of Christmas Town, there wasn't a lot she could do to hide them.

So, okay. Yes! I still have feelings for Kurt, just as he says he's got them for me. Tonight, we're going to explore them and see where those might lead. To a goodnight kiss, perhaps? Savannah sure hoped so! She'd nearly melted in Kurt's arms at the theater on Tuesday, and the only thing he'd done was hold her. That didn't mean she couldn't recall what a dynamite kisser Kurt was. He'd laid a whopping one on her at Olivia's wedding, and had completely undone her outside of Carter's cabin... The years had only improved his remarkable skill.

Savannah danced toward the door in giddy anticipation, but when she pulled it open she found Liz standing there, not Kurt.

"*Jumping jelly beans!*" Liz said. "You look terrific!"

"Oh gosh, I'm sorry, Liz," Savannah told her. "I'd ask you to come in, but I'm kind of on my way somewhere."

"I know." Liz's light brown eyes sparkled merrily. "That's what I heard."

"Heard from who?" Savannah asked, astounded.

"My brother, Stan!"

"Stan? But how did he…?"

"Kurt Christmas dropped by the Candy Cane Barbershop on his lunch hour today, and do you know what he wanted?"

"A haircut and a shave?" Savannah guessed lamely.

"An extra close shave," Liz confided. "The old-fashioned kind with a straight razor!"

"They do that there?" Savannah asked, wondering if she should be amazed or retroactively concerned for Kurt's safety.

"Oh, yeah. But almost nobody asks for it anymore. Except for on special occasions." Liz stepped a few inches closer as snow pounded the porch railing behind her. She'd thrown on her coat, but had neglected to zip it up. "This is—apparently—a special occasion," she said in low tones. "Kurt said he was taking a 'special lady' to the Peppermint Bark." She eyed Savannah astutely when Savannah's cheeks warmed. "Am I correct in guessing that 'lady' is you?"

"Well, yes. All right," Savannah whispered excitedly. "We are going out, but he'll be here at any minute, so—"

"That's why I brought this by!" Liz stated proudly. She held out a small package that had been gift wrapped in plain brown paper and tied up with twine. "It's the 'Pure Pleasure Pack,'" she confessed quietly. "Guaranteed to turn him on."

"Oh! Oh my!" Savannah's face burned hot. "Gosh, Liz. I don't know what to—"

"They're essential oils," Liz continued hurriedly. "From Della's shop, Mystic Magi. Three little bottles that will do the trick: organic lemongrass, jasmine absolute, and peppermint. Just don't use them all together." She dropped her voice in a husky whisper. "That might be too much."

"I'm afraid you've got it wrong, Liz. I don't need a... I mean, Kurt and I... It's not like that between us."

"Of course it's not!" she said, as if this were obvious. "That's because you haven't applied these yet!" She shoved the small package into Savannah's hands. "Only a few drops, now," she cautioned. "A little goes a long way! And don't start with all three; just choose one." Then she smiled brightly and was off.

"Liz, wait!"

Liz paused with her hand on the front doorknob and the door partially ajar.

"I wanted to say...er...thank you! Thanks for the gift!"

"No problem." Liz beamed her way. "I know you've had the hots for him forever."

"What?"

"Savannah," Liz said seriously. "You might have fooled some of the other folks in town. But, I know the difference between 'performance art' and a *true confession*," she finished with a wink.

Savannah set the small package down on her entryway table and unwrapped it. There were three tiny bottles inside, nestled in tissue paper and with handcrafted labels. An aphrodisiac? Ha! She wouldn't need any help with Kurt! Nor would he, obviously. Not that things were going to get *that* steamy between them tonight anyway. The cold hard truth was, Kurt might even lead her on again like he did at the theater. Bring her to the brink of ecstasy…causing her to yearn for his kiss… And then, *a big fat nothing.* Hmm.

Savannah lightly fingered the oil bottles, thinking she didn't want heavy action, but a hearty goodnight kiss would do. Maybe adding a few drops of an essential oil would help? Not as an enticement, but more like…insurance! Yes! That was it! She studied the labels carefully, deciding that peppermint was most fitting to the season. Savannah picked up the small bottle and twisted open its cap, and a sweet pungent aroma filled the air tickling her nostrils. Just a couple of dabs here… She used the wand attached to the cap to apply two little dabs to her wrists. And another drop there… Savannah gave the tiniest brush of the wand at her cleavage, and her skin warmed and tingled at every affected pulse point.

The doorbell rang, and Savannah hurriedly recapped the bottle, dropping in back in the box and closing its fold-down lid.

Kurt stood outside Savannah's door at Sisters' Row, gathering his courage. If dinner went well with Savannah tonight, he was going to tell her. It would be better to get things out in the open. Once Savannah had adjusted to that, she could share whatever secret she'd been keeping. Though it was hard to imagine it was as devastating as Savannah thought, it was true that Kurt and she had been out of touch for many years. So, Kurt understood that a number of things might have happened during that interim. No matter what it was, he was prepared to be there for Savannah and support her. Kurt hoped that sharing these truths would only bring them closer, and not, as he secretly feared, drive them apart. Nothing Savannah said could push Kurt away. He wasn't so sure she'd feel the same. Kurt swallowed hard and rang the bell again, thinking Savannah could be upstairs and might not have heard him.

She opened the door seconds later, an absolute vision in a long flouncy skirt and a pretty pink sweater. Her hair was long and loose, pulled back in one small section on top by...*it can't be but it is...a sweet little Commitment Cookie barrette.* A grin warmed Kurt's face, his hope blooming. "Savannah, wow," he said. "You look lovelier than ever."

Her gaze swept over his car coat and fedora and Kurt immediately removed his hat. "You look nice, too," she said, apparently spying the hint of Kurt's red Christmas tie at his collar. It was dotted with Christmas trees and had been a gift from his nephew Kyle last Christmas. Kurt wore a starched blue shirt with it, dark gray chinos, and a navy blazer, with his better loafers and of course his stylish reindeer socks. Those he'd purchased himself at the men's shop in town, Santa's Suited Up. "Do you want to come in?"

"Not if you're ready to go," Kurt said.

"I am!" she returned brightly. "Just let me grab my coat." Kurt stepped across the threshold to help her slip into it. As he did, he caught a whiff of her heady perfume and his nose twitched heartily. What was that familiar scent causing his senses to tingle? It was acerbic yet sweet...almost...

Peppermint! Kurt quickly turned away, sneezing into the crook of his arm.

"Sorry Savann—" He felt another one coming on and reached into his jacket pocket, extracting his freshly laundered handkerchief. Kurt unfolded it just in time to catch a rapid succession of three more sneezes.

"Bless you! Bless you! Bless you!" she repeated, clearly concerned he might never stop. When he did, Savannah worriedly searched his eyes, which burned and itched fiercely. "Are you all right?"

"Yes, I…" He pinched the bridge of his nose and turned away, forestalling another sneeze. He viewed her through blurry eyes. "Are you wearing…peppermint?"

She flushed in the porch light. Savannah had already locked her door and they were preparing to leave the stoop and walk to Kurt's SUV. "Er…peppermint?"

"Perfume?" he ventured, his throat growing scratchy. "Oil, perhaps?"

Savannah cupped her hand to her mouth. "You're allergic?" she asked with evident horror.

"Sadly, yes."

"Oh, *dear*. Since when?"

"Monday, I believe."

"This past Monday?" She scrutinized him oddly. "That's weird."

Kurt folded his hanky and shoved it back in his pocket with a sniff. "You don't know the half of it." His nose twitched again, and Savannah dug into her purse and pulled out her key.

"Let me…go and wash it off!" she stammered, jimmying the door open.

Kurt followed her inside and Savannah raced up the stairs still wearing her coat.

"I'm so sorry, Kurt!" she cried, making a hasty retreat. "I didn't know!"

When she disappeared from view Kurt noticed the small brown package on the entryway table. The box's design was oddly familiar. It looked like something that had come from that organic shop owned by Della Martin. He picked it up to examine its label and nearly sneezed again. *Mystic Magi. Huh.* Kurt carefully pried back the fold-over flap of the box, peering inside. A collection of three tiny bottles of essential oils sat side by side. On top of them and lying slightly askew was a small, stylized card that read: Pure Pleasure Pack. *Whoa.*

Heat warmed the back of his neck. Savannah didn't seem the type to resort to aphrodisiacs, but that just proved what Kurt already suspected about women. You never really knew what they were thinking, until they surprised you with something new.

Kurt heard the water running in the upstairs bathroom sink shut off, and he quickly closed the box, placing it back on the table.

"All freshened up!" Savannah told him as she traipsed down the stairs. "And, peppermint free!" She'd removed her coat and now held it in one arm. "My apologies again. I honestly had no idea! It was just…a new…" Savannah bit into her bottom lip, apparently concocting an excuse. "Perfume I thought I'd try! Holiday scented!"

"It wasn't a bad thought," Kurt said with a smile. "Just maybe unnecessary."

"Oh?" Savannah's gaze darted nervously to the box on the entryway table, which she probably was hoping he hadn't seen.

"You're enticing enough just as you are." He helped her back into her coat as Savannah blushed.

"Thanks, Kurt."

"Besides," he teased warmly. "You're already wearing a Commitment Cookie barrette."

Her hand shot to the accessory as her color deepened.

He twinkled at her and then added, "How much *insurance* does a woman really need?"

Savannah burned with embarrassment all the way to the Peppermint Bark. Fortunately, it wasn't a very long trip. Once there, Kurt opened her car door like a gentleman and escorted her up the restaurant's front steps. The hostess seated them at a reserved table for two near a front window and kitty-corner from the gently roaring fireplace. A candle flickered in the center of their table and they'd each been handed elegant menus to study.

"Would you like something to drink?" Kurt met her eyes over the top of his menu and Savannah's heart raced. Who knows what kind of evening he thought she'd been attempting to orchestrate? "Maybe some wine to go with dinner?"

"All right, thanks."

"Red or white?"

"What are you thinking of ordering?"

"I'm not sure yet. How about you?"

Savannah's eyes roved over the menu and all the selections looked delicious. "It's a hard decision, but maybe the crab and shrimp crepes?"

"Those are very good, I hear."

"How about you?" Savannah asked him.

"I'm thinking of the wild mushroom gnocchi."

246 The Doctor Orders Christmas

"Yum. That one tempted me, too."

"Maybe we can share?" he suggested.

"Now there's an idea!" she said, brightening at the thought.

Kurt drank her in with his eyes and warmth pooled in Savannah's belly. "Thanks for coming out with me, Savannah."

"Thank you for inviting me." She glanced around the elegant bistro, where the only other diners appeared to be couples out on dates. "This place is great."

Their waiter arrived to take their orders, and both asked for mixed green salads to start as well. When he'd retrieved their menus and gone, Savannah asked, "What made you say the word 'insurance'?"

"Insurance?" A puzzled expression crossed Kurt's face.

Savannah had been stewing on it ever since they left Sisters' Row. "You said that Sandy was the mind reader."

Kurt coughed into his napkin. "What are you telling me, Savannah? That I hit the nail on the head?"

Heat warmed her cheeks. "The peppermint oil was a gift, you know."

"Oh?"

"From Liz Martin."

"Imagine that? Who knew Liz had it in her?"

"Oh, she does all right," Savannah said with a giggle. "Liz is far more interesting than most folks know."

"You've gotten to know her pretty well, huh?"

"Better each day. We're going to lunch tomorrow."

"I think that's awesome. It's nice you're making friends in Christmas Town."

A wine steward arrived and after a brief interval of wine tasting, he filled their wineglasses and left. Kurt had selected a Pinot Noir that seemed like it might go well with both dishes. It was flavorful yet smooth with hints of cherry, black currant, and dark chocolate.

"This wine is excellent," Savannah told him. "Nice pick."

Kurt sipped from his glass, his mind apparently still on their previous conversation. "So, Liz Martin stopped by with the Pure Pleasure Pack?"

"Shhh," Savannah warned. She quickly scanned the room, but she was giggling. "Someone will hear you."

"Well, it won't be the first time the mysterious oils of Della's shop have been put to use."

Savannah's mouth dropped open. "By you?"

Color streaked his temples. "Of course not." Kurt cleared his throat and took another sip of wine. "I've never needed anything like that—personally." His gaze roved over her. "What about you?"

"Me?" Savannah's heart hammered with humiliation. "I…er…no!"

"Never?"

"Never!"

Kurt set down his wine. "Until tonight."

Savannah's face steamed. "It wasn't my idea. I told you—"

"Very thoughtful of Liz, yes. Even if a bit misguided." Savannah watched as his gaze traveled to the ornament in her hair. "Seems like you'd already made plans of your own."

Savannah's fingers gently stroked the barrette as she swept back her hair. "For your information, this happens to match the colors of my outfit."

"It's the perfect complement, it's true."

"Besides," Savannah said lightly. "Nobody really believes in that Commitment Cookie lore." She curiously observed his eyes. "Do they?"

"Not me." Kurt shook his head. "But I'm aware that others believe in the legend."

"Well, if you *don't*, then why were you in such a hurry to give your cookie away?"

"I didn't want it."

"Because you don't eat sweets," Savannah said doubtfully. "Or desserts…"

"Those, either," Kurt agreed.

"So," he asked as their salads arrived. "Have you eaten it?"

"No." Savannah dug into her salad with her fork. "I'm saving it for a certain occasion."

"Like what?" Kurt asked, starting in on his salad as well.

"Eating it with somebody special," Savannah teased.

"That's fine by me," Kurt said unconcernedly. Then he added as a twist, "As long as that 'somebody special' is me."

Savannah looked up to find him grinning at her.

"I thought you didn't believe?"

His dark brown eyes twinkled. "You're not the only one who likes to take out insurance, Savannah."

"How *did* you know that, by the way? About the insurance?"

"I didn't. I just guessed." He shrugged mildly. "Maybe you and I think more alike than you know?"

Savannah chewed thoughtfully as the wine steward arrived to top off their wines. "It doesn't matter anyway," she finally said. "It's not like things are going to go that far."

Kurt's brow shot up.

"Between us," Savannah added haltingly. "This is our first official date in forever, and I'm not—"

"I know that, Savannah," Kurt said kindly. "You don't have to explain about the oils. I believed you when you said Liz brought them by. I'm sure she thought she was doing you a favor."

"Yeah."

He surveyed her eyes. "You're different now from how you were before, aren't you?"

"Less promiscuous, you mean?" she asked, growing indignant.

Kurt reached out and took her hand. "I never would have called you that."

Savannah's fingers trembled in his hold. "No?"

"What we had wasn't like that. I know it and you know it, too."

"Kurt, despite what you think, I'm not ready—"

"I know you're not." He kissed the back of her hand. "I knew that the night of Olivia's wedding." He lowered his voice into soft soothing tones. "You asked me to just hold you, remember?"

Savannah ducked her chin.

"That's all I wanted, too." He observed her longingly. "All I've ever wanted is another chance. We don't need to rush things. We can take it slow."

He squeezed her hand and she held on tight in return. "Thank you," she said, her words faltering. Her throat felt raw and moisture brimmed in her eyes. "Thank you for understanding."

"Savannah," he said very seriously. "What happened all those years ago changed me. And I mean *changed* in a significant way."

She blinked back her tears, her heart aching. "Our relationship changed me, too."

He reached across the table and cupped her cheek in his hand. "I knew at the time there could never be another. It's you—or no one—Savannah. I can't help what I feel any more than what I know. It's written in the stars."

"Which stars?"

"Ours. Our destiny. Our fate," he said huskily. Kurt leaned across the table and very tenderly brought his lips to hers. Savannah nearly fainted at his satiny smooth kiss. "Just don't run away this time, okay?" he whispered warmly. "Promise me you'll stay…" He tightened his grasp on her hand. "Stay with me and stick it out, until we know where things will lead."

But Savannah already knew what she was hoping. She was hoping things would lead to forever with Kurt. Because she'd never loved anybody else, either. Way down deep in her heart, it had always been him.

Chapter Twenty-Two

As Kurt walked Savannah to her door, she turned to him. "Thanks for a wonderful dinner. The food at the Peppermint Bark was superb and the company—even better."

Kurt smiled softly. "I'm glad you enjoyed it. I had a good time, too."

"Want to come in for a drink?" She indicated the white paper sack in his hand. They hadn't finished their wine at the restaurant, so their server had bagged it for them.

"I'd like that, Savannah," he answered warmly. Kurt removed his hat and she opened the door, letting them both inside. He perused the decorated Frasier fir in the back corner. "I like what you've done with the Christmas tree," he said. "I didn't take time to notice it before."

Savannah shot him a sassy look. "Too busy paying attention to other things, I'd venture." She nabbed the box from Mystic Magi off the entryway table and carried it across the room. "Maybe I should take this upstairs?"

Kurt chuckled loudly at this. "Probably the farther away the better."

"Good thing I didn't put any candy canes on my tree," Savannah quipped.

"Yes."

She spun his way when she reached the bottom of the stairs. "Has it really only been since Monday? Your allergies?"

"That's the first time I had a reaction, yeah."

"Why do you suppose the sensitivity came on so suddenly?" Since he was a doctor, Savannah guessed Kurt must have some speculation.

"That might take some explaining."

She waited expectantly, but he shooed her along with his hands.

"*After* we're both settled with our wine…"

"You'll tell me, then?"

"Maybe more than you want to know."

She blinked hard, but Kurt just pointedly stared up the stairs.

"Er…right! I'll go tuck this away somewhere. In the meantime, feel free to make yourself at home." She glanced briefly at the coatrack and then toward the kitchen. "The wineglasses are in the upper cabinet to the left of the sink."

Kurt hung up his coat and hat and carried the wine to the kitchen. He was about to open an upper cabinet, when an odd glowing caught his eye. It appeared to be coming from the freezer above the refrigerator. He tried to ignore it, but when he looked away it seemed to glow brighter, demanding attention in his peripheral vision. *Now, that is weird.*

Kurt peeked back into the living room, seeing Savannah was still upstairs. Next, he stealthily opened the freezer. Almost nothing was in there except for ice cube trays, a small carton of gourmet chocolate ice cream, and…*whoa… A shimmering paper bag from the Christmas Cookie Shop?* Kurt gaped in awe at the glittering object. The simple brown paper bag sparkled like it was composed of millions of grains of bright beach sand. The sort that nearly blinds you at high noon. Kurt blinked and stared again, noticing something else. A fine ribbon of rainbow colors seemed to be leaking out of the bag, right at the point where it was folded closed and underneath its crease.

"What are you doing?"

Kurt slammed shut the freezer door and whirled on Savannah, who stood in the doorway. "I…uh…" Kurt scratched the side of his head, wondering if he'd imagined it. But that didn't seem likely. His imagination wasn't that good. The only spectacular things Kurt thought of were things that had actually occurred. Even when normal people might question them. Kurt knew magic when he saw it, and he had an inkling he'd just witnessed it for real. "I was wondering if you wanted ice in your drink?"

"My red wine?" Savannah asked, as if that was a silly question. Which it was, naturally. Pretty lame.

"No, your water." Kurt gathered his wits, thinking fast. "I thought you might like a glass of that, too?"

Savannah shrugged happily. "Sure, why not? It's good to stay hydrated!"

"Hydrated, yes." Kurt's eyes darted back to the freezer that still appeared to be emanating light. Somehow, though, Savannah had failed to notice.

"Want me to get it?" she asked, reaching for the handle to the freezer door. She pried it open slightly, and Kurt slammed it shut.

"Don't bother!" he said hurriedly. "Let me get the water!"

"O-kay." She eyed him curiously. "Are you all right?"

"Just fine and dandy! Why?"

"You look a little... I don't know. On edge, or something."

Sure, he was on edge. Kurt didn't need Savannah coming across an activated Virginia Cookie, before he'd even told her about *him*. One dose of magic at a time was probably enough. In Kurt's expert opinion... Kurt quickly mulled this over, deciding the Commitment Cookie's powers must have become unleashed due to him and Savannah passing that bag back and forth between them. Clearly, they were meant to eat it and share it. And stay together indefinitely, of course. But Kurt couldn't lay that on Savannah yet. There were other important things they needed to discuss first.

"I'll get the wine then," she said, trying to step past him. Kurt stopped her by shoving the bottle straight at her.

"Here! Take this to the living room!"

"But the glasses?"

"I'll bring those!"

Savannah slowly backed away, not taking her wary gaze off Kurt. "Are you feeling sick?"

"No!" he said abruptly, before adding a cautious, "Why?"

"I was just wondering if this has something to do with your allergies?"

"Yeah!" he said, awash with relief at telling the truth. "It does!"

"Oh!"

"The water will help!"

"If you're sure…?"

"And, the wine!"

"It might not be good to mix that with medication. I think there might be some allergy tablets in the medicine cabinet upstairs." She surveyed him worriedly and deposited the wine on the coffee table. "Let me just go and—"

"Don't bother!" Kurt said, growing a bit breathless. "I don't need pills for this!"

"No?"

"Nuh-uh. No meds." He stared at her earnestly, hoping to transmit his sincerity with the look in his eyes. "You'll understand better once I explain."

"Explain what?"

"About me!"

"Oh Kurt… Oh, gosh." Her face fell appreciably and Kurt knew what Savannah was thinking. She assumed he was cracking up.

"What can I do?" she petitioned sweetly. "Tell me how I can help you."

"Just sit!"

"Sit?"

"On the sofa, Savannah."

She glanced uncertainly over her shoulder then took a seat on a sofa cushion. "All right."

The last time Kurt had told her to sit, Savannah had taken offense, deducing that he'd been ordering her around. At present though, Savannah was happy to follow Kurt's orders. Something was obviously wrong with him, although she didn't know what. She anxiously chewed her lip, hoping this didn't have to do with Kurt's delusional bent. He had been rather convinced that Walt had made those Christmas trees grow instantaneously. Who knew what other sorts of wacky stuff he believed.

Savannah drew in a deep breath to calm herself. This was Kurt she was thinking about, the man she truly cared for, and was determined to help. She'd dealt with people in crisis before. She could handle this. Definitely. All she needed to do was stay neutral and hear Kurt out in a nonjudgmental way. Afterward, she could decide whether or not to recommend serious counseling.

Savannah sadly hung her head, wondering what could have happened. The evening had being going so well, and Kurt had been the perfect gentleman. All night long, he'd been attentive, gracious, and kind. The dinner with him had been fantastic, and when he'd kissed her sweetly and said even sweeter words, Savannah's heart had absolutely melted. Now, here she was being jerked back into reality.

Kurt had issues he obviously hadn't dealt with. But nobody was perfect, Savannah reasoned. Just look at Olivia and Nick! They both shared some unusual beliefs and yet seemed ideally suited to one another. Savannah swallowed hard, understanding this comparison didn't necessarily bode well for her and Kurt. Mainly, because she didn't share Kurt's belief in magically maturing Christmas trees. What did he imagine Ray had done? Sprinkle fairy dust on them?

"Here you are!"

Savannah looked up to see Kurt handing her a glass of wine with one hand and a glass of ice water with the other. "Thanks, Kurt." When she took them, he replied that he'd go grab his drinks and be right back.

In another few minutes, Kurt was settled on the sofa beside her. He took a long drink of water then set his glass down on the coffee table, picking up his wine. Next, he yanked Mr. Noodles off the back of the sofa and placed him in the armchair. "You don't mind?" he asked Savannah.

Savannah gripped her wine goblet with two hands. "No, not at all."

Perspiration swept Kurt's brow and he loosened his necktie. "Savannah," he said hoarsely. "I think it's time we had a talk."

They both set down their wine.

"I'm so glad you said that." Savannah leaned toward him and reassuringly patted his leg. "Because I think so, too."

"You do?" He stared at her with mild surprise. "Well, good. That's good. No. Excellent, really." He paused to remove his jacket, laying it on top of Mr. Noodles. "Savannah," he said, meeting her eyes. "Do you know who I am?"

She nodded cautiously. "Kurt Christmas?"

"Yeah, and I… Well…" His gaze landed on the oil painting over the mantel: the winter scene that Sandy had done. "Have some unusual relatives."

"Like Sandy?" Savannah asked, following his line of vision.

Kurt turned back to her. "And, Nick, and my dad and my brothers…"

Oh dear, he was warming up to the magic Christmas tree story. Savannah just knew it. Well, she might as well help him along. The sooner they got things out in the open, the sooner they could deal with them. "Like Ray, you mean?" she prodded gently.

"Ray, sure. But Walt's got it, too."

Savannah squinted, trying hard to follow. "Allergies?"

"No. I mean, yeah. Hmm." He appeared distant a brief moment then he locked on her gaze. "It sort of depends on how you look at it."

"Look at what, Kurt?"

He heaved a breath and ran a hand through his hair. "You know my last name is Christmas."

"Yes."

"And Nick is a Claus."

"I know."

"So was Sandy, and she still is in a way."

"Of course."

"Our two families are related."

"That's what I've heard."

"Savannah." Kurt latched onto her hand, startling her. "We're not like other people. We're spe—"

"—cial," she finished for him, Olivia's words resonating back to her in an odd way. "I see."

"Do you?" He stared at her pleadingly. "Can you really understand?"

"Kurt," Savannah began in her most professional tone. "You're a remarkable man."

"Maybe more remarkable than you believe."

Well, talk about ego! Not that Savannah didn't always know he had one. "Self-confidence is important," she replied encouragingly. "It's good to have faith in yourself."

"It's not just in me. It's in my abilities."

"Abilities, ah." *Okay, here it comes.* Savannah braced herself for the worst.

"I told you I can tell when people are lying."

"So can I," she said pertly. "My Pinocchio detection skills are generally pretty good." Which was one reason she was certain Kurt was having emotional troubles. He certainly didn't exhibit the signs of a person who was being willingly deceptive.

Kurt laid a hand on her arm. "Savannah, look at me."

When she did, he asked, "Do you believe that I'm sane?"

"Sure!"

He viewed her doubtfully. "Oh, wow."

Savannah blinked in innocence and withdrew her arm. "Oh wow, what?"

"You don't, do you?"

"Of course I believe you're sane." He was certainly at least high functioning. He'd been through medical school and ran his own practice, after all. Both were encouraging signs. Savannah was hopeful that whatever had gone wrong with Kurt's thinking still could be fixed. He was such a great man in nearly every way—except for this minor quirky one.

Kurt set his elbows on his knees and rested his head in his hands. "I'm not sure how I can convince you," he said, mumbling his words. The next thing

Savannah knew, he stared up at her with brightly shining eyes. Savannah wasn't sure, but she feared they appeared borderline manic. "I've got it!"

"Got what?" she asked, just as casually as humanly possible. Under the circumstances.

Kurt's voice was rough with emotion when he said, "Seeing is believing, Savannah."

She watched him, stunned, as he got to his feet and strode to the coatrack.

"Er… What are you doing?" Savannah gingerly asked.

He returned with his overcoat and hers. "Here," he instructed bossily. "Put this on."

"Why?" Savannah asked, determined not to move from her chair. "Are we going somewhere?"

Kurt held out her coat in reply, but instead of taking it Savannah let it drop in her lap. "Kurt, you're starting to worry me."

"Are you afraid?" he demanded with bold dark eyes.

"Of you?" Savannah thought hard, then realized that she wasn't. Kurt would never do her harm, delusional or not. "No."

"Then come with me." Kurt held out his hand and after a moment's hesitation she took it.

"Where are we going?" she asked as he pulled her to her feet.

"Where would you like to go?"

"That's silly."

Kurt soulfully searched her eyes. "Is it?"

Savannah slipped into her coat, thinking she must be mad for going along with this. "Are we…planning a road trip somewhere?"

"Not a road trip. Exactly."

Savannah started toward the door but Kurt stopped her. "Not that way," he said.

She stared at him in alarm, fearing this was far worse than she thought. "Not that way?" Savannah asked, and her voice shook. "Then, where?"

Kurt held out his arms. "Here, Savannah."

She unsurely inched toward him. "There?"

Kurt wrapped his arms around her and held her close. "Here."

She gazed up at him in incredulity and Kurt arched an eyebrow. "I've never tried this with anyone else before. I hope it will work."

"Oh gosh, Kurt!" Savannah's heart hammered and her senses started tingling.

"Shhh…" He brought his finger to her lips and said warmly, "Close your eyes, Savannah."

She humored him, though her pulse was pounding. "Then what?"

"Imagine where you want to be."

"What?"

"Anywhere. If you could be anywhere."

"Alone?" she asked nervously, "or, with you?"

His words crashed over her like an ocean wave. "With me."

"Oh!" A sharp blast of air hit Savannah in the face and Kurt tightened his embrace. Then the earth spun all around them and they were sucked in with a *whoosh*— of crazily spinning stars. Savannah's head reeled and her body felt lighter than air. So light, she was on the verge of delirium—or passing out. Savannah wasn't sure which. A split second later, her legs grew heavy and her boots hit the ground. *Oomph!* But the earth was uneven, lumpy… She opened her eyes to see she was standing on sand!

Winds howled around them, riffling their coats and threading through Savannah's hair, as a bold moon rose high over the tumbling waters. "The ocean!" Savannah gasped in in disbelief. "You've brought us to the beach?"

Kurt steadied her in his arms and gazed down at her with longing. "Not just any beach."

She questioned with her eyes and he nodded toward a faraway pier. Savannah recognized its outline from so very long ago. "You didn't…?" She caught her breath, her heart pounding wildly. "Couldn't have. None of this is real!"

"It's never too late, Savannah." Kurt cupped her face in his hands. "To believe in magic."

"But, I can't! Don't…" but even as she said it, her resolve crumbled. How had this happened? How could she and Kurt be here?

"How do you think Santa travels the world?" he asked huskily. "So many countries in such little time?"

"Er…reindeer?" Savannah asked, her head spinning.

"The reindeer can't do it alone," Kurt said. "They need a bit of help."

"You're not telling me you're—?"

"Nope. Not me."

"One of his helpers?"

Kurt laughed warmly at this. "He has plenty of those in the Maritime Provinces."

"Canada?" Savannah thought quickly, though her mind was still murky. "Wait a minute… Isn't that where Olivia and Nick—?"

"It's as simple as inheritance, Savannah. Family DNA."

"So…you can do other things, too?" Savannah caught her breath because this trick was pretty spectacular. Even if she was fantasizing this somehow, Savannah was cogent enough to realize that.

Kurt's dark eyes sparkled. "Why don't we take things one step at a time?"

Savannah glanced around the empty shoreline still unable to believe her eyes. "When did this start for you?"

Kurt tightened his embrace. "When I was about sixteen, after you and I…" He gazed into her eyes. "You know."

Savannah flushed at the thought. "Do you think that had something to do with—?"

"I know it did. That's how these abilities work. They surface and then become stronger under one special circumstance."

She surveyed him carefully.

"When a Claus—or, in this case, a Christmas—finds the one they're meant to be with, their destiny-appointed partner, our innate abilities intensify."

"Intensify? What do you mean?"

"Develop a life of their own. It's not always possible to control them, but with time and practice you can. Being with the right person helps." He beheld her lovingly, and his dark eyes glistened. "What do you say? Do you believe me now?"

"I…I'm not sure," she admitted honestly. This still could be some kind of dream, or an odd joint delusion.

"That's okay." Kurt tenderly kissed her forehead. "Give yourself time."

He gave her a hug and glanced toward the pier. "Would you like to take a walk? I mean, as long as we're here?"

"As long as we're here?" Savannah repeatedly weakly, wondering if he'd hypnotized her. Well, if Kurt had, Savannah thought resolutely, she might as well enjoy the journey. Nothing this spectacular or surreal had ever happened to her in her life. And Savannah wasn't even quite sure whether it was happening now... "All right, Kurt," she said decidedly. "Let's go."

He tenderly released her and held out his hand. "I've wanted to come back here with you for a long time."

"Yeah," she said happily, placing her hand in his. "Me, too."

"I'm glad this is where you wanted to go, Savannah."

"How will we get home?"

"Just leave that to me."

Savannah glanced over her shoulder as they began moving along. She watched the waves lapping against the shore, and moonbeams dancing across the water, but something seemed amiss in her view. It wasn't until they were nearly to the pier that Savannah realized what it was. She and Kurt hadn't left any footprints behind them.

Chapter Twenty-Three

Savannah awoke to a distant ringing. *What is that familiar sound? My cell phone!*

Her eyes popped open and she stared at the ceiling. Bright noontime light shone between the closed slats on her window's plantation blinds. Her phone rang again and Savannah fumbled for it on her nightstand. *What time is it, anyway?* She accepted the call as her gaze landed on the clock. *Twelve forty-five! My lunch date with Liz!*

"Hello, did I get the time wrong?" Liz's perky voice ran down the line. She didn't sound accusatory. More like, confused.

"Time? Er…no!" Savannah sat up unsteadily in bed wondering what on earth had happened. She never slept past noon. Ever! "Liz, I'm so sorry—"

"What's wrong, Savannah? Are you sick?"

"Sick?"

"You seem a little…I don't know. Befuddled."

Now, there was a word that seemed to fit. Savannah stared around her bedroom at Sisters' Row feeling like she'd just stepped out of a time warp. Last thing she recalled, she was strolling along the beach with Kurt. *Their beach.* But, no! That was crazy. Couldn't have happened. Not in a million billion years. "Where are you calling from?" she asked Liz.

"The café at the Elf Shelf Book Shop. I thought we said twelve-thirty, but I could have been mis—"

"No," Savannah said, cutting her off. "You were right! And, I apologize. I got caught up with things this morning and…" Savannah perused her empty room again, blinking. Someone had draped her coat over the bedroom chair, and her unlaced boots were on the floor beside her dresser. She peeked under the covers seeing she'd slept in her clothes. "Lost track of time."

"No problem!" Liz replied good-naturedly. "That *often* happens to me." After a beat, she inquired, "So! Are you still coming? I'm holding a table near the register if you are."

"Yes, of course." Savannah swung her legs over the bed and her feet met the floor. Something felt gritty on her instep, and she cocked her foot sideways to glance at the sole portion of her leggings. Miniature taupe beads were stuck to the stretchy fabric lining the bottom of her foot. For the life of her, they looked like grains of sand!

Savannah's head spun as she tried to pull herself together. "I, uh… I'll be there in a bit! Ten minutes, tops!"

"Ten minutes? Okay, good. Because things are getting crowded and I'd hate to hold the table for too long."

"Thanks, Liz! You're the best!" Savannah leapt from the bed and raced to her dresser, setting down her phone. She didn't have time to shower. She'd do that when she got home. For now, she'd toss on some jeans and a sweatshirt. She'd also pull her hair into a ponytail and quickly wash her face. The bookshop was close by, so she should make it there in no time. Savannah scooted around the corner of the dresser toward the hall bathroom. In her haste, she kicked over one of her lace-up boots. She looked down and jumped in shock. *Gingerbread snap!* It couldn't be but it was. A whole handful of beach sand had just spilled out onto the carpet.

Kurt and Walt sat sharing an afternoon coffee at Jolly Bean Java. Walt had phoned this morning to ask Kurt if he wanted to meet up after closing his clinic at one. Walt didn't get out much, so Kurt was happy to oblige him. Though, the minute he and his big brother sat down with their coffees, Kurt got the notion that Walt had something on his mind.

"How are you feeling today?" Walt asked, sipping from his coffee.

"Fine. How about you?"

"I'm doing okay." Walt shifted in his chair. "But, I've been worried. You know…" He shot Kurt a telling look. "Since Monday."

"The peppermint bark?"

"Yeah, that."

"I think we both know what that means," Kurt answered.

"Sure," Walt said. "It means you can't mess with Mother Nature. Or, in this case, what's in our genes."

Kurt knew that certain members of the Claus and Christmas families were prone to develop unusual abilities once they reached "mating age." When they found their perfect match, those abilities intensified. The only thing known to tamp those abilities down was the ingestion or application of peppermint. And yet, if you were very strongly fated to be with someone, the peppermint wouldn't work around them. In rare cases, it even caused severe allergic reactions.

Kurt leaned toward him and asked quietly, "Did it happen to you?"

"The allergy thing? Yeah."

"I thought that was pretty rare."

"I don't think it happens to the Clauses," Walt told him.

"How do you know?"

"I asked Nick." Walt set down his cup and continued, "He basically said it had a neutral effect, but didn't cause any distressing symptoms."

"But it did in you?"

"With Rose?" Walt appeared thoughtful a moment. "Yeah, and very early on, too." His face took on a serious cast. "Actually that's something I wanted to talk to you about. I…" He twirled his cup around in his hands, stalling. "I think I put something together on Monday night after you left."

"What's that, Walt?"

"You know when Rose and I met?"

"Sure, in college."

"You were still in high school."

"Of course."

"It was the fall after our last beach summer."

"So?" Kurt asked, perplexed.

"So…" Walt appeared extremely regretful, almost like he wanted to cry. Kurt hadn't seen him like this in years. Not since he'd lost Rose, and that had been an understandably hard blow.

Kurt laid a hand on his brother's arm. "Level with me. What's going on?"

Walt's deep blue eyes met his. "I think I might have had something to do with it."

"It?"

Walt's face burned red beneath his beard. "What happened to you and Savannah."

"What? How?" Kurt was completely thrown by this. It didn't make any sense.

"It wasn't intentional," Walt protested hoarsely. "I couldn't have known it would happen."

"Walt," Kurt said sternly. "What did you do?"

"You know about my abilities."

"And?"

"But maybe not all of them. There's one I haven't thought about in a long time, because—frankly—it hasn't been much use. Not since Nick's grandpa developed that new communication app. Plus, he gets the drone delivery."

Kurt shook his head. "You're losing me completely."

"The truth is," Walt stated bluntly. "I haven't been in love in a very long time. Certain skills have sort of atrophied."

"What does that have to do with apps and drones?" Kurt questioned.

"I'm talking about communications, Kurt."

"Communications?"

"There's a strong vein in our family."

"You mean like writing? I know Noelle's studying to be a journalist—"

270 The Doctor Orders Christmas

"Not just writing," Walt told him. "Sending."

"Sending?"

Walt viewed him seriously. "Getting things from Point A to Point N.P."

Kurt gave a hushed whisper. "N.P. meaning the—"

"*Yes*," Walt whispered back. "There."

"What on earth does that have to do with me and Savannah?"

"Maybe everything." Walt scooted his chair closer to the table and Kurt leaned forward. "Those letters that went missing?"

"Yeah?"

"And the e-mails? Instant messages?"

"What about them."

"I think it was me, man," Walt croaked hoarsely.

"You?"

"All sorts of wacky stuff starting cutting loose when I began dating Rose. Over Thanksgiving, I heard Mom and Dad talking about how they weren't getting any mail. At the same time, Nick made some joke to me that his grandpa was getting an overabundance at the…well, there."

"Are you saying you caused that to happen?"

"You've heard of the dead letter office at the U.S. Post Office?"

"You're talking about all those letters addressed to Santa that never go anywhere?"

"Oh, they went somewhere all right. That's the year they all disappeared."

"What?"

"It was in the papers," Walt said. "But it never became a front page story. Maybe if it had happened at Christmastime, but this was in the fall… Speculation was some practical jokers had organized a country-wide hoax, or that a group with a grudge against the Post Office had been able to throw them all away."

"What does that have to do with Savannah's letters to me? Or mine to her?"

"Anything marked 'Christmas' or 'Claus,'" Walt confided, swallowing hard, "was fair game."

"For the tricksters?"

"There were no tricksters, Kurt. It was all me. I sent those missives winging to the Maritime Provinces."

"You what?"

"I didn't mean to. It just happened! Rose and I were talking about Christmas one time and she lamented the fact that so many poor kids write letters to Santa that never get seen. I tried to insist they did, but she wouldn't believe me. In any case, my hormones were going haywire, and all this Christmas mail got suddenly redirected. Anything to do with Nick's family or ours—"

"Went to the N.P...." Kurt said in slow understanding. "How long did this go on?"

"Until I finally convinced Rose to marry me."

"How many months later?"

"Eight." Walt eyed him apologetically. "But, that was already too late for you and Savannah, wasn't it?"

"This happened with cyber communications, too?" Kurt asked, dumbfounded.

"Apparently, yes."

"And, all this time I thought it was Mom... Or maybe her and Savannah's mother." He observed Walt with dismay. "Walt, how could you?"

"I never knew, Kurt. Never knew what had happened between you and Savannah. One summer you were hitting it off as boyfriend and girlfriend at the beach. The next thing I knew our family vacations with the Livingston family abruptly ended. Maybe I should have paid more attention to my little brother and his woes, and I'm sorry for that. I truly am. But I was a college kid then. In my own sphere and into my own heady romance with Rose. Plus, I was trying to figure out how in the world to cope with my crazy birthright—without pushing Rose completely away."

"I can hear what you're saying there," Kurt answered honestly. He sat back in his chair surveying his brother. "What happened to those errant letters, do you suppose? The ones that went north, but that weren't supposed to?"

"They're probably still around Nick's grandpa's workshop somewhere. According to Nick, his granddad is not extremely well organized. That's one reason he needs Nick's help."

"So those letters could still be around?" Kurt asked in hopeful tones. "You mean, Nick could actually find them?"

Walt issued a reminder. "I'd say he's pretty busy right now."

"Yeah, but Olivia isn't!" Kurt suddenly shot to his feet, stunning Walt. "At least, not as busy as Nick!"

"Kurt, where are you going?"

"To Sandy's gallery," Kurt said, slipping on his coat. "I want to see if she can help me get a message through to Nick."

Walt appeared thrown off base. "But, you haven't even told me how it's going? With Savannah?"

"We're getting there," Kurt said with a wink. "And what you just told me could certainly help!"

Walt stared at him uncertainly. "You're not mad at me, then?"

"Mad?" Kurt gave a hoot and hugged his brother's shoulders. "No, man! I'm actually pretty thrilled. And, now—thanks to you…" He stared confidently at Walt. "I have a definite plan!"

Once Liz and Savannah had their soup and sandwiches, Liz asked cheerily, "Well, how did everything go last night?" Her eyes sparkled with mischief. "Did you use the Pure Pleasure Pack?"

"Gosh, Liz." Savannah felt herself flush. "That's a bit personal."

"*Jumping jelly beans*, Savannah!" Liz said with a big grin. "I'm just razzing you." Then she lowered her voice with a giggle. "You don't have to tell me unless you want to."

Savannah couldn't help but grow excited about confiding in someone. While she could talk to Gloria on the phone, she missed having a face-to-face friendship. "Well…to tell you the truth…"

"Ye-es?" Liz eagerly cocked an ear.

"It was marvelous, Liz!" Savannah sighed. "Just marvelous!"

"How much of the oils did you use?" Liz asked in shock.

Savannah laughed out loud. "It wasn't the oils," she whispered. "It was him. Kurt. Oh my, he was so dreamy. The perfect gentleman at dinner, and after…"

"After? Hmm." Liz playfully wiggled her eyebrows and took a spoonful of soup.

Savannah sputtered a laugh, play-swatting her in the air. "No, it wasn't like that. I just had Kurt back to my place for an after-dinner drink, that's all. We had some wine left over…" Savannah puzzled at this. "Maybe that was my problem?"

Liz eyed her with concern. "What do you mean?"

"I think I might have had too much," Savannah said with an embarrassed flush. "I'm normally not much of a drinker. One glass is my limit."

"And?"

"I had two at the restaurant."

"And after?"

Savannah's eyebrows knitted together. "That part's fuzzy."

"Uh-oh."

"Yeah." Savannah spoke confidentially. "I must have passed out or something, because I had the weirdest dream."

"You mean, you don't remember going to bed?"

"Kurt must have tucked me in," Savannah said. "Because I woke up this morning—"

Liz arched an eyebrow and Savannah quickly added, "Fully clothed."

"Whoa, that's a little scary."

"Yes. I mean, no. I wasn't actually afraid."

"About what? Passing out?"

"I'm not sure I passed out…" Savannah bit into her bottom lip. "Precisely."

"Then what happened?"

"Maybe I'll have to ask Kurt."

Liz appeared crestfallen. "Well, I apologize if the essential oils had that sort of effect on you. They might have been too strong. I'm sorry, Savannah. Sorry I even suggested—"

"Liz," Savannah said, stopping her. "It wasn't the oils, I promise."

"But, how do you know?"

"Because I…um…haven't even tried them yet," Savannah fudged. The last thing she wanted to do was hurt Liz's feelings by letting Liz know her entire plan had backfired. Liz would likely be horrified to learn the peppermint oil had caused such a negative reaction in Kurt.

"Maybe you were over-fatigued?" Liz ventured. "You have been working mighty hard at the theater."

"I know, but I don't think it was that."

"You mentioned a dream?"

"It was silly."

"No way was it silly, Savannah!" Liz sighed heavily. "A girl should always be encouraged to dream."

Savannah chuckled warmly, feeling so at ease with her new friend. "All right, I'll tell you about it. But just a little."

Liz's brown eyes sparkled. "I understand wanting to keep some of the magic to yourself."

Savannah sat bolt upright. "Magic?"

"It was just a figure of speech, Savannah. Why do you look so pale?"

"Oh, I…I'm just hungry, probably." She took a voracious bite of her sandwich. "Low blood sugar, I guess."

Liz viewed her doubtfully. "Low blood sugar, okay."

"Anyway," Savannah began. "The dream was really cool. Kurt and I were on a beach."

"Which beach? Did you recognize it?"

"Yes! It's where we went as kids. And, also..." Savannah admitted with a blush. "Where Kurt and I first fell in love."

"How sweet!"

"Yeah."

Liz eyed her astutely. "Well, I guess that says something, doesn't it?"

"Oh?" Savannah asked her. "What does it say?"

"That you want to go back," Liz said with assurance. "To the way things were—between you and Kurt."

"No one can turn back the clock, Liz."

A smile played about her lips. "Are you one hundred percent sure?"

Chapter Twenty-Four

On Sunday after church, Kurt went to see his parents. Most specifically, his mother. He'd searched for Lou at the Fellowship Hall coffee hour, but she and Buddy hadn't been there. Kurt surmised they'd perhaps attended early church as they often did during the holiday season, when things remained busy for the two of them. He found Lou in her kitchen, pulling a tray of freshly baked gingerbread slabs from the oven.

"Why, Kurt! What a happy surprise," she said, setting the hot tray on a trivet. Kurt spied more confectionary construction pieces on the breakfast room table and guessed his mom was building more gingerbread houses.

"Looks like you've been busy," he said, unwrapping his scarf. Buddy had greeted him at the front door, but Kurt had been forced to hurry down the front hall toward the kitchen. The scent from the peppermint candles in the parlor was too much for him. Even unlit, they gave off a pungent aroma.

"You'll never believe it!" Lou's smile sparkled. "An anonymous buyer put in an outstanding bid on my gingerbread village!"

"Oh, really?" Kurt asked, feeling the corners of his mouth twitch.

"Five hundred dollars!"

"Wow, he must have thought it was worth it!"

Lou surveyed him curiously. "I never said the bidder was a 'he.'"

"I was using the term loosely, Mom. In the generic sense."

"Oh right! Right, of course!" She beamed sunnily and dusted her hands on her apron. As was her custom this time of year, she still wore that Santa hat on her head. "In any case, I was truly stunned! Overwhelmed by that person's generosity."

"It's all going toward a good cause," Kurt said.

"Yes, but even so…" Lou's brown eyes twinkled. "I decided to go one step better!"

"Oh?"

"Reward my benevolent donor with an annex town!"

"Oh wow. Gee, Mom. That's probably unnecessary."

"What?"

"I mean, how much gingerbread can one person need?"

"We don't know it's one person, Kurt!"

"But between this…" Kurt gestured around the kitchen. "And what you made earlier, you've probably baked enough to feed the whole town."

"Don't be silly," Lou said lightly. "This isn't nearly enough for everybody. Maybe I should send Buddy to the store for more—"

"Mom," Kurt said. "Really! I'm sure this is plenty. More than ample for your…" He cleared his throat.

"Anonymous benefactor to deal with." Kurt casually removed his coat. "Any idea who it is?"

"No, Pastor Wilson wouldn't say."

"Well, I'm sure he—or she—found your gingerbread village very impressive."

"Thanks, Kurt!"

"Because it's certainly one of a kind."

She glowed proudly. "Yes."

Lou was such a good person and with such a kind soul, Kurt felt horrible for misjudging her regarding his break-up with Savannah. That's the main reason he'd come here today. To apologize to his mom and make amends.

"Would you like a cup of coffee?" she asked him. "Or maybe a sandwich? Your father and I were just about to have lunch in a bit."

"No, thanks. I'm not staying." Kurt took a seat at the breakfast table and Lou joined him wearing a worried frown.

"Is something wrong, dear?"

"No, not exactly." He met his mom's kind brown eyes. "I just came here to apologize."

"Apologize?" she asked, flummoxed. "For what?"

"It's about Savannah."

"Savannah?" Lou asked with alarm. "Is she all—?"

"Yeah, fine. It's not that. It's about…" A lump formed in this throat. "Back when I was in high school."

"Go on?"

Kurt heaved a sigh. "I was wrong, Mom. So very wrong to suspect you of having something to do with our break-up. And, I'm sorry."

Lou's eyes glistened. "I said it wasn't me."

"I know you did, and I feel like a heel for not believing you. I just couldn't fathom... I mean, guess who else might have interfered."

"But you know now?" Lou questioned.

"The individual didn't mean to," Kurt replied. "It was just one of those things."

"Stopping the mail?" Lou's face lit in understanding. "It was a Claus thing, wasn't it?"

"You're in the ballpark," he told her.

"Christmas?"

"I really don't want to say."

"But everything's okay now?"

"Hope so." He shot her a tentative smile. "At least, I intend to make it so. To the best of my ability."

She fondly patted his hand. "That's my boy."

She studied his eyes a moment before asking, "How's Savannah?"

"Doing better, I think."

"With...?"

"Everything."

"Well, she should, you know. Each and every one of my sons is a spectacular catch, and you're no exception."

"Thanks, Mom."

She laid a hand on his arm, when he stood to go. "Kurt."

He met her gaze and she said, "I really hope that it works out for you. For you and Savannah. Something tells me it was meant to be."

That afternoon, Savannah phoned Gloria. "So," she asked, inquiring about Gloria's brother. "How was David's service?"

"The best!" Gloria said proudly. "He's really so gifted. Such a strong speaker. And, honestly?" Savannah waited during the pregnant pause. "I think a number of ladies in his congregation have crushes on him."

Savannah laughed at this. "You mean the younger ones?"

"The older ones, too!" Gloria reported brightly. "I have to be careful with my baby brother," she joked. "He might get cougared."

"That wouldn't be the end of the world," Savannah said.

"No," Gloria responded thoughtfully. "It might even be good for him."

"I guess he's used to having an older woman tell him what to do," Savannah ribbed.

"Hush! I'm not the mother hen I used to be."

"Right."

"Okay, okay. So maybe I insert myself too much into his business. But, seriously. I just wish he'd find a nice girl."

"He probably thinks the same about you?"

"What? That I'll find a nice girl?" Gloria teased.

"That you'll find somebody special," Savannah corrected.

"I have found someone special," Gloria bantered. "Myself! And, until I find better company, I'm sticking with me. Thank you very much."

"It's worse to be with the wrong partner than with no one at all," Savannah said, thinking of James.

Her comment must have made Gloria think of him too, because next she asked, "Have you heard from him?"

"James?" Savannah asked intuitively. "No. Not that I was expecting to."

"I wasn't sure what to expect, either," Gloria said. "It just seems that…after so many years…"

"I think when we ended it, we both knew it was over. There's no point in rehashing things now."

Gloria paused reflectively. "That's true."

"Yeah."

"Since it wasn't going anywhere."

"No. Never."

Gloria adopted a chipper tone, changing the subject. "How's Kurt?"

"Doing very well," Savannah said without giving too much away.

"And, how was the date on Friday?"

"Dreamy."

"Sounds good."

"It was! Only…"

"Only, what?"

"I'm not sure. Something happened that I… Well, anyway..."

"Something good or bad?"

"Good! Most definitely good. Only the tiniest bit confusing."

"Sounds like true love to me."

"Gloria."

"I'm happy for you, Savannah," Gloria said. "Glad that you're there in Christmas Town and that you've reconnected with Kurt."

Savannah's heart fluttered. "Yeah, me too."

"When will you see him again?"

"I'm not sure."

"Well, you'd better do something to fix that! Christmas is right around the corner."

Savannah chuckled warmly. "Now, who's mother henning *me*?"

"You know it's because I care."

"Yeah, and I care about you, too. Which is why I've been thinking about someone you should meet."

"Me?" Gloria sounded surprised. "Now, hang on, Savannah. Now's not the time. I already told you that I can't travel this Christmas."

"I don't think this eligible bachelor is going anywhere."

"Why not?" Gloria asked skeptically. "What's wrong with him?"

"Nothing, you big goof!" Savannah giggled. "The man is nearly perfect. He's intelligent, thoughtful, runs his own business, too. He is a single dad, though."

"That part doesn't bother me." In spite of herself, Gloria sounded intrigued. "How old are the kids?"

"College age."

"So he's an…older gentleman?"

Savannah belly-laughed. "Not much older than you, Gloria. He just got started on his family young."

"Ex-wife?"

"Late wife."

"Tragic."

"Yeah." Savannah could tell Gloria was dying to ask, so she decided to inform her. "He's drop-dead gorgeous, too. Tall, with dark hair, a beard and a mustache…"

"I don't mind facial hair."

"And the most stunning blue eyes."

"Whoa."

"And, here's the bonus!" Savannah felt herself smiling with glee. "He's also Kurt's big brother!"

"What?"

"Just think, Gloria! If things work out with me, and you work out with—"

"Savannah!" Gloria nearly shouted. "Stop yourself right there. Do you even hear yourself? Do you know what you're saying?"

"Yes! That I'd love for you to meet Walt."

"That's not all you said," Gloria replied cagily. "You've just admitted to me you want to marry Kurt."

"Did *not*."

"Did so!"

"Gloria."

"Have you picked out a ring yet?"

"Gloria!"

"Planned your honeymoon?"

"Will you cut it out?" Savannah asked, but she was giggling.

"Sure, I will. The moment you stop suggesting I marry Kurt's brother."

"I never said marry. The *m* word I used was 'meet'!"

"Hmm," Gloria mused. "Let's try this one on for size… Savannah Christmas. I like it!"

The truth was Savannah kind of liked it, too. Savannah Christmas did have a certain ring to it. But she'd never admit this to Gloria. Not when her friend was teasing her so badly.

"I am *not* marrying Kurt, okay?"

"Why not?"

"Because he hasn't asked me."

"Then you ask him!"

"Don't you think it would help if we had a second date?"

"Oh yeah. There's that."

"And, maybe a third one, and then a fourth…?"

"Come on. You've known each other forever."

"And, we've been out of touch."

"So, great! Now you're back in it! I'm so happy for you, Savannah. Because, even though you won't admit it, I can already see where this is going."

"Don't say it!"

"Okay, okay. I won't. Gee."

"Not one little peep."

"About you and—?"

"Nope!"

"Getting *mmmm*d."

"Stop."

"Married, married, married!" Gloria quipped happily. "My best friend's getting married!"

"Now you're going over the top."

"Just do me one favor?"

"Huh?"

"Invite me to the wedding?"

"Gloria!" Savannah shouted, but Gloria had already hung up.

Savannah gaped at her silent cell then it rang seconds later. It had to be Gloria calling back, either to apologize—or tease her mercilessly again. "I am *not* marrying Kurt! All right?"

"You sure know how to burst a guy's bubble." His deep voice rumbled down the line and Savannah's face burned hot.

"Er…Kurt?" she asked meekly.

"Hi, Savannah."

"Um…hello."

"It's nice to know you were thinking about me."

"I was just talking to my good friend, Gloria," she said, her cheeks steaming.

"Your friend in Miami?"

"Uh-huh."

"How's she doing?"

"Great!" Savannah said with a squeak.

"Well, that's good to know." After a beat, he added, "I'd like to meet her sometime."

Savannah exhaled deeply, her nerves jangled. "I'm sure she'd like to meet you, too. And…and, your brother."

"Ray?" Kurt asked, surprised.

"The other one."

"Walt. Ah, I see," he said, apparently putting something together. "Gloria is single, I suppose?"

"Yes, and highly attractive. Big brown eyes, beautiful dark hair… Ultra smart and talented!"

"It's not me you have to convince," Kurt told her. "You'll have to talk to Walt."

"Right."

"The only thing is, Walt hasn't dated in years. So, your friend might be out of luck."

"I never said she was interested," Savannah answered, growing a little haughty on Gloria's behalf.

"But you just said she'd like to me—?"

"All of it was my idea!" Savannah proclaimed defensively. "Gloria had nothing to do with it."

Kurt clucked his tongue. "So, whose idea was it that you were going to marry me?"

Savannah swallowed hard, feeling caught out. "Neither of ours, actually. It just sort of…um…came at us from out of thin air."

"Thin air? Hmm."

"Speaking of air, and wind and such…" Savannah said, deciding to brave it. "There's something I wanted to ask you about concerning our date."

"Can it wait until tomorrow night?"

"Why? What's happening tomorrow night?"

"I was hoping to cook you dinner at my place," he said. "What do you say?"

Savannah couldn't help her heart from pounding when she said yes. "Is there anything I can bring?"

"Just yourself. I can pick you up on my way home from the clinic. Will six-thirty be too early? We can visit over drinks while I fix the dinner."

"Just one drink, all right?"

"Whatever you'd like."

Savannah gathered her nerve. "I'd like to talk to you about a couple of things."

"That's great," he said jovially. "Because, I'd like to talk to you, too. I also have some news to share," he said temptingly. "I hope you'll be just as pleased by it, as I was."

"Kurt!" Savannah protested. "You can't keep me in suspense."

"It's for less than twenty-four hours," he told her. "Besides, I want to tell you in person."

Chapter Twenty-Five

Savannah was working at the theater the next day when Jade dropped by. Apart from the armoires, Savannah had purchased a couple of cozy couches for the dressing room and a few end tables. She was in there working on her laptop with her legs propped up on the couch when Jade rapped on the doorframe.

"Knock-knock!" she said, grinning warmly. "I hope you don't mind. The main door was open."

"No, not at all! Please, come in."

"I thought I'd drop by and see if you wanted to walk with me to lunch?"

That's right, Savannah suddenly remembered. *Our girls' date!* She'd been so preoccupied with curriculum planning, she'd totally forgotten. However, she decided not to mention this to Jade.

"That's very nice of you. Thanks! Let me just save this file, and I'll grab my coat."

"What are you working on?"

"A schedule of plays and puppet shows for the first quarter of the year. These will correspond with the new theater camps for kids."

"That sounds fantastic," Jade said. "I wish my boys were old enough to participate."

"Well, Josiah might be a little young," Savannah said. "But Alexander can certainly join in."

"Yeah?"

"How old is he?"

"Eight, now."

"Then there are several roles he can play," Savannah assured Jade, grinning. "Plus, he has experience as a wise man."

Jade smiled sunnily in return. "Yeah, that's true." She observed the main theater area. Savannah had lined up the chairs in a seating arrangement and mapped out where the stage would go on the floor with masking tape. "It looks like things are coming along! Where are you getting your stage?"

"Buddy Christmas is building it."

"How nice!"

"Yeah, it was sweet of him to volunteer."

"Buddy's very handy. He made the little toy train and the Santa's workshop display in my bookshop's front window."

"I saw it the other day," Savannah said. "It's so cute!"

"I know," Jade answered. "I love it, too."

Savannah flipped shut her laptop and put on her coat. "Nick says the renovations can get started here after the first of the year. But, they will be minor." She told Jade about them as they headed out the door, and Jade responded with enthusiasm, saying she couldn't wait to see the finished space.

They traipsed down the curved staircase of the Grand Hotel and the studios on either side of them were all busy as they passed by. The various artisans were merrily at work, as shoppers browsed their wares.

"Savannah," Jade said as they descended to the building's front foyer, which divided the ballroom from the Main Street Café. The bistro was packed with animated customers chatting happily while having lunch. "With Christmas coming up, I wanted to make sure you know that you're included. Wendell and I host a Christmas dinner each year. Nothing fancy. Just a potluck for family and friends... But it's at Sisters' Row—so convenient to you! We invited Liz, but she always eats with her brother's family. My dad will be there though, and our two boys, of course. Hannah and Carter can make it with Amanda for dessert. They'll be at Ben and Sandy's for the main meal, where Hannah and Ben's dad will be joining them. But Nick and Olivia are coming, and can be there the whole time."

"Nick and Olivia will be back for Christmas?" Savannah asked with an excited grin. "How awesome!"

"Yeah," Jade said. "Nick apparently spoke to Kurt—"

"Kurt?" Savannah wondered how this was possible, since Olivia had assured her they'd be out of cell phone range. Then, she guessed Nick might have e-mailed Kurt somehow. Maybe from one of those cyber cafés? If they had such places that far north...

"Yes, and he told him they're returning. As soon as they possibly can, which will likely be around noontime on Christmas Day."

"That's wonderful, then!" Savannah was about to accept Jade's kind invitation when she thought of Kurt.

Jade must have sensed this intuitively because she said, "Kurt's certainly welcome to join us. I plan on asking him, too. Though that may be a tough one since his family always has Christmas dinner together."

"Hmm, yes." Savannah considered this, understanding there could be a conflict. "I can talk to Kurt, if you'd like?" Next, she admitted shyly, as they exited the Grand Hotel's front door and were greeted by a torrent of snow, "I'm seeing him tonight."

"Are you, now?" Jade had a pleased gleam in her eye as both women popped open their umbrellas, holding them over their heads. "Well, don't spill all the details just yet!" she said with a grin. "I'm sure that Hannah and Sandy will want to know them, too."

As they scurried carefully down the steps, Savannah decided then that there was no point keeping secrets in Christmas Town. At least, not happy ones, anyway... "All right," she said, with a sassy twang once they were on the sidewalk. "I'll tell everyone all about it at lunch."

And Savannah fully intended to. Only, she planned to leave out that little tidbit about Kurt beaming her to the beach. No sense having her new friends think she was Looney Tunes. And, Savannah *was* making friends here, she realized, with a joyful smile. Not just Jade, Sandy, and Hannah, but Liz Martin, too. She was starting to see why Olivia loved Christmas Town so much. It really was a very welcoming place.

After a companionable lunch at Santa's Sandwich Shop, Savannah parted ways with her friends and strolled back through the snow toward the Grand Hotel. As she did, she passed Kyle Christmas holding a bag from her sister's gift shop.

"Well hello, Kyle!"

"Good afternoon, Ms. Livingston."

"Is school out for the holiday?"

"Yes, ma'am."

"You must be excited about that."

"Yes, ma'am!"

Savannah studied his package as they walked along, both heading in the same direction. "Out Christmas shopping today?"

Kyle colored appreciably. "I was just getting one of those Christmas barrettes." He eyed Savannah's hair, and she recalled she wore a Charity Cookie barrette, decorated with a blond-haired, blue-eyed angel. "Like the one you're wearing, there."

"Your friend's likely too young for the other kind," Savannah teased with a wink, and Kyle's shade of red deepened.

"Yes, ma'am."

"Kyle," she said sweetly. "You don't have to keep calling me 'ma'am.' Savannah will do."

"Yes, ma…uh…Miss Savannah, ma'am."

Savannah grinned warmly. "Your folks are pretty strict on manners, huh?"

Kyle nodded at this, then Savannah said, "Well, I'm sure that whoever you bought that present for is going to love it."

"You really think so?" Kyle asked with a hopeful look.

"I know so," Savannah said. "If there's anything women love, it's accessories!"

Savannah scuttled up the steps to the Grand Hotel, chuckling to herself. She'd have to tell Kurt she'd seen his nephew in town. Apparently, Christmas shopping for a very special friend. Savannah was just thinking about young love when the Jolly Bean Java barista, Devon, barreled out the door, arm in arm with a beautiful young blonde with pretty blue eyes, who favored Walt Christmas.

"Joy, hello!" Savannah said, recognizing Kurt's pretty niece. "Merry Christmas!"

Joy's blue eyes sparkled. "Merry Christmas, Savannah. It's great to see you!"

"Love your exhibit in there," Savannah said, mentioning Joy's art. "Your work is outstanding."

Color warmed Joy's cheeks. "Thank you."

Devon held the door open for Savannah, addressing her with a grin. "Christmas Mud Mocha, right?"

"That's me!" Savannah said pleasantly.

Joy shot a secretive look at Devon. "Savannah's my Uncle Kurt's friend."

"Yes, that's right." Savannah's face warmed. "Kurt and I are friends. Old friends. From a very long time ago."

"That's what I *hear*," Joy said tellingly. Her eyes shone brightly as she issued a woman-to-woman smile. "Don't be too hard on him, now! He's one of my favorite uncles!"

As she and Devon headed down the steps, Devon whispered over his shoulder, "She's only got two," and Savannah laughed, her heart feeling light.

So, word was getting around Christmas Town, at least within Kurt's family, that Savannah and Kurt were connected. From the look in Joy's eye, the college girl had supposed that Savannah and Kurt were *romantically* connected. Which they actually were...

They might not be getting "married, married, married" as Gloria had teased, but she and Kurt were definitely dating each other. On a casual basis, anyway... Though, in her heart, nothing about Savannah's relationship with Kurt felt casual. The bond she and Kurt were forming felt authentic, rich and promising. If only Savannah didn't have that horrid secret from her past standing in the way things would be perfect.

The moment Kurt got over his persistent delusions, that was...

And, quit foisting them off on her.

Savannah couldn't wait to see Kurt tonight. She had so many questions to ask him, starting with, "What's your good news?" He'd been careful in guarding his secret, in a way that made Savannah think Kurt was hiding something big. She'd experimented with many different scenarios trying to guess what that might be. In the end, she'd given up and had decided she'd just let Kurt surprise her.

Chapter Twenty-Six

Savannah opened her door that evening with butterflies in her stomach. Kurt arrived looking his usual dapper self in his car coat and fedora, and Savannah was all ready to go. She wore her coat, hat, gloves, and scarf over nice black jeans with a ribbed, emerald green turtleneck sweater. She'd chosen the Clemency Cookie barrette due to its dainty Christmas tree matching her top. Fur-lined snow boots kept her feet and calves warm, as she knew they were in for a walk.

Though Kurt's place wasn't far away, wintery winds were blowing and it was still below freezing out. The snow-covered streets and sidewalks were marred by tire tracks and footprints, as a cascade of snowflakes twirled beneath the streetlamps' glow.

"I hope you don't mind walking," Kurt said with a warm smile. "I'll drive you home later, of course. It will be even darker—and colder—then."

Savannah nodded and locked her door. "Thanks for having me over tonight."

"I'm hoping you like barbeque spareribs?"

"Love them."

"With au gratin potatoes and greens?"

"Yum!" She studied him curiously as they descended her stoop. "When did you learn to cook?"

Kurt grinned graciously. "Oh, somewhere along the way."

When Savannah reached the bottom step, Kurt held out his hand, helping her down to the sidewalk. Once they were there, however, he didn't let go. Heat warmed Savannah's cheeks as they strolled along, hand in hand.

"You know you're still holding my hand, don't you?"

He answered without turning to look at her. "Yep."

Savannah spied Frank and Victoria Cho approaching from up ahead. "People might get the wrong impression."

"What impression is that?"

"That, we're…you know." She conspiratorially squeezed his glove and spoke in low tones. "Boyfriend and girlfriend."

He gave her a cursory glance and there was mischief in his eyes. "Would that be wrong, Savannah?"

"I…I don't know! Nobody's exactly…" She was awash with heat from her head down to her toes. "…*asked* me."

Kurt stopped walking and made a dramatic show of slapping his forehead beneath the brim of his hat. "And they say professors are absentminded. How about doctors?" He stunned her then by stepping right in front of her and taking her in his arms. Over his shoulder, Savannah saw the Chos drawing nearer. "Savannah

Livingston!" Kurt proclaimed as snow dusted his hat. "Will you go out with me?"

"I am going out," she replied in a hushed whisper.

"I don't mean just for tonight."

She angled closer. "Shhh!"

Kurt leaned toward her with a devilish look. "Why are we whispering?"

"Well, look what we have here, Victoria." Frank's cheery voice boomed from behind them. "Two little lovebirds out in the snow!"

"Good evening, Savannah!" Victoria said with a twinkle as they passed by. She nodded cordially at Kurt. "Kurt!"

Savannah's blush deepened but Kurt just called out, "Top of the evening to you both!"

Savannah defiantly met Kurt's chocolate-brown eyes. "You know this will be all over town now?"

"I have a little secret for you," Kurt said. "It already is."

"Oh? Since when?"

"Since a very devout woman I know made her proclamation to the church."

Savannah play-pounded his chest. "That's not fair!"

"No?" He took her hands in his and held them captive. The next thing she knew, his mouth was moving in on hers. "Then, how about this…?"

"What are you doing?"

"Trying to kiss you."

"But, why?"

His dark gaze smoldered. "Why do you think?"

"Good evening, good citizens!" Savannah looked up with alarm and she wanted to melt into the snow.

Pastor Wilson was approaching, gripping a brown grocery bag from the Merry Market.

"Good evening, Pastor," Kurt said, not letting Savannah go. She squirmed in his hold trying to break away but he pulled her closer.

Pastor Wilson gave Savannah a curious look. "I hope you're enjoying your stay in Christmas Town, Savannah?"

"Uh-huh! Very much!"

"That's wonderful, my dear."

"We were just going to my place for dinner," Kurt informed the minister.

"How grand!"

"Cooking a meal for my new girlfriend is the least I can do."

Savannah nearly swallowed her tongue, but Pastor Wilson beamed appreciatively. "My congratulations to you both." He sighed wistfully. "Old love made new! And just in time for the holidays!"

"Yes, indeed!" Kurt said and Savannah wanted to kick him. The only thing was she was afraid she might slide and fall on her keister while making the effort.

Kurt tugged Savannah closer and shot her a longing gaze before addressing Pastor Wilson. "Did I tell you she loves me?"

"No, my boy!" Pastor Wilson's eyes sparkled. "I heard it straight from the horse's mouth!" He reined himself in quickly. "Not that you're a horse, my child," he said hastily to Savannah. "Extremely far from it!"

"And the best part is…" Kurt's voice grew husky and he got that dazed look in his eyes. "I love her, too…"

"Yes, well!" Pastor Wilson said, apparently embarrassed by Kurt's spectacle. "I guess I'll leave you both to it," he rasped hoarsely before shuffling away.

"Kurt Christmas," Savannah said, her veins filled with fire. "I can't believe that you did that."

His brow rose in mock innocence. "Did what?"

"Embarrass me in front of Pastor Wilson!"

"You were embarrassed?"

"Yes, Kurt! And, so was he," she said, her eyes on the retreating minister. "What do you think?"

He gave her a predatory stare and Savannah's heart stuttered. "Here's what I think," Kurt murmured friskily. "I meant every word that I said."

Kurt's lips brushed over hers and Savannah whimpered. He was so strong, so commanding, so *Kurt*... And, she'd wanted Kurt for a very, very, very long time.

"Kurt, I..." she said, catching her breath. "We..."

"Hmm, yeah." He tenderly kissed her again. "I like the sound of that." Kurt trailed kisses down the side of her neck then he sexily nipped her earlobe and gooseflesh cloaked her skin. Beneath her coat...under her sweater...inside her jeans... *Oh...my...goodness.*

Savannah gasped. "We're in the middle of the sidewalk!"

"That beats being in the middle of the street." He brought his mouth down on hers and Savannah saw stars of the most glorious kind. They were bright red and green with shimmering silver streamers and cloudbursts of glittery gold sparkles.

Whoa! Savannah wondered when Kurt had learned to kiss like this. She even questioned briefly if this was another one of his magic tricks... But, ultimately, she

didn't care. All Savannah wanted to do was surrender.
Let go. She didn't even know where they were
anymore.

Kurt's hat became dislodged and catapulted to the
ground, and before Savannah knew it her fingers were
in his hair... Stroking his manly cheekbones, gripping
his rock-solid shoulders... Massaging that manly chest!
Ooohhh, wow.

Her knees caved and her arms went limp, but Kurt
bolstered her in his arms to support her. Then, he kissed
her again. And, again, as snow pelted her cap and
prickled her cheeks, until Savannah felt warm all over.
Way warm. Like it was impossible to believe she was
standing outside in below-freezing temperatures—until
a car horn blasted loudly.

Kurt and Savannah abruptly broke apart to find a
red pickup truck idling by the curb beside them. The
flashing blue light on top sent bands of flickering light
streaming across the sidewalk and bouncing off the
buildings at Kurt's back.

Carter lowered the driver's side window and tipped
his sheriff's hat. "Hey, you two!" he said sternly,
though he was grinning. "Ever hear the phrase, 'get a
room'?"

Savannah giggled all the way to Kurt's place. They
ran hand in hand down the sidewalk, and Savannah felt
like a kid again. Being with Kurt—most especially
tonight—made her feel reckless and free. Almost like a
carefree teen, but in the very best way. Because now
she was an adult—with a grown-up perspective and a
fully matured heart.

They went inside Kurt's cute bungalow and he took her coat and things, offering to hang them with his in the hall bath to dry. The pelting snow had soaked their outer clothing but Savannah didn't mind. She was having the time of her life. Apparently, Kurt was too. He was still chuckling when he returned to the cozy living room, outfitted with a leather loveseat, matching chairs, and a very high-end stereo system. It also had a wood-burning hearth and Savannah noted Kurt had put up a Christmas tree. Not one single candy cane was on it.

"Well, I must say, Savannah," he told her. "You certainly got us running from the law."

"Me?" Savannah contended. She set a hand on her hip. "I'm not the one who started it."

"The kissing?" Kurt arched an eyebrow. "Maybe not. But you didn't seem to want to end it, either."

"Shush!"

Kurt smiled happily. "What can I get you to drink?"

"Water to start."

"Water?"

"I'm taking it slower tonight."

"All right."

"Is there something I can do to help?" she asked as he walked toward the kitchen.

He sent her a petitioning look. "Come with me and keep me company?"

"Love to."

Savannah was impressed by the selection of copper-bottom pots hanging from the ceiling over Kurt's gas range. "You really are cooking now, aren't you?"

"With gas!" he quipped and she laughed.

"I had no idea."

"Last time, you didn't stay long enough to look."

"Kurt..."

"It's okay," he said warmly. "I don't blame you. Things were different then from how they are now."

"Oh? How are they now?"

"Different." His dark eyes danced. "More comfortable between us."

"Okay, I'll admit it," Savannah agreed. "You're right. Things were awkward at Olivia's wedding."

"They felt all right to me," he said.

"You know what I mean."

He viewed her thoughtfully. "Yeah, I think that I do." Kurt opened a cabinet and grabbed a couple of tall glasses. He filled each with ice and water and handed one to Savannah.

"Winded after your sprint down Main Street, are you?"

"Coupled with my race up Church Street?" she asked with a laugh. "Absolutely!"

Kurt sipped from his water. "Some important things were different then..."

"You're talking about last summer?"

Kurt nodded seriously. "You were with James—"

"No, I wasn't!" Savannah said. "If I had been, I never would have come back here with—"

"You know what I mean, Savannah. Not *with* him, but with him. You hadn't completely cut free."

"Just like how you hadn't totally finished things with Eliza."

"Exactly."

"I like things better now," Savannah said in a flirty tone.

Kurt beheld her warmly. "Yeah, so do I."

"I can't believe you asked me to be exclusive in front of Pastor Wilson!" she said, but she was laughing.

"I was trying to make honest people of us both," Kurt teased.

"I have a feeling it's hard to hide things in Christmas Town," Savannah said.

"Certain things? Yes," Kurt answered. He set his glass down on the counter. "Others, though? Not so much."

Savannah considered this a moment before asking, "So! Are you going to tell me about the big news you have?"

"Definitely," Kurt said. "But not until I fix dinner."

"Argh! You're trying to vex me!"

"No, I'm not, Savannah. Just trust me." His gaze was sincere. "I'm not much of a multitasker, so let me get the meal together. Then, over dinner?" The warmth in his smile resonated to her soul. "We'll talk."

Kurt and Savannah sat down to a beautiful meal in Kurt's quaint dining room. It was barely large enough to accommodate the maple dining room table, which he said had belonged to his grandmother on Lou's side. A pair of brass candlestick holders with holly leaf and berry designs near their bases held dark green tapers that matched the dark green placemats with gold piping. Kurt's everyday china was ivory colored with a thick forest green band around the perimeter of each plate.

Kurt pulled out Savannah's chair for her and she thanked him for the invitation.

"Everything looks so pretty!" she said, surveying the romantic table set for two. "And, so elegant."

Kurt gave a self-deprecating laugh. "I hope it tastes as good as it looks."

"I'm sure it will," Savannah replied, savoring the delicious aromas of roasted beef, wilted spinach sautéed with garlic, and extra cheesy au gratin potatoes. Kurt had offered her wine with dinner and she'd accepted, determined to take better care with her limits this evening.

Kurt took a seat in the chair opposite hers and raised his wineglass to hers. "Here's to new beginnings."

Heat warmed her face as she clinked her glass to his. "To new beginnings, Kurt."

Several minutes passed while Kurt asked Savannah about her progress with the theater, and they both enjoyed the wonderful meal. "Thank you for everything," she said. "It's delicious."

Kurt's dark eyes sparkled. "I'd cook for you every night if you let me."

"Would you really?" Savannah purposely added a saucy edge to her voice, as she imagined what that would be like. Playing house with the unbelievably handsome Kurt Christmas day after day. "What would my job be?" She laughed teasingly. "Cleaning up?"

"Nope. I've got an elf app for that."

"Right."

Kurt finished chewing a bit of beef and set down his fork. "I'm not joking. Nick gave it to me. It's in its

pilot phases, but still." Kurt shrugged mildly. "I haven't
lost any dishes yet."

Savannah laughed heartily. "You also haven't lost
your sense of humor."

He studied her wistfully, apparently caught up in
his own thoughts. "Why don't we try it?"

"Try what, Kurt?"

"I cook, you eat."

"That hardly seems fair."

"All right then…" His lips tipped up in a grin.
"You can bring dessert."

"You don't eat it."

"Maybe you'd like to?"

"Maybe I'm watching my girlish figure," Savannah
said with a flirty edge.

"It's certainly worth watching." Kurt cocked an
eyebrow. "If you'd like, I can keep an eye on it, too."

Savannah leaned back in her chair. "All right, Mr.
Shameless, but only if I can keep an eye on yours."

"I'll show you anything you'd like…" Kurt said
leadingly. "You'll be pleased to know that certain
attributes of mine have…" He coughed lightly.
"…matured over the years."

"Kurt Christmas!" Savannah cried, tossing her
cloth napkin at him. It sailed above the tabletop, its
corner skirting a candle's flame. The fabric smoldered
then burst into flames.

Savannah yelped in horror and leapt to her feet,
knocking over her chair. Her napkin landed in a fiery
heap beside the open wine bottle and then the
ornamental wreath that served as a centerpiece caught
fire, its brittle twigs crackling loudly as the charred
scent of pine filled the air. A dark cloud of smoke rose

up, stinging Savannah's eyes. At that precise moment, the smoke alarm in the kitchen began blaring.

To her dismay, Kurt hadn't moved a muscle, likely because he was in shock. Savannah grabbed for her water glass and was just about to douse the flames when Kurt calmly raised a hand, his extremely intense gaze fixed on the fire. Savannah watched slack-jawed as the individual flames stretched tall then—*poof! poof! poof!* —completely extinguished themselves, one by one, leaving behind small puffs of smoke and a blackened spot on the tabletop. The smoke alarm suddenly shut off, leaving nothing but an eerie quiet in the room, offset by the faintest flickering sound of the candles.

Savannah gaped at Kurt in awe. "Wha-at just happened?"

"I think you threw your napkin at me and it caught fire," Kurt said, sounding equally dazed.

Savannah slowly picked up her chair, righting it. Then she took a seat to get off her wobbly legs. "No," she said, blinking. "I mean, with *that*." Savannah pointed to the charred napkin balled in a heap beside the wine bottle.

He slowly looked up and met her eyes. "I couldn't just let it burn. That would have been dangerous. For you, for me, and the—"

Savannah's heart pounded. "You put out the fire?"

"Savannah, I…" Kurt appeared lost a moment, then he seemed to find his course somewhere deep within her eyes. "I have so much to tell you." He held out his hand. "Come. Will you sit on the sofa with me?" His gaze roved over their plates. "We're pretty much finished, anyway."

"Yes, Kurt," she answered, desperate to know what he had to say. "I'll hear you out." As much as she'd worried about Kurt's sanity, now Savannah feared that perhaps her grasp on reality was slipping as well. But those seemed like awfully long odds, for the two of them to lose their mental capacities together.

They left the table as it was, and Kurt led Savannah to the red leather loveseat in the living room. "Should I light the fire?" he asked, indicating the hearth that had been laid with logs, kindling, and starter paper.

"You just put one out," Savannah said on soft breath.

"This one won't hurt anyone," he assured her.

Savannah shared a shaky smile. "All right." She had no idea where Kurt was going with this, but there was obviously something pretty major going on here.

Kurt took the box of matches from the mantel and lit the tower of candles on it. Next, he tossed the remnants of the burning match into the hearth and the fireplace bloomed with instantaneous warm light.

"A one-match fire?" Savannah asked, impressed.

"It's in my skill set," he said, walking back over to the sofa.

"An ability?" Savannah wondered, thinking over what had happened during their date.

"Nope." Kurt gave an ingratiating grin. "Just a talent."

"I'm not sure I understand the difference," Savannah said, as he sat beside her.

308 *The Doctor Orders Christmas*

"A talent is like a honed skill," he answered. "If you work at something, you can generally get pretty good at it."

"You've got to have some good base material to work with, though," Savannah contended. "Some people have no gift for music, for example. No matter how hard they work, they'll never become Mozarts."

"Don't tell that to Lou." Kurt's eyes sparkled playfully. "She's still has ambitions."

"Stop."

"No, really."

Savannah smiled encouragingly. "So, how about you, Dr. Christmas? What are your ambitions?"

"They're really pretty simple. A good life with the woman I love." He took her hand. "Someday, hopefully a family."

Savannah's heart pinged at this. "A big wedding, or small?"

"Intimate." Kurt fell into her eyes. "Only those who are closest to us will be there."

Her pulse quickened as she realized what he was saying. "Kurt, I…"

"But I'd still like to have it at the Corner Church, if that's all right. And, for Pastor Wilson to perform the ceremony. He christened all three of us boys, and married my mother and father."

Savannah was a little breathless when she said, "I'm not sure we should be talking weddings when there's no engagement yet."

"You're absolutely right." Kurt kissed the back of her hand. "But here's the thing, Savannah. What I'm going to tell you tonight is highly personal. So personal that I never thought I'd share it with anyone but my wife. Or, the woman who would become my wife one day… And it's not just about me being private, it's part of my family code."

"Family code?" Savannah said. "I'm not sure I understand."

"I told you about the Christmases and the Clauses. You do remember that part?"

Savannah nodded. "The long-ago family connection."

"Some of those connections might not be as distant as you think."

"You're talking about those 'abilities'?" Savannah searched his eyes, so badly wanting to understand, but not trusting she would fully believe whatever it was he was going to tell her.

"I have three." Kurt's Adam's apple rose and fell. "As far as I know."

"You can tell when someone's lying."

Kurt squeezed her hand. "Yes."

"And, the other night…? With the beach…?"

"Yes."

"But how?"

"It's a matter of focus. Beyond that, I'm not sure. I think the molecules get disassembled then reassembled somehow."

Savannah gasped in slow understanding. "But in a different place?"

"At first, I couldn't go far." Kurt gave a pained laugh. "Just from one room in the house to another. Then, over time, I started experimenting."

Savannah was trying to wrap her head around it, but she just couldn't. Even though she'd experienced it herself. "Wow."

"Though skills and abilities are different, abilities can be perfected, too. It's easier when…"
He gave a soft smile. "You're with the right person. That's how I knew it was you, Savannah. Even all those years ago. Once you and I had been together, things started changing. I began changing… All of a sudden, I could do things I'd never done before. Rare things. Spectacular things—"

"Like put out fires…" Savannah said, blinking at the distant memory. When they were teens, she and Kurt had snuck down to the beach and built a late-night bonfire behind the dunes. They'd been making out too close to the flames and a log popped sending a shimmer of sparks into Savannah's long red hair. The horror of the moment was vivid still. Savannah feared the fire would consume her within seconds. And yet, it was suddenly blown out by a blast of icy cold air that seemed to materialize from nowhere. Savannah had escaped the mishap mostly unscathed, with only a few strands of her hair singed slightly at their tips.

She'd counted it as a miracle at the time.

Savannah slowly met Kurt's eyes. "The bonfire at the beach? That was you?"

"My love for you was so strong." He swallowed hard. "Is strong. That part never changed.

"It wasn't just young love or hormones." Kurt searched her eyes. "Savannah, it was you. I didn't even know I possessed that ability, but I couldn't let the fire hurt you."

"And, tonight?"

"How can Santa go down a chimney when a fire is lit?"

"But you're not Santa?" she asked unsurely.

"*No-ho-ho,*" he said, with a teasing smile.

Savannah caught her breath. "Your dad says that, doesn't he? *Ho-ho-ho?*"

"Yeah."

"But, he's not…?"

Kurt shook his head.

"That would be on the Claus side," Savannah said, getting it in an odd sort of way. In some fashion none of it made sense. But then, in another peculiar manner, there was a certain logic in the absurdity of it all. The Clauses and the Christmases were related, so they shared common DNA. Some things had been passed down through the generations, along one vein of the family or the other. The trick was, one had to believe in Santa to buy it. But if Santa was just a myth, how else could these incredibly fantastic things that had happened to her be explained? Savannah had witnessed them with her own two eyes!

She recalled the sand spilling out of her boot onto the carpet and her heart hammered. "You really did take me to the beach, didn't you?"

Kurt viewed her tenderly. "That's where you wanted to go."

"But, I woke up the next morning in—"

"The return trip was too much for you," he told her. "You're not used to it." Kurt raised his brow. "I guess you could say you were jet-lagged."

"But without the jet," Savannah said.

"Right."

She stared at him in wonder. "This was the surprise you were keeping?"

"Not quite. Those are old secrets." He slid closer to her on the sofa. "My good news is something new!"

Savannah wasn't sure how much more she could process in one night. Already her head was exploding from information overload. At the same time, her heart ached with joy. Kurt had confided in her by sharing some ultra personal things—if she could find a way to believe that they were true. And, strangely, Savannah found herself starting to do just that. Little by little, she'd found kernels of truth among Kurt's statements that were difficult to ignore.

"Savannah?" he asked with a soulful look. "Remember those letters? The ones that we thought were lost?"

"From high school?" she guessed. "They were lost. Or—taken. Something happened to them for sure, because neither of us—"

"That's because," Kurt said with a handsome glow, "they went north."

"North?"

"Were mistakenly redirected."

"By who?"

"Somebody else with abilities."

"Your mom?"

"Not her."

"Buddy, then."

"No, but I'd rather not—"

"Ray?"

"Savannah, please."

She gasped in understanding. "Your brother Walt?"

Kurt shifted on the sofa. "You've got to believe me, nothing was on purpose. He has abilities, too. And, when he started seeing Rose—"

"Oh, gosh." Savannah searched Kurt's eyes. "What does this mean? Where did the letters go?"

"To Santa's Workshop."

"O-kay," Savannah said, thinking that didn't sound any more absurd than the rest of it.

"But, here's the good news." Kurt brought his arm around her. "I talked to Nick and he's going to try to find them."

"Find them?" Savannah suddenly felt very, very pale. "Maybe now's not the best time for that," she said in a small thin voice.

"Not the best time?" Kurt viewed her perplexedly. "Savannah. Sweetheart. Not getting those letters is what drove us apart. Can't you see? It's a way to make things right. Resolve those old hurts."

A jagged memory tore through her soul, searing her gut and sending tears to her eyes. "Resolve them?" she asked, her lips trembling. "What if they open up new ones?"

"Savannah. Honey." Kurt turned toward her and gently gripped her shoulders in his hands. "What is it? What's wrong?"

Tears poured from her eyes and burned trails down her cheeks. How could she ever tell him? How?

"But, I…" Hurt and confusion brimmed in his eyes. "Thought you'd be so happy?"

"Happy, Kurt?" she asked, her words faltering. "Why can't we just let bygones be bygones?"

"Because I wanted you to know…believe that I…" His voice cracked harshly, then he studied her with new understanding. "There's something in those letters you don't want me to see, isn't there?"

Savannah sniffed and dragged the back of her arm across her face to wipe her tears. Black mascara marred her sweater sleeve.

"Whatever it is," Kurt said gently. "It can't be that bad."

She sent him a defeated look. "Yeah, well. Maybe it is."

Kurt stroked back her hair with his fingers. "Even if you weren't wearing that pretty Clemency Cookie barrette," he said, mentioning the accessory in her hair. "You've got to know I'd forgive you anything."

"Almost anything," she said through her tears. "But probably not this."

A few hours later, Kurt glumly cleaned up his kitchen after carrying the dishes in from the dining room. He had some lemon oil in the garage he could apply to the damaged table. Kurt wasn't as sure about fixing the ache in his heart. He didn't know what had gone wrong, but he'd apparently made an enormous blunder in asking Nick to bring him those letters. Just the mention of recouping that correspondence had sent Savannah into an emotional tizzy. She wouldn't even tell him what was wrong. She'd only insisted he take her home shortly afterward.

Perhaps it was his fault for trying to lay so much on her at once. First, there was the girlfriend thing in front of Pastor Wilson, then the marriage talk… *Hoo, boy.* Kurt hung his head in shame, realizing he'd laid it on too thick. Too much too fast was not the right way to go with Savannah. But, in some ways, he hadn't been able to help himself. He'd been bursting at the seams to tell her everything.

Though Kurt had denied it for years, the people he was close to knew he still carried a torch for Savannah.

It wasn't just a prolonged bout of unrequited love. It had been an interminably painful journey of holding out until the right moment when Savannah could once more be his. Kurt had to believe this would be possible again someday. If he hadn't, he wouldn't have been able to move forward. To function day to day... Much less...breathe. Kurt sighed heavily and set his hands on his hips, hoping he hadn't blown it. Fate had given him one more chance with Savannah. But the principal challenge remained: for Savannah to open up her heart.

Once she did, she would trust him. Then, she would tell Kurt what was weighing on her mind. So he could help her, and hold her... And, love her, as he wanted to do—forever.

Chapter Twenty-Seven

Savannah was unable to sleep for the third night in a row. While her theater work kept her busy during the day, she was her own worst enemy in the evenings. Sandy had called to ask her out for coffee, but she'd declined, saying she was crunching on her deadline of getting a chunk of her consultant work completed before Christmas. Liz had dropped by, but she'd made the excuse she wasn't feeling well. Which was actually the truth. Savannah's emotions hadn't felt this upended in decades. This was the primary reason she'd let Gloria's last two calls go directly to voice mail. Savannah didn't trust herself to talk to her best friend without completely breaking down. Besides, what would she tell her? *I've learned something cool about Kurt! He can put out fires—literally! No props involved!*

Savannah sighed and punched her pillow, rolling onto her right side. A few seconds later, she flipped over facing the other way. Her overturned lace-up boots were still on the floor by her dresser, and Savannah hadn't bothered to clean up the sand. If she did, she would have to acknowledge that it had to have gotten there somehow. And, there was nothing around here for miles and miles and miles except for fluffy white snow.

Savannah shut her eyes, recalling the feel of the ocean breeze on her face and in her hair, and the warmth of Kurt's touch as they strolled hand in hand toward the pier. It had seemed so real—perhaps because it was. She definitely hadn't imagined the episode with her burning napkin, and there was no way to explain it without giving Kurt some credit for influencing the outcome. Savannah thought of Olivia, wishing she had her here to talk to. If everything that Kurt said was true, Olivia must have gone through similar turmoil when she learned more about Nick and his family. That had to mean that Nick had abilities like Kurt's…

Savannah reflected on those wacky phone conversations she'd had with Olivia when Olivia had started falling for Nick. She'd claimed Nick could do all sorts of unusual things to the point where Savannah had become worried about her sister, and had even gone so far as to suggest counseling. *Now who needs help?* Savannah sighed heavily and flipped over onto her belly, but that was uncomfortable so she flopped onto her back. She thought of the saying, "Physician heal thyself…" wondering if it was possible for a counselor to counsel herself? She'd tried it but hadn't been exactly successful. Each time Savannah tried to get to the root of her troubles, everything came back around to her relationship with Kurt. And, it honestly wasn't so much about what he'd told her. It was much more about what Savannah *hadn't* told him.

That's where the comparison between her situation and Olivia's broke down. Olivia didn't have any buried secrets as far as Savannah knew. Then again, Olivia didn't even know about what had happened to Savannah, because Savannah had never told her. The truth was Savannah had never told anyone. Not her mother, or father, or Carter. Not even Gloria.

Savannah realized with a bolt of clarity that maybe she'd been right about not confiding in other people. Because the information was way too sensitive to share with someone else, when she hadn't shared it with the person who would be affected by it the most. Savannah wiped back the tears that had pooled in her eyes, understanding what she had to do. And, she needed to do it now before she lost her nerve.

She pushed herself up into a sitting position in bed and propped her pillow behind her back against the headboard. Then, she reached for her cell with a shaky hand and called Kurt.

Kurt sat up with a start at the sound of his cell ringing, his mind whipping into instant mental alertness. His years of practicing medicine had conditioned him so he could transition from deep slumber to being totally awake within a matter of seconds. Kurt never knew when an emergency might arise that would require him to grab his medical bag and hasten out the door to somebody's aid. Kurt employed an answering service full-time, but that was not the number that was displayed on his phone. The person calling was...

"Savannah?" Kurt asked, keen with worry. He blinked and checked his watch on the nightstand, seeing it was just after 3:00 a.m. "Are you all right?"

"I'm sorry…" It sounded like she was crying. "Sorry to wake you."

"What's wrong?"

Savannah drew in a breath. "I need to see you… Talk to you."

Kurt's throat felt raw and his heart pounded. He'd been trying to reach Savannah for days, but she hadn't been taking his calls. "When?"

"I know it's late—" She sputtered a sob.

Kurt ran a hand through his hair, surveying the rumpled sweatpants and undershirt he'd slept in. "Do you want me to come over?"

There was silence down the line, but he could hear her weeping.

"Savannah?" he asked gently. "Just say the word, sweetheart. And, I'll be there. You know I will."

"Can you come now?" Her voice shook, and her plea was followed by more tears.

Kurt ended the call and glanced down at his bare feet thinking he should put some shoes on. But the carpet beneath him wasn't his own. It was the rug in the downstairs of Savannah's rental at Sisters' Row. Wow, he hadn't even felt that. Savannah's pull on him was that strong. Kurt scanned the darkened living room, surmising that she was in a bedroom upstairs. He strode to the staircase and laid his hand on the banister. "Savannah," he called hoarsely. "I'm here!"

The upstairs hall light clicked on and she appeared at the top of the staircase, looking dazed. She wore pajama pants and a tank top, and her long red hair spilled past her shoulders in wild disarray. Her eyes were red and puffy and she clutched a tissue in one hand. "Kurt?" She sniffed and dabbed her eyes. "But how—?"

He took the steps two at a time toward her. "How do you think, Savannah?" Kurt reached the top landing and took her in his arms. His gaze poured over her when he said, "I got here as soon as I could."

She stared at him beseechingly. "You didn't drive, did you?"

Kurt slowly shook his head.

"Or, walk?"

He cocked his chin, waiting for her to say it but she didn't. Instead, she just softly murmured, "Thank you."

He worriedly searched her eyes. "Have you not slept?"

"Not well," she admitted. Then she added, "In days."

"Oh, Savannah." Kurt hugged her up against his chest. "What's wrong, sweetheart?" He kissed the top of her head. "Is this about what I told you?"

"No, Kurt," Savannah whispered and Kurt's heart thundered. "It's about me."

He pulled back to view her sorrowful face. "Want to talk about it?"

"Yes."

"Up here or downstairs?"

In response, Savannah took his hand and led him to the back bedroom. Kurt saw that the bedclothes were rumpled, and noted the pair of lace-up ankle boots Savannah had left on the floor. Fine grains of sand spilled out of one of them.

The light beside the bed was on but turned to its dimmest setting. Savannah's cell phone and a small alarm clock were beside it, along with a box of tissues. Savannah sat down on the mattress and he sat beside her.

"I'm sorry you're so upset," he said. "I hate seeing you like this."

"I'm sorry that I waited, Kurt." Her chin trembled and tears filled her eyes. "Waited so long to tell you."

"Tell me what?"

She turned to look at him and her face registered pain and sorrow. "The truth."

Kurt reached out and stroked her cheek. "Is it really that bad?"

Savannah hung her head. "I'm afraid so."

Kurt draped his arm over her shoulder. "Whatever it is, Savannah, I'm sure—"

She stared into his eyes and hers watered. "We had a baby, Kurt."

A red-hot arrow shot straight through his heart. "What?"

Savannah shut her eyes and tears streamed down her cheeks. "I lost it."

"Lost?" The room seemed to spin around him. "What do you mean?"

Her voice shuddered when she said, "It was all my fault." Savannah buried her face in her hands, and Kurt wrapped his arms around her. Kurt could tell that's what she thought, but in his heart he couldn't believe it to be true. Savannah did, though. She completely held herself responsible, and the guilt was destroying her.

Kurt's world was crashing and burning, too. Coming apart at the seams. *A child? Mine and Savannah's?* His throat swelled shut, making it difficult for him to speak. "What happened?" he asked huskily.

Savannah met his gaze, teary-eyed. Kurt nabbed a tissue from the box by the bed and gently wiped back her tears. "You can tell me, Savannah. I'm here."

"I didn't know… I mean, didn't think—for a while."

"A while after that last summer, you mean?"

She nodded and he dabbed her cheeks again. "We only—"

"One time, I know."

"Well, apparently," she said sadly, "once was enough."

Kurt's pulse pounded in his ears. "Oh, Savannah. I wish I'd known."

"I tried to tell you."

"The letters?" Kurt asked, crestfallen, understanding she must have believed that he'd received them and didn't care. "Savannah, I never would have ignored you. I certainly wouldn't have ignored that." He wondered who else knew. "Did you tell your mother?"

"No one."

"Not even Olivia?"

The mention of her sister's name brought forth more tears. Kurt hugged her up against him. "You must have been terrified. Felt so alone."

She nodded numbly and he held her closer.

"I did one of those tests," she said. "You know, like you get at the store."

"Savannah," he said soothingly. "You can't blame yourself. Miscarriages happen."

"Maybe I made it happen." She harshly bit out the words.

Kurt sat there stunned, not sure how to interpret her confession.

She sniffed then locked on his gaze. "I took…" Savannah pursed her lips, apparently unable to continue, and Kurt held her face in his hands.

"What did you take?"

She blinked back her tears. "Olivia's horse."

"Her horse?"

"Jezebel," Savannah said weakly. "I wanted to ride and ride…or maybe run away. Go as far as that mare could take me." Her voice quaked. "Me and our baby."

"You felt you had no one," Kurt intuitively said.

"The weather turned… An October storm…
Jezebel hated lightning." The scars from the harrowing ordeal were reflected in her eyes. "But I wouldn't turn back. I made her keep going. Galloping faster…and faster—until we hit the edge of our property."
Savannah's chin quivered. "And, the split-rail fence."

"She jumped it," Kurt whispered hoarsely.

"No," Savannah said as tears streamed down her cheeks. "She tried."

"You were thrown, weren't you?"

"Jezebel stumbled and fell. I had to run back for help through the rain, and leave her…" She bit into her bottom lip.

"How horrible for you, Savannah."

"It was more horrible for that poor horse. My father had to put her down."

"That must have been hard on Olivia, too."

"It was awful, Kurt. I could hear her crying through the bedroom wall for weeks. But, you know what she did?" Kurt waited patiently for her to continue. "She forgave me. Said she knew it was an accident and not really my fault."

"The pregnancy ended then?" Kurt guessed.

"I was so sore from the fall," Savannah rushed to explain. "Everything ached all over. My mother gave me some aspirin and suggested I take a hot bath, a very hot one. And…"

Savannah quit talking, haunted by the devastating memory.

"I'm so sorry, Savannah." Kurt's heart ached for her, but his was breaking as well. How irresponsible he'd been, and his lapse in judgment had caused her to endure so much pain. It had been after their secret wedding and he had used protection. Obviously, that had failed.

"If anyone's to blame, it's me. We never should have—"

"Kurt," she said, stopping him. "I wanted it, too." She latched onto his hand. "As I recall, it was my idea."

He searched her eyes. "And, the baby?"

"It was very early on. Just a couple of months. If I hadn't taken that home test, I might not have known. Might have thought I'd had a really heavy period, brought about by the fall."

"Did you see a doctor?"

"Not for a couple of years."

"Years?" he asked with dismay.

"I waited until I was in college and could see someone on campus."

"You didn't want your parents to know."

"It was nobody's business, but ours." She met his eyes and Kurt locked on her gaze.

"I'm glad that you told me."

"The doctor said there was no lasting damage. I was young and my body recovered. There's no reason to think that I…" She looked distant a moment, like she was far away. Savannah disconsolately lifted a shoulder. "Someday."

Kurt squeezed her hand.

"There's something else… Something else I wanted to tell you."

"Yes?"

Savannah's green eyes glistened, but this time she held back her tears. "There's never been anyone but you."

Kurt swallowed hard. "You mean…?"

She gathered her resolve and continued bravely, "I haven't slept with anybody since then. Not since the beach."

Kurt's head reeled. "Savannah…"

"That became a bit of a problem with James." She rolled her eyes.

"I'm sorry."

"I couldn't take a chance, Kurt. Can't you see? After what happened, I was petrified to have something like that happen again. But that wasn't the main reason."

"No?"

She placed her hand on his cheek. "I was waiting for you."

"Savannah," he said, tenderly. "My sweet Savannah…"

"And, now that I've waited this long, I think I finally understand why. I don't want something that important to be casual, Kurt. I want it to mean forever."

"No one deserves forever more than you."

He reached for her and she told him, "I won't sleep with you again unless we're married. For real, in a church and with a license."

Kurt cocked an eyebrow. "Then, we'll have to do something about that, won't we?"

"I mean it, Kurt."

"I know you do."

"It would devastate me if…" But she clearly couldn't revisit the memory again. It had been agonizing enough for her to share it the first time.

"Come here and let me hold you." He wrapped his arms around her and Savannah sagged against him. "I'll hold you all night, if you want me to. Just like I did after Olivia's wedding." He paused in thought. "Is that why you ran out on me? You couldn't face me the next morning, because you felt you'd need to explain?"

There was agreement in her silence.

"It doesn't matter that you didn't tell me then," he said soothingly. "The important thing is you've told me now."

He softly stroked her hair and her body relaxed further in his embrace.

"There's nothing we can't face, Savannah. The two of us together. As long as we're honest with each other. Me with you, and you with me…we'll work through it. All right?"

She nodded and he held her tighter.

"Do you want me to stay?"

She looked up and met his eyes. "I never wanted you to go."

He tenderly kissed her lips with a promise. "I'll never leave you again." Kurt gently laid her down, carefully settling her head on a pillow. Then he switched off the light and reclined behind her, snuggling the covers around them.

"I love you, Savannah," he said, holding her close. "I always have."

She whispered in the darkness and her words warmed his heart.

"I love you too, Kurt. I always will."

Chapter Twenty-Eight

Savannah felt like a fairy princess getting ready for the Christmas Town Ball. She'd been bubbling over with excitement ever since Kurt had invited her to accompany him to the Christmas Eve event. Though Savannah had planned to go anyway, the prospect of being with the man she loved and now considered her boyfriend made everything so much better. Though their relationship obviously wasn't the focus of the ball, the soiree was a coming out party for her and Kurt in a way. It would be the first formal event the two of them had attended together, and Savannah couldn't wait to have the handsome Christmas Town doctor on her arm.

Liz zipped up her sparkly white strapless dress and grinned. "You look positively gorgeous!"

Savannah did a small pirouette in the strappy gold high-heeled sandals that matched her small clutch handbag. Her hair was up in a loose chignon at the base of her neck and occasional tendrils spilled forth. Her beautiful gown fell nearly all the way to the floor, barely grazing the tops of her shoes. She wore a Charity Cookie barrette as an accent piece in her hair, and when she glanced in the mirror she almost could have sworn that the tiny angel winked at her.

"Thanks, Liz." Savannah stared at her reflection, marveling at the fact that she appeared to be glowing— yet it wasn't just due to makeup. Blusher swept her cheeks, and she'd taken care applying pale pink lipstick and mascara. "I feel amazing."

She turned to her friend with a pout. "I sure wish you were going."

"I'm babysitting for Sandy and Ben, remember?" Liz shrugged. "Besides, nobody wants to attend a soiree like that by going stag."

"That's what Walt told Kurt, too," Savannah said.

"Walt took a heavy hit," Liz commented. "Even though it was years ago, I've got the notion he still misses Rose."

"Yeah," Savannah said, thinking briefly of Gloria. She'd called her friend this afternoon to wish her an early merry Christmas and update her on how things had been going with Kurt. Since Savannah and he had their heart-to-heart talk, the two of them had been practically inseparable. While they each had jobs to do during the day, they routinely met for lunch at the Main Street Café.

In the evenings, Kurt cooked for her as he'd said he would. And, little by little, she'd convinced him to let her help. Ultimately, they'd developed a cozy routine of preparing dinner together then settling down to read or watch holiday movies on Kurt's sofa by a roaring fire. At the end of each night, Kurt drove Savannah home then kissed her passionately on her porch before going back to his own place.

Savannah told Gloria all this, but didn't share the particulars about what had initially driven her and Kurt apart. Gloria, being the caring and gracious friend that she was, never pressed Savannah on the details.

Gloria quipped that Savannah and Kurt's relationship sounded *incredibly domestic*—but not without telling Savannah how very happy she was for her. Though Savannah had never said so outright, Gloria had long suspected that a smoldering flame still burned between the old high school sweethearts. And, she'd been absolutely right.

Fortunately for Savannah, the only thing burning between her and Kurt these days was the bright light of their love and the sexy heat of their mutual desire. Kurt hadn't needed to put out one single fire since that incident with the napkin.

"Will you help me with this necklace?" Savannah asked, handing Liz the heart pendant. She already wore her pearl stud earrings.

Liz draped the gold chain around Savannah's neck and the gold heart landed just above her cleavage. "Kurt's going to pass out when he sees you," Liz said, smiling.

"Hope not!" Savannah giggled. "If he does, then how will he escort me across the street?"

"Yeah, and it's such a long walk," Liz teased.

The doorbell rang downstairs and Savannah's heart fluttered.

"Thanks for everything, Liz," she said, giving her friend a hug.

"I hope you have the time of your life, Savannah. Merry Christmas."

Savannah opened the front door and Kurt took her breath away. He was dressed in the tuxedo he'd worn to Olivia's wedding and he wore it incredibly well, beneath his charcoal gray overcoat. Kurt removed his fedora and his dark eyes sparkled. "Wow, Savannah. You're a knockout."

She shot him a sassy smile. "You clean up pretty well yourself."

He stepped inside and gave her a kiss. "Merry Christmas Eve."

"Merry Christmas Eve to you," she said, as he helped her put on her fancy coat.

Liz had stayed upstairs to keep out of the way. She told Savannah she'd let herself out after the couple had gone.

Kurt peered at Savannah's heels as she walked outside. "Are you going to be okay in those shoes?" Snow lightly drifted outdoors as streams of well-dressed couples paraded toward the Grand Hotel across the way, bathed in the streetlamps' glow. There was a merry mischief in the air as laughter and good tidings resonated up and down the street.

Savannah hooked her arm through Kurt's. "As long as you hang onto me, I should be all right."

Kurt leaned toward her and whispered, "Sweetheart, I'm never planning to let you go."

Savannah's heart felt light as they approached the fabulous historic building that her sister and Nick had helped renovate. Then, she experienced a pang of sadness that the two of them weren't around to witness this. "I'm so sorry that Olivia and Nick couldn't be here."

"I know you are, and so am I." Kurt tightened his hold on her arm as they crossed the crowded street. "But they have other important work tonight."

"I understand," Savannah said, at last trusting that she did. It wasn't necessary for her to comprehend all the wonders of Christmas Town, or even discern every truth about Kurt's family. Kurt had helped her see that having faith was enough.

Kurt loved her and he'd let her into his world. As time went on, she would learn more. Just as Kurt would learn more about her... Savannah was betting that Olivia had come to similar conclusions when she'd opened her heart up to Nick. Though many people didn't believe in the magic of Christmas, what could possibly be more magical than love? The longer Savannah experienced it with Kurt, the more anything seemed possible.

Kurt was respectful and genuine and kind... Thoughtful and supportive, as well. He was also the sexiest man on the planet—anywhere. The best-looking guy, too. And, hands down—without question—the world's most phenomenal kisser. Savannah sighed as he ushered her along and they approached the steps to the Grand Hotel.

Jade and Wendell were ahead of them, and turned to say hello. When they reached the top of the stairs and entered the foyer, Savannah spotted Hannah at the far end of the hall. She'd donned a beautiful red velvet dress with a fitted bodice and off-the-shoulder cap sleeves. A gorgeous compass charm necklace on a golden chain glimmered brightly against her alabaster skin. Carter took her hand and led her into the ballroom.

Savannah couldn't help but think that her older brother looked very handsome in his formal attire. And, oh! There in the milling crowd stood Lou and Buddy Christmas. Lou had outdone herself in a simple black dress that was cocktail length and outlined her youthful figure. Poor Buddy's tuxedo vest barely fit, his girth testing its buttons.

An attendant took their tickets and Kurt tucked a check into a donation jar on a table near the front door. The proceeds from the ball tonight, along with any extra gifts, would go to benefit the Lena Winchester Good Works Memorial Fund, named in Hannah's great-grandmother's honor. Next, another event employee offered to take their coats.

Savannah entered the glittering ballroom with Kurt trailing her as they held hands. "It's fabulous," she said, catching her breath on the sight.

Everywhere she looked, people mingled about holding champagne flutes and selecting choices from platters of hot hors d'oeuvres carried on silver trays. Servers wearing sharp black trousers and starched white shirts circulated throughout the room, picking up empty glasses and providing full ones, in addition to offering steaming treats.

"Shall we get something to drink?" Kurt asked.

"I wouldn't mind a bit of champagne."

Kurt playfully cocked an eyebrow. "But, only one glass?"

Savannah laughed lightly. "We'll see. Maybe I'll be daring tonight and have two!"

"Anything your heart desires."

Later in the evening, dancing began in the ballroom to holiday tunes played by a string ensemble. Kurt took Savannah in his arms, thinking he'd never seen her look more beautiful than she did tonight.

"You know," he said, as he whirled her around the dance floor, "we never did eat that Virginia Cookie."

"How do you know I didn't eat it myself?" Savannah teased.

"Because I peeked in your freezer."

"Kurt Christmas!" she said in mock scolding tones. "When?

He thought on this. "The night we first went to the Peppermint Bark." Kurt shot her a sheepish look. "And maybe one or two times after…"

Savannah arched an eyebrow. "Been checking up on me, have you?"

"I was just making sure you hadn't shared it with someone else."

She laughed lightly. "Not on your life!"

"Well, good." They took another turn, spinning around near the flickering hearth and the gold-framed mirror above it. "Because I was hoping you were saving it for me."

"I am saving it for you. The only thing is…" She shot him a saucy smile. "You don't eat desserts."

"I could probably make an exception."

"Oh yeah?" Savannah challenged. "When?"

"How about tomorrow at Christmas?"

"I thought we were having pumpkin pie at your parents' place, after eating dinner at Jade's?"

"Why don't we scrap that whole plan?"

Her face registered surprise. "Skip Christmas?"

"Not skip it. More like, have a private celebration…just us two?"

"I don't know, Kurt," she said, but she looked tempted. "I'd hate to let your family, or our friends, down."

"I'm sure they'll understand." Kurt held her closer. "We'll have a good excuse."

Savannah's face flushed. "Oh?"

He pulled her even nearer and whispered in her ear, "We have some reading to do."

She stared at him agape. Nonetheless she appeared the tiniest bit excited. "Nick found the letters?"

Kurt nodded. "I heard from him right before I picked you up. He's bringing them by my house in the morning."

Worry filled her eyes. "Are you sure that we should go back there? Dig up those old hurts?"

He'd pondered this himself, so he tried to reassure her. "I think it might be good for us, don't you? None of my letters were bad ones. Mostly, I proclaimed my undying love for you."

She considered this a beat then her face brightened. "Yeah, me too."

"I can make us a very nice dinner…?" he said, still trying to convince her.

"Only if I get to help."

"Not if that means getting your hands dirty."

"My hands?" Savannah appeared flummoxed. "Whatever do you mean?"

Kurt stopped dancing to pull a ring box from his pants pocket. Savannah's mouth dropped open and Kurt's heart hammered. "You told the whole town how you feel about me…" He winked at her. "Now, it's my turn to make a proclamation."

Heat warmed her face. "Kurt Christmas," she admonished playfully, but her smile sparkled brighter than new-fallen snow.

"You're the most wonderful woman in the world," he said, undeterred. "Talented, intelligent, sweet... I can't bear the thought of you going back to Miami to take up your old life there. I understand that you have things to settle, and maybe your academic year to get through. But after that?" He drew in a breath then pressed ahead. "I want you to stay here, Savannah. Stay with me in Christmas Town."

Others around them stopped dancing when they saw what was going on. Kurt spied Sandy's jubilant face nearby, as she grinned and grabbed Ben's hand.

Kurt dropped down on one knee and a hush fell over the crowd. The musicians also stopped playing, as Kurt longingly gazed up at Savannah. Her green eyes glistened and he'd never seen a more beautiful woman.

"I love you more than life itself," he said. "From the very first moment I saw you, you bowled me over, and you still have that same effect on me now. Nothing would make me prouder than you doing me the honor of becoming my wife."

Tears brimmed in Savannah's eyes but she wore a happy blush.

Kurt flipped open the ring box, exposing a brilliant solitaire, and gasps were heard around the room. His voice grew raspy when he asked, "Savannah Livingston, will you marry me?"

A slow grin graced her face. "Kurt Christmas," she answered solidly. "I absolutely will!"

The room exploded in cheers and happy laughter as Kurt slid the ring on Savannah's finger, and she tugged him to his feet.

Savannah sighed joyfully in his arms, examining her ring. "It's beautiful, Kurt. Thank you."

He held her closer. "Thank you for saying yes."

"Let's not make it a long engagement." Happiness and affection danced in her emerald green eyes. "I've already waited half my life."

"Savannah, my dear," Kurt huskily agreed. "So have I."

"And, the honeymoon?" she asked with a playful smile.

"You've got to know I'll take you anywhere in the world you want to go."

Savannah's merry laughter filled the room. "Oh Kurt, I love you so much."

Her face was bright pink and her lips lush and lovely. Kurt couldn't wait to kiss her and seal this phenomenal deal. "Here's a little secret," he said, as his mouth moved in. "I love you, too."

The End

A Note from the Author

Thanks for reading *The Doctor Orders Christmas.* I hope you enjoyed it. If you did, please help other people find this book.

1. This book is lendable, so send it to a friend who you think might like it so that she (or he) can discover me, too.

2. Write a review at the site where you purchased this book and at Goodreads.

3. Sign up for my newsletter so that you can learn about the next book as soon as it's available. Write to GinnyBairdRomance@gmail.com with "newsletter" in the subject heading.

4. Come like my Facebook page: https://www.facebook.com/GinnyBairdRomance.

5. Follow me on Twitter: @GinnyBaird.

6. Visit my website for details on other books available at multiple outlets now: http://www.ginnybairdromance.com.

This Christmas won't you come home to Christmas Town? If you haven't already read them, I hope you'll check out the first three books in the Christmas Town series. Details follow.

New York Times and *USA Today* bestselling author Ginny Baird brings you the start of a brand new holiday series…

THE CHRISTMAS COOKIE SHOP
(Christmas Town, Book 1)

Hannah Winchester is down on her luck and disillusioned with love, but her fortunes are about to change. When Hannah inherits a defunct bakery in East Tennessee, her first thought is to sell it and settle her substantial debt. Then the townsfolk welcome her warmly and she's taken with the joyful spirit of the place, where stores employ holiday themes and residents have surnames like Christmas and Claus. After a handsome lawman comes to her aid dressed as Santa, Hannah learns he's more than a hot guy in a red suit and shiny black boots. Sheriff Carter Livingston has joined in the cause of rejuvenating the town, and he's encouraging her to do her part. Hannah's great-grandmother, Lena, sold special holiday cookies that brought hope and renewal to the people of Christmas Town. Yet Hannah has plans elsewhere and isn't looking to stay. Can she possibly reopen the shop known for kindling romance—without sacrificing her heart?

THE CHRISTMAS COOKIE SHOP
(Excerpt)

The last turn she took was supposed to lead straight to the town roundabout, the one that connected with South Main Street. Hannah had been told to watch for a flagpole, the courthouse, a library, and a big town sign. But all she saw ahead of her in these near-whiteout conditions was more snow! That's when a flashing blue glimmer in her driver's side mirror caught her eye. *Thank goodness! Help has arrived.* It had to be a cop figuring her for a distressed motorist. Hannah certainly couldn't get any more distressed than this.

Hannah hadn't journeyed to Tennessee for a leisurely visit. She'd inherited a business she knew absolutely nothing about, and she was determined to sell it at the first opportunity. She tried to imagine herself running a cookie shop, but just couldn't. The only picture that came to mind involved huge plumes of black smoke curling out an open doorway. Where some people had a brown thumb in the garden, Hannah wore a charred oven mitt in the kitchen. She couldn't even microwave popcorn without the bag catching fire.

Hannah spun in her seat to better view the approaching figure in dark clothing. *No, wait. It's a matching red tunic and slacks worn beneath an open field coat.* The full silhouette of a man emerged from a snowy swirl and Hannah's heart thumped. It wasn't just any outfit; it was a Santa suit. Though she'd never seen

Old Saint Nick looking quite like *that*. Rather than being short and stout, he was tall and built, with an obviously solid chest and a manly jaw thinly disguised by a fake white beard. A Santa hat sat slightly askew on his head, partially covering short brown hair. He strode to her driver's side window in shiny black boots and tapped on the glass. Hannah goggled at the apparition, then lowered her window a crack.

Evergreen eyes peered in at her and Hannah caught her breath. She didn't even know eyes came in that color. They reminded her of Christmas trees: the really fresh kind, not the plastic sort that normally stood on an end table in the corner of her apartment.

"Everything okay in there? I saw that you'd pulled over. No wonder, really." Little lines crinkled around his eyes, lending them warmth beneath the wind's chill. "Given the weather." He tugged off his fake beard and stuffed it in his pocket, exposing a rugged face.

Whoa, he was a good-looking Santa. She judged him to be a few years older than her but not more than five. As if his age mattered! Hannah wasn't in Tennessee to stay and she certainly wasn't in the market for a man. She'd had enough boyfriends to last her, thank you very much. And every…single…*one* of them had let her down. *Love.* Just one more four-letter word that had been canned from her vocabulary.

~ * ~

The Christmas Cookie Shop
Available now!

Come home this Christmas to…
CHRISTMAS TOWN, TENNESSEE
Where everyday dreams come true!

New York Times and USA Today bestselling author Ginny Baird continues her heartwarming holiday series…

A MOMMY FOR CHRISTMAS
(Christmas Town, Book 2)

Northern Virginia attorney Ben Winchester has spent the past four years being the best single dad he could be to his eight-year-old daughter Lily. Yet, last Christmas, he was unable to give her the one thing she asked for: a mommy. Since his late-wife's death, Ben has scarcely dated at all. He's also had a hard time with the holidays. When Ben and Lily venture to Christmas Town, Tennessee for Ben's sister's December wedding, they discover a village infused with holiday joy. Upbeat Sandy Claus runs the Snow Globe Gallery…loves sleigh bells, winter and kids. She has a special way about her, and is the most caring and intuitive person

Ben has ever met. When Ben finds himself falling for the beautiful blonde with big blue eyes, she hesitates about becoming involved due to some unusual family history. Despite complications that ensue, will true love prevail with Ben making his—and Lily's—fondest Christmas wishes come true?

~ * ~

A Mommy for Christmas
Available now!

Come home this Christmas to…
CHRISTMAS TOWN, TENNESSEE
Where everyday dreams come true!

***New York Times* and *USA Today* bestselling author Ginny Baird continues her heartwarming holiday series…**

ONLY YOU AT CHRISTMAS
(Christmas Town, Book 3)

Former interior designer and store owner Olivia Livingston followed her brother to Christmas Town, Tennessee two and a half years ago and never looked back. It was the perfect place for purchasing the holiday knickknack shop, All Things Christmas, and an ideal spot for hiding from heartache. Olivia's broken engagement to a Virginia vintner three years before shattered her illusions about love. So when a hot, young architect comes to town to restore the Grand Hotel, Olivia has no qualms about working with him on the project. Nick Claus might be tall, dark and exceedingly handsome—with spectacular blue eyes. But that doesn't mean Olivia's even mildly attracted to the really nice guy, who can totally fill out a pair of jeans. And, seriously? What is the *deal* with him thinking he can tell when she's been naughty or nice?

~ * ~

Only You at Christmas
Available now!

~*~ Keep up with new releases! ~*~

Visit www.ginnybairdromance.com.